Boys  of Summer

Boys

of

Summer

JESSICA
BRODY

SIMON PULSE
New York London Toronto Sydney New Delhi

This book is a work of fiction. Any references to historical events, real people, or real places are used fictitiously. Other names, characters, places, and events are products of the author's imagination, and any resemblance to actual events or places or persons, living or dead, is entirely coincidental.

SIMON PULSE

An imprint of Simon & Schuster Children's Publishing Division

1230 Avenue of the Americas, New York, New York 10020

This Simon Pulse edition April 2016

For information about special discounts for bulk purchases, please contact Simon & Schuster Special Sales at 1-866-506-1949 or business@simonandschuster.com.

The Simon & Schuster Speakers Bureau can bring authors to your live event. For more information or to book an event, contact the Simon & Schuster Speakers Bureau at 1-866-248-3049 or visit our website at www.simonspeakers.com.

Cover designed by Russell Gordon

Interior designed by Steve Scott

The text of this book was set in Cochin.

Manufactured in the United States of America

2 4 6 8 10 9 7 5 3 1

Library of Congress Control Number 2016930599

ISBN 978-1-4814-6349-2 (hc)

ISBN 978-1-4814-6348-5 (pbk)

ISBN 978-1-4814-6350-8 (eBook)

For Charlie,

with whom I will never stop chasing eternal summer

Oh simple thing, where have you gone?

I'm getting old and I need something to rely on

—from "Somewhere Only We Know" by Keane

Boys

of

Summer

GRAYSON

CHAPTER 1

As soon as I spot the lighthouse rising from the rocky slope of the north-side cliffs, I start to wonder if I'm a total idiot for coming back here.

I lean against the railing of the ferry and watch the tiny island grow closer with every subtle swell and dip of the water. Winlock Harbor is like my second home. It's been a safe haven for as long as I can remember. A perfect escape.

But I'm kidding myself if I think a summer on an island could possibly erase the horror of the past few months.

My phone vibrates in my pocket, stopping the incoming flood of memories. I pull it out to find a text message.

> Welcome back! First official clambake of the
> season tonight. See you at the club?

Mike Metzler. Winlock local and always the first one to know about a party on the island . . . official or otherwise. Also always the first one to *leave* the party to hang out with his wet blanket of a girlfriend.

I smile, tap out a reply, and put the phone back into my pocket, releasing a deep sigh.

1

Yes. *This* is exactly what I need. Parties and beaches and cute girls in sundresses. Mike and his laid-back attitude about everything. Ian and that acoustic guitar he drags around with him like a child with a smelly stuffed toy.

A carefree summer on an island far, far away from Bridgeport, Connecticut, and all the bullshit of the past three months.

This is the reset button I've been looking for. Something to reboot me back to the person I used to be. There's no better place to do that than in Winlock Harbor. And no better people to do it with than Mike and Ian.

The ferry docks at the pier, and as I follow the line of tourists waiting to disembark, I can just make out my father's sailboat parked a few slips away. He came early to get the house ready while I finished up senior finals and my last few rounds of physical therapy.

I step onto the dock, relishing the familiar sights and sounds of the island's tiny marina. My father is waiting at the end of the pier with the convertible. I throw my bag into the backseat and jump in without bothering to open the door. But I regret the move as soon as I land in the passenger seat and my arm screams out in pain.

"Hey, champ." My father greets me with a friendly punch. Mercifully, it's on my *other* arm. "How's the wing?" he asks.

I grit my teeth and smile. "Good as new."

He nods his approval. "That's my boy."

I haven't told anyone—including my doctor—that my arm still feels like someone ran over it with a semi. I don't want to give them any excuse to keep me captive in Connecticut all summer.

My dad shifts into first gear, but then thinks twice and eases back into neutral. "Wanna drive?" he asks.

I turn toward the open window and shake my head. "Not today."

I can feel him staring right though my skull, trying to dissect my thoughts in search of weaknesses.

I decide to head him off at the pass, before he can come to any conclusions about why I still refuse to get behind the wheel. "I'm exhausted from the ferry."

I hold my breath, silently pleading for him not to push it any further. Because the truth is, the ferry ride really *did* take a lot out of me. And I'm way too tired to come up with any more lies.

Later that night I stand barefoot in the sand in front of the Coral Bay Beach Club, with a frosty plastic cup of beer in my hand and the warm seaside breeze rustling my linen shirt.

I stare into the bonfire, breathing in the smells of the clambake. Smoke seasoned with salt from the ocean. Spices wafting up from the large pots of boiling seafood. It's exactly as I remember, and I'm hoping the familiar scents will smooth out the frayed edges of my nerves.

Everything about this scene is nostalgic. It should feel like home. Nine months ago I couldn't wait to get back here. I couldn't wait to dig my feet back into this very sand and inhale this very air.

But a lot can change in nine months.

We've been at the party for less than an hour, and already the guys are placing bets.

"I've got twenty on Miss America with the red, white, and blue top," Ian says, setting the stakes. He's tall and lanky like a ski pole, with dark hair that always looks like he went at it with a chain saw.

"No way," Mike counters. "It'll be the blonde with the seashell barrette."

Mike towers over both of us, but sometimes his expressions make him look like he's still the little kid that I met building sand castles on the beach twelve summers ago.

"Dude," I cut in, and take a sip from my drink. "Just the fact that you said the word 'barrette' scares me a little."

Usually I don't mind playing this game. Placing wagers on who I will end up leaving the party with has become a summertime staple—like midnight swims, watching *Crusade of Kings,* and the secret handshake we made up as kids—and I know I should be relieved that the guys are talking about something so normal. God knows there are so many other, less fun topics we could be discussing. But for some reason tonight the whole thing is making me antsy. I try to play it off. I don't want them to know that it's taking every ounce of strength I have not to jet down this beach like a three-hundred-pound linebacker is chasing after me.

"You see," I go on, nudging Mike with my elbow. "This is what happens when you're chained to one woman for six years. You start using words like 'barrette' without a second thought."

"What can I say?" Mike replies with his boyish grin. "I speak the language of the ladies."

Ian nearly chokes on his beer. "More like you speak *like* a lady. Plus, you're totally wrong. Seashell Barrette isn't leggy enough. It's the first clambake of the season. Statistics show that Grayson always goes for the longest pair of legs first and then works his way down."

"'Statistics show'?" Mike fires back. "Seriously? Have you been scoring Grayson's scores?"

"Aren't you supposed to be working or something?" Ian asks, sounding scorned. "Isn't there a coffee cup for you to refill or a trash can for you to empty?"

Mike guffaws like this is the funniest thing he's heard

all day. He's held just about every job there is to hold on the island. This summer he's doing ground maintenance at the beach club.

"I'm off tonight," Mike explains.

"Plans with *Mrs.* Metzler?" I jump back into the conversation. "How is the old Harpoon, anyway?"

Mike hates when I call her that. But I've always found the nickname so fitting. No matter what is happening between those two, no matter how far she wanders just out of reach, Harper Jennings always seems to have one sharp spear safely impaled in Mike's leg.

Mike scowls at me from behind his cup. I grin back, unfazed. Because this is just what we do. We bag on each other. It's what makes us . . . us.

See, I tell myself. *This is good. Nice and casual. No one is asking questions. No one is whispering. It's just a normal summer night on Winlock Harbor.*

Fake it till you make it. That's what my father always says.

Maybe he didn't fake it well enough. Maybe *that's* why my life fell apart.

"She's on the mainland visiting her brother. And we're taking a little breather."

"Another one?" I blurt out, and immediately regret it when I see Mike flinch ever so slightly. It seems like Mike and Harper are constantly taking a breather. Sure, they always get back together in the end, that's just what they do, but the incessant up-and-down has to bother him. Even if he swears it doesn't.

I give him a hearty slap on the back, trying to recover from my misstep. "Well, perfect timing, then. It'll give you a chance to test the waters. See what you've been missing out on. Hey, I'll even let you have non-leggy Seashell Barrette."

Mike shakes his head at my antics. "I'm not going to cheat on my girlfriend."

"We know," Ian and I say flatly in unison, and then break into laughter.

"My money's still on Red, White, and Blue," Ian says, pushing his shaggy hair from his face. "I mean, look at her. She's hot *and* patriotic. What more could you want?"

"Is that the name of your next love ballad?" Mike teases. "'Hot and Patriotic'?"

"You joke." Ian points with his beer. "But that's just the kind of song that will turn me into a YouTube sensation."

As I listen to my friends go back and forth in their usual jeering banter, I take another sip and peer over the rim of my cup at the two girls in question—a tall redhead in an American-flag top and shorter-than-short denim cutoffs, and a medium-height blonde in a sexy white sundress with a small seashell clipping back some of her hair.

No doubt, both of them are cute. No doubt, one year ago I would have been happy to show either one of them the inside of my father's sailboat.

But that person feels like a ghost now. A fun-house mirror reflection of myself.

Yet it's that very reflection I need so desperately to get back. A suit of armor I need to slip back on. Especially if I'm going to survive this summer in one piece.

I wince and rub my right arm. I downed four aspirin before I left the house, and my arm is still killing me. I need something stronger. Something that requires a prescription. But, unfortunately, prescriptions require honesty about how much pain you're actually in.

Seashell Barrette catches me looking and interprets it as an invitation to make her way over. Mike and Ian, still ribbing, instinctively take a few steps back, clearing the way for her like jesters at my court.

The girl sidles up and tucks a strand of hair behind her ear. The breeze immediately blows it right back into her face. "You're Grayson Cartwright, aren't you?" She bites her lip and rocks gently back and forth on her heels. Her intention for coming over is clear. It's written all over face. She's not here to sell me insurance.

My mind wants so desperately to turn her down, walk away, take off running, and not look back. But I remind myself that *this* is exactly why I'm here. For a distraction.

And God, does she smell good.

Just like summer.

The charm turns on automatically. Like a light bulb that responds to a double clap. I smirk back at her. "The one and only."

She giggles and sips coyly from her cup. "I've heard things about you."

"Good things, I hope?"

She tilts her head from side to side. "Just . . . *things*."

I flash another grin, making sure this one triggers the dimple. They all love the dimple. "Lies, I tell you. They're all lies."

She laughs again, tipping her head back. Her neck is long and slender, her skin the color of honey. When she looks back at me, her eyes actually sparkle.

"When did you get to the island?" she asks.

"Just today. You?"

"A few days ago. It's my family's first time here."

I snap my fingers. "I knew I would have remembered you."

Her smile broadens. And what do you know? She has a dimple too. "We used to summer on Nantucket, but my dad thought it was getting too mainstream."

"Well, I can tell you with authority that Winlock Harbor is anything but mainstream. We like to think of ourselves as classy but eccentric. And it's a very tiny island. The kind of place where everyone knows everyone's name and everyone's business."

"Oh," she says, pouting a little. "That's too bad."

I frown. "Why?"

"I'm not a huge fan of tiny."

I clear my throat. "Which reminds me. I still don't know *your* name."

"Sorry. It's Nicole. Short for Nicolette."

"Pretty," I remark, not because I have any affinity for those particular letters, but because that's what you always say when girls tell you their name.

"Your family has that big place down by the marina, right?" she asks.

I cock an inquisitive eyebrow. "You sure know a lot about Winlock Harbor for having just arrived a few days ago."

She blushes. There's no denying she's adorable. And sexy. Her little white sundress is tight enough that the margin of error for imagining what's underneath is negligible. "Someone gave me a very extensive tour," she explains.

"Was this the same someone who was saying all those nice things about me?"

"Maybe."

"So what else did you learn on your little tour?"

She shrugs with one shoulder. "Lotsa stuff."

"Like what?"

"Like how you're attending Vanderbilt in the fall as the first African-American starting quarterback in history."

My smile collapses. "Not the first," I mumble as I grab her cup a little too brusquely. "Let me refill that for you."

"But I wasn't—" she starts to protest. I don't let her finish. I turn and plod toward the bar. She staggers after me, her wedge heels sinking into the sand with each step, making it difficult for her to keep up.

I place the nearly full cup down hard on the surface of the tiki-themed bar. Beer sloshes over the sides. "Top it off, please," I say, nodding to the cup.

The bartender gives me a strange look. Not because I'm only eighteen—the Coral Bay Beach Club seems to operate by its own set of rules—but because there's barely enough room in the cup for more than a few drops.

He decides not to argue, though, and squeezes a dribble of beer from the keg's faucet until the cup is full again. I hand it to Nicole, who is now standing behind me. "Here you go."

The charm is gone. My tone straddles the line between hostile and annoyed. I need to rein it in, get back to the easy breezy guy I seemed to have such a solid handle on just a few seconds ago.

She forces a smile. Totally fake. "Thanks," she murmurs, but doesn't drink.

"You know," I begin in a measured voice, trying to regain control of the situation. "It's really getting crowded out here. Do you wanna go someplace quieter? My boat is just a few minutes down the beach."

She nods, her expression brightening. "Sure!"

I wonder if her extensive tour of the island included commentary on Grayson Cartwright's boat. If it did, she certainly isn't dissuaded by the implications of the invitation.

She sets down her untouched beer and reaches for my right hand. I flinch at the pain that shoots up my arm and quickly switch to her other side, hiding my grimace with a smile as I entangle my large dark fingers with her slender pale ones.

As I lead her away from the party, I can't help but notice how wrong and unnatural the whole thing feels, like I'm walking in a stranger's shoes. A stranger who just happens to look like me.

Fake it till you make it.

That's the plan, anyway.

When we pass the bonfire, out of the corner of my eye, I see Ian begrudgingly hand a twenty-dollar bill to Mike. Mike holds up his winnings to me like he's toasting my send-off.

I make a mental note to pay Ian back later.

CHAPTER 2

The house is its usual state of disaster when I get home. Someone let the dog onto the couch—whose idea was it to take in a stray dog?—and now there's more sand on the cushions than on the beach I just left.

I place the leftovers I scored from the clambake on the table and step over a pile of wet swim trunks and plastic shovels, just as a blur of bare skin and fur comes barreling past me, nearly razing me. Jake and Jasper have apparently invented a new game. It's called Tornado.

The boys—who are wearing nothing but their super-hero underwear—jump onto the sofa, trying to get away from the matted, sandy creature chasing them. The dog—I think his name is Frank this week—jumps up after them, and there's a chorus of squealing and barking.

I shake my head. "Who's hungry?"

This gets their attention. It's the only thing that does. They leap off the couch in simultaneous kung fu kicks and come over to see what I've brought. The dog follows. He's clearly an optimist.

"Jasper, feed Frank," I say.

Jasper lets out a whine and stomps his foot. "I fed him last night."

"His name's Walter now," Jake informs me.

"Fine. Jake, feed Walter."

"I fed him this morning. It's Jasper's turn."

I look from one identical pout to the other, trying to figure out if they're doing that twin prank where they trick me into thinking Jake is Jasper and Jasper is Jake until I finally get so confused that I just feed the dog myself. You would think after six years with these little villains, I would always be able to tell them apart, but you'd be surprised.

"You did not!" Jasper argues.

"Did anyone feed the dog this morning?" I ask, looking down at the brown-and-white wire-haired mutt sitting patiently at the foot of the table, waiting for his share. I should reward him for being the quietest of the bunch.

Jasper and Jake look at each other and then at me with blank expressions.

I laugh and uncover the plates of food. "You eat. I'll feed him."

I scrape a portion of food onto a separate plate for Dad before the twins can devour it all, and place it on the kitchen counter. They may be miniature, but they can put away steamed clams like no one's business. Then I pour a bowl full of kibbles for Walter. He gobbles it up immediately, and I feel myself soften toward the poor guy. We found him wandering the streets behind Coconut's Market, looking for scraps. It's odd to find a stray dog on the Locks. Especially one who looks like him. All of the tourists bring their designer, pedigree, purebred show dogs to the island and wouldn't dare leave them behind at the end of the summer. The origins of this little mongrel are as mysterious as his breed.

"Mike!" I hear one of the boys scream from the family room. "Jake is hogging all the corncobs!"

"Share!" I call back, and then disappear into my room and close the door, temporarily blocking out the sound of the Metzler Twins' Last Stand.

I slip off my flip-flops and collapse onto my bed. Between a full-day shift maintaining the endless grounds at the club and the clambake, I'm totally beat and my feet are killing me.

I get exactly ninety seconds of peace before someone knocks.

"Come in!" I say.

I expect the boys to come barging in to tell me the dog swallowed a clamshell or something, but instead it's my dad who steps inside. "You think maybe you can keep them quiet? I'm trying to sleep."

I snort out a laugh, and he flashes his typical goading grin as he hobbles into my room favoring one foot and sits next to me on the bed. I notice he's not using his crutches. I would bring it up if I thought it would do any good.

"You think maybe I could spike their milk with cough syrup tonight?" I joke back.

"Already tried that," he deadpans. "The villains are immune."

"Don't worry. I'm sure it's just a phase."

Dad cracks up. It's a little private joke between my parents and me. We've been saying it since the twins were six weeks old and wouldn't stop crying all night. "It's just a phase." When they turned two and were throwing dual temper tantrums in the middle of the grocery store, that was just a phase too. And when they were five and first learned the word "sex," they thought it was *hilarious* to say it to every person they met. That was one of the more awkward phases.

I bet when they're forty-five and still running through

life like it's a giant playground, my dad and I will be giving each other the exact same empty reassurances.

"Mom home yet?" I ask.

He shakes his head. "She took an extra shift."

I hate thinking about my mom working so hard at a job that's so labor-intensive, but I admit we could really use the money. And she won't have to clean houses forever. As soon as Harper and I move to New York at the end of the summer and I can get a job that pays a decent salary, I'll be able to send money home.

The thought of Harper instantly makes my stomach twist, but I quickly push it away, reminding myself that our most recent separation is just a short-term thing. Like all of our separations. She'll come around. She always does. These "breathers" of hers never last long.

Harper just likes to know that she can run when she needs to. That I'm not an anchor weighing her down. I just wish I didn't have to keep proving that to her. I wish she'd realize that even when we're together, I would never hold her back. Her ability to fly is what I love most about her.

Part of the problem is this town. This island. It's suffocating. But things will be different when we move to New York and start our life together. I mean, our *real* life. We've been planning this move since we were fourteen. Harper is going to star on Broadway, and I . . . Well, I haven't quite worked out what I'm going to do yet. But I'm not worried. I'm sure the right opportunity will smack me across the face as soon I step off the train.

"So," Dad begins with a grimace, and I know he's about to ask me something I won't like and definitely won't agree to. "My buddy Dave gave me a heads-up about a big roofing job starting soon. Good money. Two months minimum. It's one of those rich mainlander mansions on the beach. I thought maybe I'd pick up the job. The mortgage payment is coming up, and—"

"Are you crazy?" I interrupt. "You can barely walk on solid ground, and you want to go traipsing around a poorly shingled roof?"

"It's not so bad. I'm pretty much healed."

"The doctor said you're supposed to stay off that leg for another month."

Dad swats this away like it's an annoying fly. "Eh, what do doctors know?"

"A lot, actually. They know a lot. That's why they're doctors."

"Maybe I could just—" he begins, but I cut him off.

"No. Absolutely not. We don't need you messing up your other leg too. Besides, someone has to stay here with the twins. We can't afford to put them in the kids' camp at the club. They're charging a fortune this year."

"But—" he starts to argue.

"I'll take the roofing job," I tell him. "I've helped you with enough of them through the years. I can move some shifts around at the club so I can do both."

I know it's what has to be done. Dad's right. The mortgage payment is coming up, and we need the money. But this is my last summer on the Locks with Grayson and Ian. And I can feel it slipping away by the minute.

"Mike," Dad says, and I can hear the break in his voice. He hates that I have to pick up the slack around here since his accident, but I don't care. That's what families do. They pick up slack.

My phone vibrates in my pocket, and I glimpse at the screen. It's a text from Harper.

I'm back. Can we talk? Meet me at the Cove?

I hide a knowing smile and slip the phone back into my pocket.

Like I said, the breathers never last long.

Standing up, I slide my feet back into my sandals and tell Dad, "I'll call Dave first thing on Monday and work it out. Can you hold down the fort for another hour or so? I'm going down to the beach. The boys are fed. So is Walter."

Dad frowns back at me in confusion.

"The dog," I clarify.

"I thought his name was Frank."

"That was yesterday."

Dad nods, struggling to get up from the bed. I reach out a hand to help him, but he ignores it and pushes himself up with a grunt.

I head into the family room. Jasper and Jake have already polished off the leftovers and are now lying in a food coma on the couch, staring dazedly at some Disney movie playing on the TV.

Wow. That worked even better than cough syrup.

I clearly need to feed them clams more often.

The quiet alcove tucked away from Coral Bay's main beach, hidden by a large clump of tall grass and uninviting brush, is my best-kept secret on the island. It has the perfect view of the water, and it's far enough away to stay clear of the surf but close enough that you can still hear the music of every wave.

Hardly anyone knows about it, including the locals.

It's been Harper's and my place for as long as we've been together.

When I arrive, she's already there, standing barefoot in the sand, staring out at the ocean, holding her sandals in one hand. She looks like a scene from a movie, her yellow sundress billowing in the breeze, her hair windswept and wild from the ferry.

"Hey," I say quietly so I don't scare her, but she startles anyway.

She laughs to cover up her surprise. "Hey."

I walk up to her, leaning in to kiss her. She hesitates and then ducks away at the last minute.

And that's when I know.

She's not ready.

She still needs more time.

I take a step back. "What'd you want to talk about?" My voice is light. Easy. Unattached.

"I . . . ," she begins, but then obviously thinks better of whatever she was going to say. "It's pretty, isn't it?" She turns back to the water. "I've always loved the first waves of summer."

I nod and angle my body toward the surf, keeping one eye on her. "Yes."

The memories of a half dozen summers flash through my mind at once. Lazy, moon-drenched nights with Harper and me sitting in this very alcove. Her leaning back against my chest. Me kissing her bare shoulder. Her twisting her head to meet my lips.

"Mikey," she says remorsefully, and I feel my heart sink. She only calls me Mikey when she's apologizing or breaking bad news.

"It's fine," I assure her. "We can wait it out. We don't need to decide anything tonight."

She bites her lip, looking like she's about to cry. "I'm sorry. I can't." Her voice shatters.

I pull her into me. That's when her tears break loose. Her sobs shake her entire body. I try to absorb them with my arms. "It's okay," I whisper into her hair. "You need more time. I get it."

She pulls away and rubs a finger under her nose. "No. It's not that. I don't need more time."

I'm not following. She must see it in my face, because she starts crying again. I reach for her, but this time she takes a step back. "I can't keep doing this to you. These breathers. These in-betweens. They're not fair. To either of us."

I stand, speechless, comprehension starting to trickle into the corners of my brain. "What are you saying?" I ask, even though I'm pretty sure I already know.

She sniffles. "I'm saying it needs to be over. For good."

My head settles into a thick fog. I try to shake it clear. "You don't mean that," I say with the same conviction I feel every time she talks like this. "You're just nervous because of New York. It's getting close and everything is feeling too real. I get it. I'm nervous too. But this is what I've always wanted."

"No," she says quietly. "It's not. You don't want to go to New York. It's never been *your* dream. It's always been mine. You'd just be following me there, and I can't let you do that. I can't let you make that mistake."

I feel my teeth clench in frustration. "I'm a big boy, Harper," I snap. "I can make my own mistakes." I tug my fingers through my hair, trying to calm myself down. Why is she doing this again? Why can't she just accept the fact that I love her and I want to be with her?

"And you're wrong, anyway," I go on, my throat thick. "It's not a mistake. I *want* to go. I want to—"

"Mike," she interrupts brusquely, her tears put on pause long enough for her to say, "*I* don't want you to go."

I fall silent, feeling like a meteor has just crashed into

my chest. I recognize the certainty in her voice and know it doesn't matter what I say now. Harper has made up her mind. At least for today. And nothing I do or say is going to change it now.

But tomorrow is always another story.

"I'm sorry," she says quickly, and I can tell from her voice that she really does mean it. She always means it. "You're my best friend. And I love you too much to watch you do something you'll regret." She's crying again now.

"I won't regret it!" I say, my voice rising rapidly. "Why do you keep trying to tell me how I feel?"

"I'm not!" she shouts back, sobbing so hard that the tears swallow up her words. "I'm trying to tell you how *I* feel."

She sniffles, struggling to catch her breath. "I just . . . ," she begins. "I just . . . I think this is for the best."

I feel my hands clench into fists at my sides, my ears ringing inside my brain. I can't stand here any longer. I can't watch her cry over something that doesn't have to be this way.

I push past her and stride over to the fallen log where I keep my surfboard.

"Whatever you want, Harper," I mutter, tucking the board under my arm.

It's what I always say. It's what I always mean. I've just never walked away from her as I said it.

CHAPTER 3

oral Bay's main beach is so crammed with people, they should call it a "human bake." It's the same old, same old party with the same old, same old contradictions. Red-checkered tablecloths offset by crystal champagne glasses. Corny plastic lobster bibs protecting designer dresses that cost more than some people's rent. Beach club employees in pristinely pressed uniforms serving seafood and corncobs from banged-up metal pots.

Welcome to a Winlock Harbor clambake.

The quintessential summer event. The mainlanders all want an authentic island experience. They just don't want to give up their Veuve Clicquot to get it.

"Tourists," I mutter to myself as I take a sip from my beer and gaze out at the sea of human crustaceans.

This little island shindig was supposed to cheer me up. Grayson and Mike seemed to be counting on that. Not that either one of them would admit it directly. But Grayson left an hour ago with some pop tart with a shell in her hair, and Mike had to scurry away to deliver dinner to his little brothers. It's probably for the best, anyway. I'd started to zone them both out. I've been doing a lot of that lately. Zoning out. I've become a real pro at it. In school, at home, in my therapist's office. Which I find ironic, since the zoning out is what landed me in the therapist's office to begin with.

I'm not even sure what I'm doing here. Not only at this lame party but also on Winlock Harbor. Does my mother really think that coming here will make everything okay? That we can just sail back to Fantasy Island, where life used to be good, and forget about everything that's happened in the past year?

Surrounding yourself with memories of happier days doesn't automatically *make* you happier. It just reminds you of how drastically *unhappy* you've become, how life can go from pretty okay to pretty shitty in less than six months.

A minute later my mother is beside me. As if she can actually *feel* me brooding. She downs the final sip from her glass of red wine—which I swear was full only a minute ago—and smiles into the bonfire.

"Isn't this great?" she asks whimsically. "Your father always loved these clambakes. He was such a joiner."

Yeah, he joined the army, and look where that got him.

I roll my eyes and finish off the rest of my beer.

"Are you *drinking*?" she asks, scandalized.

She should talk.

"Yes, Mom. I'm drinking. I drink. I'm an eighteen-year-old alcoholic."

She shoots me a disapproving look. "Don't take that tone with me, Ian."

"This is the only tone I have, Mom."

"Your grandparents are standing right over there," she hisses. "I don't think they'd appreciate seeing you drink."

I glance over at Nana and Papa, dressed in their matching khaki shorts and tropical-print shirts. They're sharing a plate of clams. Papa catches my eye and grins at me, toasting me with an empty clamshell.

I force a smile and avert my gaze. I can't look at him. I don't even see him anymore. All I see is my dad. *His* eyes, *his* nose, *his* crooked smile. The way *he* would look if he'd been able to grow old here, just like his parents. Just like he always wanted.

We've only been here a few days, and already the island is suffocating me.

A waiter walks by with a tray of drinks, and my mom trades her empty glass for a full one. I can't watch this. If she's had as many as I think she's had, things are about to get not pretty.

And she doesn't want my grandparents to see *me* drink?

I turn to walk away, but she grabs me by the wrist. For a woman who barely passes the five-foot-one mark, she's impressively strong. Being an army wife will do that to you. "Where are you going?"

"Home. Down the beach. To the lighthouse. I don't know. Anywhere but here."

She releases me. "But the party just started. We haven't even roasted marshmallows yet!"

Marshmallows? Seriously?

This is her solution to recently being widowed? What's her solution to war? Reese's Peanut Butter Cups?

I dump my empty beer cup into the trash. "Roast two for me," I tell her. "I'm going back to the house to get my guitar."

"Ian," she warns, keeping her voice low enough to not attract attention from the rest of the dancing shellfish. "Hiding in your room writing sappy ballads isn't going to help you get through this."

"Actually, Mom," I say, "that's about the *only* thing that's going to help me get through this."

She sighs and places a gentle hand on my arm. "Your therapist says—"

"My therapist isn't here," I reply tightly, feeling the end of my rope steadily slipping through my grasp. "And you are not his replacement."

I shake her loose and stride off down the beach, not bothering to say good-bye to anyone. The only people I cared about saying good-bye to are already gone.

I can hear the laughter and music grow more and more distant with every step I take, and my body slowly starts to uncoil.

How many more of those things will I be expected to suffer through?

It's not like no one around here knows what happened. Winlock Harbor is as close-knit and gossip-infested as a church. Everyone knows everyone else's business, and they *love* to talk about it. Just not to your face.

The island has an interesting assortment of people. There are the locals—like Mike—who live here year-round and somehow manage not to go stir-crazy. Then there are the vacationers—like Grayson—who come during the summer months and fill the place with an air of smugness. And then there's me. I fall somewhere in between. We certainly aren't rich enough to own a summer house here like the Cartwrights. The measly death benefits we got from the military are barely enough to cover the rent on our two-bedroom apartment in Philly, let alone a vacation home.

My grandparents built here long before it became a hot spot for wealthy tourists. And despite the many offers they've received over the years, they refuse to sell. Their beachfront property is probably worth a fortune by now. All the developers are just dying for my grandparents to tear down the unpretentious beach bungalow and build something worth putting on the front of a brochure.

We've been coming here and staying with my dad's

parents since I was six years old. It used to be something I looked forward to. A breezy getaway from the hot and stuffy army base, a place where my mom wasn't so stressed out all the time. But now I can barely stand to look at the house.

When I reach the front steps a few minutes later, I bypass the door and scale the ivy-covered trellis running up the side of the house like a green virus that's been left unchecked for too long. I squeeze through my bedroom window that I left open and roll adeptly onto my bed.

Sure, the front door is logistically easier, but it requires walking through a minefield of other dangers. Hazards of the emotional variety. Framed photographs of my dad as a kid. Knitted afghans on the couch that we used to fall asleep under. A medal of honor that's supposed to make death feel less like death and more like a carnival game.

If it were up to me, I would have taken all that shit down the moment we got the phone call.

But very little is up to me these days.

I grab my guitar and sit on my bed, strumming a few bars of the new song I've been working on. But my hands fumble awkwardly over the strings, and my fat fingers can't seem to form a single chord. It's these walls. They're prison walls in a cell that gets smaller by the second. I haven't been able to get through a full song since we arrived.

Frustrated and claustrophobic, I stuff the guitar back into the case and strap it to my back. I throw a few items into an overnight bag and toss it over my shoulder. Then I wedge myself back out the window and shuffle carefully to the edge of the roof before crouching down, swinging my legs over the side, and climbing down the trellis.

As soon as my feet hit the sand, I start to move, putting as much distance between me and those walls as I can.

There's really only one place to go. A place where the furniture isn't infested with ghosts and the walls are too far apart to ever suffocate you.

Grayson Cartwright's house is one of the largest on the island. It's about a ten-minute walk down the beach. I make it in seven, my guitar case and overnight bag banging uncomfortably against my hip the whole way.

The lights are out. Grayson is most likely still on his boat with the pop tart from the clambake, undoubtedly doing what Grayson does best. But I know my way to one of the spare bedrooms that's always empty. It used to belong to Grayson's little sister, Whitney, but she stopped coming to the island a few years ago, after she realized that Winlock Harbor didn't have a Barneys.

This is probably the only moment in my entire life when I actually *envy* the infamously shallow and materialistic Whitney Cartwright.

At least she gets to *choose* where she spends her summers.

Whitney's bedroom is on the first floor. I'm grateful for that, since I already scuffed up my palms and knees in my last wall-scaling escapade.

I try the window. It lifts easily. Hardly anyone ever locks anything on Winlock Harbor. What's the point? Unless you have a private boat, there's only one way on or off this island, and that's by ferry. Chances are, someone will catch you before you make it out with a flat-screen television.

I push the window all the way open and hoist myself onto the sill. With one more boost, I'm able to shove my way into the pitch-dark room, and tumble onto the unforgiving hardwood floor.

And then someone screams bloody murder.

CHAPTER 4

By the time the footsteps retreat down the dock, I'm already imagining the rumors the girl will spread.

Grayson Cartwright can't get it up.

Grayson Cartwright is gay.

Grayson Cartwright broke more than just his throwing arm in that car accident.

Regardless of which lie she chooses, it *will* reach the other end of the island by daybreak. That's inevitable. Winlock Harbor is too small a place, and the tourists are too desperate for gossip.

It certainly won't be the biggest scandal of the summer, but it will be the first. And that counts for something.

I want to care. I really do. The old Grayson Cartwright would care big-time.

But ironically, I just can't get it up.

I collapse onto my back and stare at the ceiling. The air-conditioning on the boat hums to life, trying desperately to compete with the humidity outside. My arm is killing me and the frigid air on my bare chest makes me shiver, but I can't muster the energy to sit up and find my shirt. So I simply grab a handful of comforter and yank it across my body.

I can hear my phone ringing somewhere on the floor, but I make no move to reach for it. I don't want to take the risk that it might be my mother calling again. Trying to apologize for ruining my life. Trying to relieve her own guilty conscience.

I haven't answered since she left.

She doesn't get to do that. She doesn't get to just walk out on us, send my entire existence into a tailspin, and then call and make nice.

I turn over and punch the mattress. *Hard.* I keep punching and punching until my arm is throbbing and I cry out in agony. Tears stream down my face.

If only my teammates could see me now. If only the head coach at Vanderbilt could see me now. Crying like a toddler throwing a tantrum.

I bury my face in the pillow. The scent of Nicole's hair is still heavy on the fabric. Coconuts mixed with something. Mint? Cream?

Who the hell cares?

The point is, I tried. I tried to be the guy that everyone on this island expects me to be. I tried to show them all that I'm fine. That people leave and cars crash and arms break, but *I* — Grayson Cartwright — am *fine*.

Nicole was exactly what I needed. Cute. Sexy. Eager. She was cut and pasted from every other summer I've spent here. An exact replica of every other girl I've brought back to this boat. Even the smell of her hair was an echo. As if the island only sells one brand of shampoo.

Which means the problem isn't her.

It's me.

Any other summer this night would have turned out differently.

Any other summer she wouldn't have left here with her

shoes in her hands and a colorful variety of curse words on her lips.

But it's not any other summer.

It's *this* summer.

And I'm no longer the guy who left Winlock Harbor nine months ago with a bagged future and a cocky smile. I'm someone else. Someone I barely recognize. Someone I'm desperate to get away from.

Which is why I eventually shove off the comforter, slide my feet into my shoes, step onto the dock, and start running. I bow my head to hide my face, and cradle my throbbing arm in my hand.

As I pass the familiar landmarks, the memories of a thousand summers come racing back to me. The Coral Bay Beach Club, where my friends and I first met when we were six years old and I (semi-purposefully) trampled through a sand castle that Mike and Ian had spent hours constructing. Ian's grandparents' house, where Ian's dad used to play army base with us when we were kids. The small Winlock Harbor Inn, where Mike lifeguarded last summer and used to sneak beers for us from the bar. The garden shed where I had my first kiss. The small marshland where Cherry Tree Creek empties into the sea and where my mom and I found the nest of baby birds and nursed them until they were old enough to fly. The rental cottages that have housed a hundred girls who walk and talk and smell just like Nicole.

I probably could run forever. I could circle this island five times before daybreak and not even feel winded.

But I don't.

I barely even make it a full lap around.

Because somewhere just past the lighthouse, I trip over Harper Jennings.

CHAPTER 5

The moon always looks bigger when you're floating in the middle of the ocean. As though you're closer to the stars out here.

I know it's an illusion. I read about it once. The moon, in fact, never changes size, no matter where you are on the planet, no matter what is happening in your life. It's your perspective that changes.

And right now my perspective is completely warped.

I lie on my back and let the swells of the tide gently rock my board. Normally I love coming out here and just floating aimlessly in the ocean, letting the waves take me wherever they want. This is where I can be alone. Where I can be me. Harper never liked the water much. She says it makes her seasick. Ironic, given that she grew up on an island. Maybe that's why she always feels so trapped.

As I drift, the usual post-Harper-breakup feelings flood through me. Frustration, disbelief, anger, before finally settling where I always settle. Somewhere near acceptance. It's like a routine now. A sick ritual.

This is who Harper is. This is what Harper does.

I know this. I've always known this. She didn't mean

what she said. It's not the first time she's said it's over for good. I just really hope it'll be the last.

I'm not sure how much longer I can keep this up.

She called out my name as I stormed off from the Cove. At least there was that. But I didn't stop. I kept going until I was halfway around the island, until the moon looked different. That was when I could finally believe that I had gotten far enough away.

Although that's an illusion too.

I know it's the same damn moon.

It's the same damn island.

And until I get her off it, she's going to be reacting the same damn way. It's a vicious cycle. She feels stuck, and I'm the easiest thing to break free of.

But what if I don't want to be so disposable anymore? What if *this* time, after she realizes that freedom isn't what she wants after all, I refuse to take her back?

The thought makes me laugh aloud.

Who am I kidding? I've been in love with Harper Jennings since the second grade, when she asked if I would split my cupcake with her. I handed over the whole thing without even batting an eye. Because I can't say no to her. I've never been able to.

I think about just leaving now. Jumping off this board, swimming to shore, banging on her door, and convincing her to go with me right this second. Don't pack any bags, don't say good-bye to anyone, let's just catch the first morning ferry, hop on a train, and go to New York. Let's get as far away as we can from this place and this moon and these vicious cycles.

Of course I know I can't do that. I can't leave my family to fend for themselves. My dad's still too injured to work, and my mother can't handle that burden alone.

Three more months, I tell myself. Work hard, save as

much money as you can, and then we can go. Assuming Harper has gotten over whatever fear is plaguing her this time. Maybe I should have stuck around longer. Asked her more questions, so I could figure out how to change her mind. How to fix it.

No. Let her fix it herself. I'll leave her to enjoy her precious *space*, and then I'll wait for the signs that she's ready to come back. There are always signs. Reminiscing about the past, gentle touches on my arm that are supposed to look accidental, laughing too hard at everything I say. No matter how many times she leaves or how many different excuses she gives me for going, the way she comes back never changes.

And when that moment comes, I'll be here ready and waiting to whisk her off to New York. Leaving the island — the only home I've ever known — may make my stomach twist, but the thought of living a life without Harper makes it downright rip in half.

I can feel the tide picking up, the swells getting bigger beneath my board. Maybe the moon really *is* shifting.

I flip onto my stomach and paddle along the coastline. I wait patiently, biding my time until the right wave comes along to bring me to shore. Surfing is all about patience. Clearly I have an abundance of that.

Just like in life, the longer you wait, the bigger your reward.

Finding the perfect wave isn't about logic or calculations or studying the patterns of the tides; it's just something you feel in your gut.

I can see my perfect wave a few feet away, gently rolling toward me. With the help of the moonlight, I track it, feeling the buildup, letting the fiery anticipation spread through my arms and legs, like I'm a jungle cat stalking its prey, waiting for the precise moment to charge.

The moment comes fast.

I paddle hard, my arms aching in protest. I align myself with the oncoming swell. When it's almost beneath me, I pop up, and land in a crouch. I lean left, angling my body into the wave, joining its energy, becoming a part of it.

The surf lifts my board up, and I start to fly.

It's the most exhilarating feeling in the world.

This is my payoff. This is the reward for all my patience and diligence and hard work.

The wave shifts, and I lean to the left to compensate. But I misread the swell. The tip of my board catches on the water, and the board shoots out from under me. I stumble and try to hold on, but it's a lost cause. I go tumbling into the water, my side hitting first. Pain explodes in my ribs as the colossal wave washes over my head.

I hold my breath and swim frantically away from the shore to escape the undertow. Water rushes into my ears as the current tugs at my feet.

I kick toward the surface. When my head breaks through, I glance around for my surfboard, but it's nowhere to be found. I don't panic, though. It's not the first time I've lost my board. It's hard to keep track of at night, with the limited light, and it always washes ashore eventually.

I tread water to keep myself afloat as I peer toward the coastline. I'm not too far out. I could easily swim back now, but I decide to search for my board first. It couldn't have gone far.

I paddle to my left, in the direction of the cluster of small rental cottages on the western tip of the island. Fortunately, I spot my board only a few yards away. *Unfortunately*, before I can reach it, I feel something in the water with me. My heart races as I try to kick away, but it moves fast. Too fast. And within seconds I feel myself being pulled under the surface.

CHAPTER 6

I stumble through the darkness, trying to find the light switch and stop the ringing in my ears.

Who is screaming?

The light comes on before I even find the wall, and I'm standing face-to-face with Whitney Cartwright as I've never seen her before. Tattered T-shirt, messy pulled-back hair, glasses, and no makeup. She's wielding a straightening iron like it's a butcher knife.

Since she turned thirteen, I've never seen Grayson's sister in anything but short shorts, miniskirts, or tight-fitting dresses. And I've *never* seen her in glasses. Did she always wear those?

"Ian!" she says breathlessly, wilting in relief. Then she starts smacking me with the straightening iron. Thankfully, it's not on. "What the hell?"

"I'm sorry!" I say, cowering and protecting my face with my hands. The girl is stronger than she looks. "I didn't know anyone was in here!"

"And you forgot what a front door was?"

"I didn't want to wake anyone up."

She guffaws and mercifully sets the flat iron on the dresser. "How'd that work out for you?"

Just then the door flies open and Mr. Cartwright comes in with a much scarier baseball bat. I instinctively duck and cover again. He looks from his daughter to me and then lowers the weapon. "What is going on in here?"

Whitney groans. "Relax, Daddy. Go back to bed. It's just Ian. He climbed through the window."

Mr. Cartwright casts another curious look between the two of us. I can tell he's trying to figure out what he missed. "Are you two . . ." His voice trails off.

"NO!" We both respond at once. I instinctively back away from her until I'm practically shoved against the wall. I brave a glance at Whitney, who happens to look my way at the exact same moment. Our eyes meet for a second, and we both shudder in revulsion and repeat the word. "*No.*"

"Then why the hell are you climbing through my daughter's window in the middle of the night?" Mr. Cartwright asks.

"It's Ian," Whitney answers for me with a hint of disdain. "Why the hell does Ian do anything?"

I sneer back at her. "Shut up."

Mr. Cartwright sighs, clearly not wanting to get in the middle. "I'm going back to sleep . . . if that's even possible at this point. Ian, use the front door next time. That's what it's for."

"Yes, sir," I say. "Sorry. Won't happen again, sir."

He shakes his head and leaves.

"Yes, sir," Whitney mocks in an obnoxious voice as soon as her father's out of earshot. "What, are you in the army now too?"

It suddenly feels like the floor has been knocked out from under me. Or that someone took Mr. Cartwright's bat right to my knees. Whitney's hand flies to her mouth as soon as she realizes what she's said.

"I — I," she stammers.

"It's fine," I say immediately, not wanting to get into this with her. Or anyone. But least of all her. How could rich, spoiled, has-everything-she's-ever-wanted Whitney Cartwright possibly understand what it's like to lose something you love? "I'll go find another room to crash in."

I head down the hallway, into the kitchen, praying that Whitney doesn't follow after me.

She does.

"Ian, I'm so sorry. I forgot. That was a stupid thing to say."

"I said it's fine," I snap.

This shuts her up. At least for a minute. She *is* Whitney Cartwright, after all. The longest I've ever seen her keep her mouth shut was five summers ago when Grayson, Mike, and I dared her to hold her breath for a minute. It was the most blissful sixty seconds I can remember.

"Do you want some tea?" she asks, holding up a stainless steel kettle. "I could boil some water."

It certainly wasn't what I was expecting her to say, but the softness of her voice is right on par. It's the same tone everyone uses around me. Like they're tiptoeing with their words. Let's all be nice to the guy with the dead dad. It makes me want to scream.

I never thought I'd prefer Whitney's annoying holier-than-thou demeanor, but right now, looking at that disgusting pity in her eyes, I'd do anything to get it back.

"Yeah, like you drink tea," I say snarkily, hoping to trigger her.

It works. She sets the kettle back down with a *clank*. "How do you know what I drink? You don't know me."

I snort in response.

"What is that supposed to mean?" she barks.

I raise my hands. "I didn't say anything."

"You snorted. It's worse. It *implies* something."

"I wouldn't dare imply anything."

"No, you just call me a slut to my face."

Suddenly, in one fell swoop, the tables have turned and *I'm* the one feeling guilty. I know exactly what she's talking about. It was three summers ago, the last time I saw her, before she stopped coming to Winlock Harbor. I was fifteen and she was fourteen and I . . . Well, let's just say I wasn't very nice to her. Grayson, Mike, and I were hanging out in the living room, watching the first season of *Crusade of Kings* with a naïve optimism (before we realized that the writers would eventually kill off every character we ever loved), and she came out of her room dressed like a medium-class hooker. She said she was going out with friends. Grayson barely noticed how incredibly inappropriate her clothes were. He was far too invested in the episode. It was the one where the heir to the House of Develin started plotting with his sister/lover to murder their father at the subtle behest of their manipulative mother. But *I* noticed. She looked ridiculous. I might have made some snide, sarcastic remark about her outfit, but it was just a joke. And she didn't seem to care. She just rolled her eyes like she does at all my sarcastic remarks. Then she lobbed some snippy retort back at me and left.

I didn't think she actually remembered that.

"I didn't call you a slut. I never used that word."

"That's right," she says, crossing her arms and looking smug. "You *implied* it."

I shake my head, laughing under my breath. "Why are you even back here? Did Dolce and Cabana close or something?"

"It's Dolce and *Gabbana*, you moron. And it's none of

your business why I'm here. This is my house. I can come whenever I want. Why are *you* here, is the better question. Don't you have a house on the other side of the island?"

I lower my gaze to the floor and fight back the rolling tidal wave of emotion that threatens to suck me under. "I like it better here." I glance at her. "Or at least I *did* until five minutes ago."

She huffs. "Nice to see you again too."

She pushes past me and starts in the direction of her room. I back up to give her a wide berth. Whitney Cartwright may be shaped like a supermodel, but she takes up a lot of space.

"Wait," I call out to her. She stops halfway to the hallway and turns back around.

"What?"

I'm actually not sure what I'm going to say to her. I didn't really think it through. I'm not even sure why I stopped her. To apologize? To clear the air? To thank her for offering to make me tea?

"When did you start wearing glasses?" I ask.

She reaches up to touch them, as if she forgot they were even there. And in that briefest moment the Whitney Cartwright facade slips ever so slightly and I see a flicker of self-consciousness underneath. But it's gone just as quickly as it came.

"Fifth grade," she says shortly.

Fifth grade?

How is that possible? I would think I would've remembered her wearing glasses all those years. She must usually wear contacts.

"How come I never noticed them before?" I ask.

She smirks. "I bet there are a lot of things you never noticed before, Ian."

And with that, she continues down the hallway, her bare feet padding unusually loudly on the hardwood floors. A few seconds later I hear her bedroom door slam.

I'm about to follow her down the hall, in search of an empty bedroom to crash in, but my gaze lands on the kettle she was holding just a second ago, and I suddenly have a really strange craving for tea.

CHAPTER 7

Of course I land on my right arm. The pain is so intense, I can actually feel it traveling through my body. As if it's too big for just one location and it has to spread. Move. Light fire to everything.

I bite my lip hard to keep from crying out. I taste blood.

It takes me a moment to get to my feet. I rest on my knees, taking deep breaths that do absolutely nothing. That's what my physical therapist told me to do. Take deep breaths. But unless the air is laced with morphine, it's not gonna do much good.

To be fair, however, I lied about how much pain I was actually in.

Every time I stepped into my PT's office, she would hold up the pain chart. You know, the one with the little faces and corresponding pain numbers on it, ranging from shit-eating grin (1) to "I want to kick someone's teeth in" (10). I always pointed to somewhere around the three or four mark—the faces that looked like they'd just swallowed something unpleasant—when in reality I was at an eleven.

Fake it till you make it.

"If you're about to give me another one of your Grayson lectures, you can save it. I'm not in the mood."

That's Harper. I almost forgot she was there.

"Nice to see you too, Harper," I say, cringing at how strained my voice sounds. Like I just finished an Iron Man race.

She must hear it. She'd have to be deaf not to. And I interpret her silence as confusion. Grayson Cartwright sounding weak? Winded? What planet is this?

"Are you okay?" she finally asks. "You didn't even fall that hard."

Another lightning bolt of pain shoots through my body, and I suck air in through my teeth. I finally give up on standing and just roll over so that I'm sitting next to her.

She didn't even move to try to help me when I fell. Typical Harper. Always too wrapped up in her own drama to bother with anyone else around her.

"I'm fine," I say, but it's the worst lie in history.

I cradle my throbbing arm in my other hand like a makeshift sling.

"Did you really hurt yourself?" There's concern on her face, but I don't believe it for a second. If I've learned anything from watching her lead Mike on all these years, it's that she's one hell of an actress. In fact, I bet she makes it in New York. Those skills have got to be useful for something.

"No," I retort bitterly. Harper Jennings is about the last person I want to confess my pain to.

The concern on her face doesn't fade, though. It actually deepens. She's suddenly moving, kneeling in front of me and gently placing a hand on my arm.

I wince, and she whips her hand back, like my skin is on fire. "Yikes. That bad? Should we get you to the hospital?"

I shake my head. "I've already been."

Now she just looks confused.

"It's an old injury," I explain.

She nods knowingly. "Football?"

My head jerks up, and I catch her eye for a moment. So she *doesn't* know. And here I thought word of my accident had already spread through the entire island.

Maybe I'm better at faking it than I thought.

I wonder who else doesn't know. Ian? Mike? I certainly didn't tell them. I just assumed word would get out some-how, that I would arrive on the island to a pity party of frowny faces. And when they didn't say anything or ask about it, I figured they were just being polite.

My father and I agreed a few weeks ago that we would keep it under wraps. All of it. My mom's departure, my accident, the broken arm. Actually, we didn't agree on it. My father suggested it, and I didn't *dis*agree.

"Why burden other people with our problems when they have their own?" he said.

Which is code for "Why let other people see our weak-ness when we can just as easily hide it?"

I think he's still convinced that my mom is coming back. I think he still believes this will all blow over.

I'm pretty sure it's that same blindness that made her leave in the first place.

But I keep those thoughts to myself.

"Yeah," I say numbly to Harper. "Football."

Let her think this was a heroic injury. Let her think I busted my arm getting sacked in the end zone as I scored the winning touchdown and won the national champion-ship. Let her spread *that* rumor around. It's better than the alternative. It's better than the truth.

She nods, and in that moment her face catches a glint of moonlight. I can see the tear streaks on her face. The smears of black around her eyes. The redness of her nose.

"What happened?" I ask. The question surprises her. It seems to take her a second to remember she's been crying, because she eventually reaches up and runs a fingertip under each eye.

"Oh," she says, forcing a laugh. "Nothing. Just, you know, trying to figure out why I'm so fucked up."

I laugh too, because the way she says it, like it's just a normal everyday activity (like gardening), is actually kind of funny.

"Come up with anything?" I ask.

She plops down onto the sand next to me again with a heavy sigh. "No."

"Damn. I was hoping to cheat off you."

She cocks an eyebrow.

"You know, copy down your answers. So I don't have to come up with any myself."

She scoffs. "Yeah, right. Grayson Cartwright already has all the answers. Grayson Cartwright was *born* with the answers."

"I think you're confusing having all the answers with never asking any questions."

She doesn't seem to follow this. I'm not sure even I know what I'm saying. I kick at a pebble lost in the sand. "Never mind."

I'm afraid she's going to press the issue, and it makes me regret even opening my mouth in the first place, but thankfully, she doesn't. She falls quiet. We both stare at the waves, and for the first time in history, I wonder what Harper Jennings is thinking.

"Mike and I are done," she blurts out.

The sound of my best friend's name on her lips makes me uncomfortable, and I instantly remember why I don't like her. I mean sure, when we were kids, it was all fun and games. She was almost one of the guys. She'd go swimming with us in the ocean, skip rocks with us in the creek, race homemade sailboats with us in my family's pool. She even joined in on a few of our pranks. Then we hit puberty and Harper got boobs—nice ones at that—and everything changed. She and Mike started having "special alone time" together. There'd be days on end when Ian and I wouldn't see either of them. Mike lost his virginity to her, and then he lost his mind to her too. That was when the games started. That was when Ian and I stopped knowing which Mike we would be getting each day. The happy-go-lucky, carefree, hopelessly-in-love Mike. Or the one who was waiting for Harper to come back.

That was when I stopped liking Harper Jennings.

"So I've been told," I mumble.

"No," she clarifies, her voice leaden. "Like, for good. I ended it."

I chuckle skeptically. "Yeah, I've heard that one before."

She doesn't respond. She's silent for a long moment. And then she breaks into tears, dropping her face into her hands and sobbing uncontrollably.

I'm so taken aback by the outburst, I don't quite know what to do with myself. I completely freeze. What is the best friend of a girl's ex-boyfriend supposed to do in this situation? Pat her on the back? Hug her? Let her cry on my shoulder?

She just admitted she broke my best friend's heart . . . *again.* Comforting her should be the last thing I want to do. And yet I can't just sit here like an asshole while she cries. She seems genuinely upset. It's confusing the hell out of me.

In all the years that I've seen Mike broken up and conflicted after Harper said she needed space, or felt suffocated, or didn't want to be tied down, I've always pictured Harper skipping off into the sunset to find some hunky tourist to grind up against at a beach party.

I never pictured her crying over him.

I never pictured *her* heartbroken too.

It doesn't make any sense. If she's this torn up about losing Mike, why did she break up with him in the first place?

"I don't know what's wrong with me!" she says, but the sobs swallow up her words and I'm barely able to understand them. She sniffles. "Sometimes I look in the mirror and I'm like, 'Who the hell is that? And why is she screwing up my life?' Do you ever feel that way?" She picks up her head and looks at me. Her face is so red. Her nose is so runny. She looks nothing like the pretty, blond, breezy Harper Jennings that lives in all of my summer memories.

I open my mouth to tell her that yes, I feel that way every single day, in every single mirror, but she doesn't give me the chance. She barks out a sharp laugh. "You probably have no idea what I'm talking about." She buries her face in her hands again. "God, I'm so pathetic. Why can't I just get my shit together? Why can't I just let myself be happy?"

I can't fight it anymore. I have to do something. I reach out to put my good arm around her shoulders, but before I can make contact, she suddenly leaps to her feet. "I'm sorry. You must think I'm such an idiot."

"Actually, I don't," I say, but maybe it comes out too softly, because she barely seems to acknowledge that I spoke.

"Don't tell Mike about this, okay?"

And there's his name again. There's the reminder of what this is all about.

She has broken Mike's heart a thousand times. She doesn't deserve my arm around her, telling her it's going to be okay. She doesn't deserve my sympathy.

"Okay," I mutter. Not because I'm on her side. Not because I owe her anything. But because I know that telling Mike about this will only make it harder on him. It will only make it that much more difficult for him to move on.

And I think it's about damn time he moved on.

CHAPTER 8

I fight to break free from the grasp of whatever is pulling me under the water. It's too dark to see what I'm dealing with, but I can't shake the hunch that it feels human. Like a hand. No, an entire arm. It snakes around my chest and yanks me back hard and fast.

My head dips under the surface and I hold my breath, but I'm too late. I swallow a mouthful of seawater and immediately start coughing.

"Don't worry!" a voice says from somewhere behind me. It's unmistakably female. "I've got you. You're going to be okay!"

I feel myself being dragged from behind. Confused, I try to turn around, but her hold on me is too tight. I struggle to break free.

"Relax!" she screams over the rush of the waves. "I've got you!"

"I don't need you to get me!" I call back, finally breaking away with one final shove. "I'm not drowning!"

I tread water and use my hands to spin my body toward my unwelcome savior. It's a girl I've never seen before. She's cute, in an elfish sort of way. Her short dark hair is wet and plastered against her forehead. She pants and pushes it clumsily away, reminding me of the way Jake and Jasper brush hair from their eyes in the bathtub.

"Oh my gosh! I'm so sorry! I saw you go under from my front porch. I totally thought you were drowning." She spits out water. "Well, this is awkward."

I peer down into the water we're both treading furiously. I can only see her from the chest up, but it looks like she's wearing pajamas.

"Sorry to scare you," I say, my pulse finally starting to slow.

"No! I'm sorry!" she's quick to retort. "I'm a lifeguard. But I just finished training, so I'm still in that extra paranoid mode where I assume everyone is drowning. They kind of drill that into you. Better safe than sorry, you know?"

She's talking a lot. And very fast. It's kind of cute. Not to mention impressive. That she can talk that fast *and* tread water at the same time.

I laugh. "It's fine. I just lost my board. I was looking for it."

"Oh!" she exclaims. "I'll help you look!"

"You don't have to—" But it's too late. She's already dived under the water like a dolphin and is swimming away from me. I stare after her for a second, a little speechless, before taking off in the other direction.

I swim a couple laps back and forth in a small area before finally giving up. I'm sure it's washed up somewhere by now. But just as I'm about to head back to shore, I hear the girl call out, "Found it! I'll bring it in!"

I try to yell back "Thanks," but a big wave takes me by surprise, splashing into my mouth, and I start choking again.

"You okay?" I hear her call. "Are you drowning this time?"

I manage to cough the remainder of water from my lungs and yell, "No!"

"Just checking!"

When I finally reach the sand, she's sitting next to my board like she's been waiting for hours. She pops up as I pull myself from the water and tug at my twisted swim trunks, which have ridden up so high that they're practically a Speedo.

"So sorry again," she says, and I now have a full view of her. She's definitely wearing pajamas. And not just, like, a random tank-top-and-shorts combo like Harper always wears to bed, but full-on, matching-top-and-bottom pajamas. They're soaking wet and clinging to her body, which I admit is kind of a turn-on. And I can't be sure, but are those little ducks on the fabric?

She notices me looking and glances down, like she forgot what she was wearing. I half expect her to blush and try to cover herself up. Most girls would if they were caught out of their house in duck pajamas. But she doesn't. She just laughs.

"I was about to go to bed," she explains. "I stepped out onto the porch to say good night to the ocean, and that's when I saw you, you know, *not* drowning."

I shake my head, certain I misunderstood. "I'm sorry, did you say you were saying good night to the ocean?"

Once again she shows no embarrassment. "Yeah. You know, like 'good night, room; good night, moon; good night, cow jumping over the moon.'"

I recognize the words. They're from a book I used to read to the twins. It was one of the few they'd actually sit still long enough to finish. But it doesn't mean I'm able to follow anything she's saying.

"So you say good night to the moon, too?"

"Sometimes. But mainly just the ocean. I've never actually slept by the ocean. This is my family's first summer here. We live in western Mass. Like, near Amherst? We're renting one of those cottages." She points up the beach. "Sometimes we go to a lake house in the Berkshires in the summer, but 'Good night, lake' just doesn't have the same ring to it, you know?"

"But *why* do you say good night to the ocean?"

She shrugs. "I just think it's a nice gesture? Like in the book. No one ever says good night to their mittens or their socks. They should."

I bite my lip to keep from laughing. This girl is a little bit crazy, but I'm pretty sure it's the good kind.

"Well, anyway," she says, grinning, "I should get back. It was nice not saving you."

"Yeah," I agree. "It was the best non-rescue I've ever had. Maybe I'll see you around."

She nods eagerly. "Totally. I'm working at the Coral Bay Beach Club all summer. In the kids' camp."

"Oh, then I'll definitely see you. I do grounds maintenance there. You know, weeding, gardening, mowing, a little of everything."

"Are you a local?"

"Yeah. Why?"

She shakes her head. "Nothing. It's just that I seem to be the only tourist here who actually has a job. I'm not really a sit-around-on-the-beach-all-day kind of girl. When we used to go to the lake house, I always worked at the sandwich shop in town. Plus, I wanted to start beefing up my resume. I'm starting Smith College in the fall. I'm studying to be an elementary school teacher."

I don't even know this girl, but for some reason I can totally see her commanding a classroom full of kindergartners. Like, the job is just stamped right across her forehead. It must be nice to know exactly what you're meant to do with your life.

"Well, you'll have your hands full at the club. The kids that come here in the summers are pretty crazy."

She giggles and tucks her short hair behind her ears. "I think I can handle it."

I laugh too, because it's kind of hard not to. "I bet you can."

She bounces a little. "Okay, well, see ya."

I watch her run down the beach toward the rental cottages, and I pick up my board and start home.

Our small, one-story, three-bedroom house is located smack dab in the middle of the island, where most of the locals live, which means it's about a ten-minute walk from any of the beaches. I've never minded it, though. I've always loved strolling through the town. The different smells and sounds. The subtle shift in scenery as you go from the tourist pockets into the local neighborhoods.

I've lived in this house my entire life. When my father was twenty-two, he came to the Locks for a summer vacation with his parents, sister, aunt and uncle, and three cousins. This was back when the island was just starting to become a destination spot. He met my mother—a local girl—on his third day, and basically he never left. I've always liked hearing the story of how my parents met, how my father gave up everything—his first big job, his apartment in the city, his life—just for my mom. It reminds me of what I promised to do for Harper. Only in reverse.

When I walk through the front door ten minutes later, the house is quiet. Jasper and Jake are both passed out on the couch in front of the TV. The title menu of the movie they were watching is on the screen, the DVD having run through the entire film and its credits.

I grab the remote and switch off the TV. I scoop up Jasper first, who hangs limply in my arms like a dead body, his head falling back over my arm, his arm flung into my face. I set him on the top bunk and return to the living room. Jake is the opposite. He curls up tightly against my chest when I lift him, like he's trying to fit into a too-small cocoon. You don't have to wonder who took up the most space in the womb.

Once they're both tucked in, I retreat to my own room and collapse onto the bed—wet bathing suit and all. It's then that I realize I left my T-shirt on the beach somewhere. There's no use in going back to find it. It's probably already a victim of the tide. Not that I have the energy to get up.

I know I should at least change out of my bathing suit, but my legs are far too sore and my eyelids are far too heavy. Just as my eyes drift closed, I catch a glimpse of the moon through my open bedroom window. Once again it looks completely different.

That fickle thing.

CHAPTER 9

I'm able to hide out in Grayson's house for more than a week before the guys stage an intervention. Mike and Grayson barge into the Cartwrights' guest room, which I've turned into my own little man cave, and rip the guitar right from my hands.

"The poetry too," Grayson orders Mike. "Search the room. Find the poetry."

"Guys," I gripe. "What are you doing? There's no *poetry.*"

"Found it!" Mike says, holding up a yellow legal pad that I swiped from Mr. Cartwright's office a few days ago.

"There's always poetry," Grayson says smugly.

I jump to my feet and try to snatch the pad from Mike's hand, but he holds it high over his head like we're still nine years old and playing keep-away with the ball. And who do you think was *always* the one they were keeping the ball away from?

Mike throws the pad to Grayson, who catches it awkwardly with his left hand.

"Give it back," I demand. "That's private."

"Don't worry. I have no desire to read your sappy poems," Grayson says. "We're just here to save you from yourself."

"I don't need saving," I tell him.

Grayson carries my legal pad and guitar down the hall, places both in a closet, and locks the door with a key that he stashes somewhere in his bedroom. "You'll get those back after the party."

I groan. "*No.* No parties."

"Fine," Grayson says, crossing his arms. "Then no guitar."

I look to Mike behind us and appeal to him with my most pathetic look. He just shrugs.

I surrender a sigh. "What's the party?"

The Mexican-themed fiesta at the beach club pool is already in full swing when we arrive. Mike grabs us beers, and we stand off to the side and watch the tourists make fools of themselves, trying to do line dances that are way too complicated, to music that's way too old.

I really don't want to be here.

I appreciate the gesture, I suppose. The guys are only trying to help. But sometimes I wish they would just talk to me. Like friends are supposed to do. Instead of dragging me to these stupid shindigs. Do they really think that a bunch of drunk tourists and outdated songs are going to help?

I spot Whitney right away. She's sitting on a lounge chair, talking to a guy I've seen hanging around the past few summers but whose name I've never bothered to learn. I've tried my best to avoid her around the house the past week. Actually, I've done my best to avoid everyone. I've pretty much stayed holed up in my room, playing guitar (or trying to) and watching reruns of *Crusade of Kings* while I wait in agony for the next new episode to air, which, coincidentally, is tonight.

I notice that Whitney isn't dressed in her usual getup. She's wearing jeans and a basic black tank top, and she still has her glasses on. And instead of the sleek, straight look she usually wears, her hair is wavy and untamed.

She probably broke her straightening iron when she was beating me up with it.

I watch the guy crack some joke and use it as an opportunity to place a hand on her knee. She laughs loudly at whatever he said, tossing her head around and accidentally catching my eye in the process. She shoots me a dirty look, and I drop my gaze to the sand.

I feel my blood pressure spike. I don't know what it is about that girl, but she completely stresses me out.

As I continue to glance around the pool, I get a nauseating sense of déjà vu. Not just because this party feels nearly identical to last week's clambake on the beach, but because it feels nearly identical to every party everywhere, going all the way back to the beginning of time. There are always two kinds of people at parties: the kind who join in and enjoy themselves—people like Whitney and Grayson and, according to my mom, my father—and the kind like me, who will never feel like they ever belong at a party.

Sure, it was fine last summer and all the summers before that when I could paint on a breezy smile and drink a few beers to loosen up and joke around with the guys. I used to be able to tolerate it. More often than not I even had a relatively good time. But everything is different this summer. Not just with me. Mike and Grayson seem different too. I can feel it in the stiff way Mike is standing, like a petrified tree, and the way Grayson is staring off into the distance while he mindlessly sips his beer.

There's a dreary fog that has settled over our little group. A weight dragging us down. I have a chilling premonition that if we keep going this way, it's going to drag us right down to the bottom of the ocean.

And I just can't bring myself to fake that smile anymore. My paint is all dried up.

"Remember that one summer when we smeared dog shit on the bonfire logs?" Grayson is the first to break the ice.

Mike laughs at the memory. "That was hilarious. Everyone was trying to pretend that the entire beach didn't smell like burning crap!"

"And remember that time we dared those tourist girls to skinny-dip and then we hid all of their clothes?" Grayson says.

"What was that?" Mike asks. "Three years ago?"

"Four," I respond tonelessly. "I remember because Grayson had just gotten his braces off and he couldn't stop licking his own teeth like a pervy porn star."

Grayson guffaws. "That's right. That was the summer I hooked up with Courtney Willows. She was hot. Whatever happened to her?"

"What's the matter?" Mike teases, nodding at the crowd. "Not satisfied with the selection tonight?"

Mike slugs him in the arm, and I notice Grayson wince just a little too much.

"Shall we start the bets, gentlemen?" Mike asks, scanning the crowd. "I spy a brunette with—"

"No," Grayson says, and I instantly hear the edge to his voice. Grayson must hear it himself, because his next words are much more playful. "Not tonight. All the best players need some time on the bench every once in a while. Even me."

Mike laughs, but it sounds strained. I wonder if he's nervous about bumping into Harper here. If he is, he hasn't said as much. So far there's been so sign of her. If she has any heart left, she'll stay far away from here and give the poor guy a break.

My gaze wanders back to the cluster of lounge chairs where Whitney is sitting, except she's not there anymore. The chairs have been claimed by a family of four sharing a plate of nachos. The guy she was talking to is gone too.

I blink and glance around the party, feeling a strange twist in my gut. I quickly shake it away. Why the hell do I care where Whitney goes or who she goes with?

I don't.

The DJ plays "Macarena" next, and the tourists cheer. It wouldn't be a summer pool party without a bunch of old white people pretending they can dance to Latin beats.

"Well, that's my cue to leave," I say, tossing my empty beer can into the nearest trash can.

"What?" Grayson says. "You can't leave yet. We just got here."

"Yeah, but *Crusade of Kings* starts in a few minutes."

"That's what DVRs are for," Grayson argues. "We can all watch it together tomorrow. Like we always do."

"You said I had to *come* to the party. You didn't say anything about how long I had to stay."

"But Mike's not even drunk enough yet to do the chicken dance."

"Hey!" Mike interjects. "I don't *do* the chicken dance." He pauses to sip his beer. "I *rock* the chicken dance."

"See?" Grayson says. "C'mon. You have to stay. We're having fun."

There's a bizarre anxiety in his voice. I know he probably doesn't intend for me to hear it, but I do. For some reason he seems desperate to act like this is just another summer. And maybe for him it is.

But it's not for me.

I feel a ripple of frustration move through me.

Doesn't he get it? My father is dead. I'm never going

to have just another normal summer ever again. Why does Grayson think he can just bring up all of these past memories—things that we *used* to do—and it will make everything okay?

Reminiscing about the good stuff in the past won't erase the bad. It will only make it hurt worse.

I know the guy is trying, but it's just too much.

"Hey, Macarena!" I hear someone yell, exceptionally loud over all the other voices. I look up to see my mother among the line dancers, one hand raised in the air, the other wrapped tightly around a plastic wineglass. She does the requisite end-of-verse hop to change directions, and chardonnay sloshes over the rim, spilling all down the front of her dress. She laughs like this is the funniest thing ever.

If I wasn't ready to leave a minute ago, I certainly am now.

I wrap a hand around Grayson's forearm and give it a squeeze. "Sorry, man. I gotta go."

I turn to leave just as my mother spots me. Her face brightens. "Ian! Where have you been? I haven't seen you all week! You have to come dance with us!"

I give her a meager wave and take off toward the beach. My mom keeps calling and calling, her voice getting angrier with each step I take. I cringe with each repetition of my name.

Ian. Ian. IAN.

By the time I'm halfway to the Cartwrights' house, it sounds less like a name and more like a dying bird.

I feel a stab of guilt as I plod down the beach, sand slipping between my feet and my sandals. I probably shouldn't have just left her there. Especially in the state she's in. But I can't bring myself to go back. Plus, I'm sure my grandparents are there. They can help her get home.

That's two disastrous parties in one week. Two nights I've left my drunk mother to make a fool of herself in front of the entire island. Two times I've retreated down this very beach to the soundtrack of fading music and rising waves.

Will every night here be exactly the same?

I don't know why I let Grayson and Mike talk me into this. If I'm going to live the same day over and over again, I'd rather do it locked in a dark room.

By the time I get to the house, I'm already planning to raid Grayson's bedroom in search of the key that will free my captured guitar from the closet, but I freeze in my tracks when I hear voices. Loud, hostile voices. Coming from the window I climbed through just a week ago.

Whitney's room.

"Stop!" Whitney cries out.

"C'mon," a male voice says. "I know you've done it with half this island."

"I have not!"

"That's not what people are saying. But don't worry about it. I like girls who know what they want."

"I don't want this," Whitney snaps.

"Sure you do."

I hear a struggle and a few grunts, and then Whitney yells, "Get off me, you douche bag!"

And that's all it takes for me to complete this déjà vu night by diving right back through Whitney Cartwright's bedroom window.

CHAPTER 10

o, how's work?" I ask Mike after Ian leaves.

He shrugs. "Same grass, different day."

I nod, taking a sip of my beer, looking out at all the people gathered around the beach club pool. "Remember that time we put laundry detergent in the hot tub, and the next day this entire area was overrun with soap bubbles?"

Mike smiles but doesn't laugh. "Yeah. That was funny."

I prod him with my cup. "And remember that time Whitney had a slumber party and we replaced all the Oreo cookie filling with toothpaste?" I let out a loud guffaw and then cringe at how fake it sounds.

He chuckles halfheartedly. "Another classic."

I blow out a breath. God, trying to make conversation with Mike is like trying to make conversation with a turtle who refuses to come out of its shell. I wonder if my attempts sound as desperate aloud as they do in my head. I don't know how many more rambunctious stories of our childhood I can rehash before I just run out.

Why is it so awkward? Between all of us? It used to be so easy. We didn't have to reminiscence about old memories, because we were too busy making new ones.

I know Ian's dealing with some pretty heavy shit with his dad passing away and everything. I've been trying to get him to talk about it all week. I've asked him repeatedly how he's doing, hoping he'll open up and tell me what's on his mind. But he always just mumbles a one-word answer and then disappears into the guest room. So I've pretty much given up.

I want so badly to forget about all this crap in our lives and just have a good summer. A last summer. Before we each ship off to our real lives. Before Mike moves to New York with Harper (if they're even back together by then). Before Ian goes off and becomes some hotshot moody solo artist. Before I start Vanderbilt in the fall as their starting quarterback.

Yeah, right.

I can barely even hold a beer in my right hand, let alone throw a perfect spiral. My future feels so derailed, it would take a miracle to get it back on track.

My dad tried to bring it up yesterday, while Ian was locked in the guest room, strumming the world's most depressing chord progression, and my sister was off traipsing around the island doing God knows what with God knows who.

The Cartwrights. If we're not known for our abundance of cash, we're known for other abundances.

"Hey, you wanna toss a few on the beach?" my dad asked. He had already fished the football out of the shed and was passing it back and forth from hand to hand. He threw it to me across the kitchen. It was a perfect throw. It sailed over the island, spiraling beautifully through the air. Apparently my dad still has it, even if I don't.

I tried to catch it left-handed, afraid if I used my other arm, I wouldn't be able to hide the pain. It was ugly. It fumbled through my useless fingers. I curled my chest around it, but it simply bounced off and knocked right into the spice rack, sending bottles of paprika, curry powder, and cumin crashing to the counter.

It still smells like an Indian restaurant in there.

I tried to pass it off with a laugh, but the suspicion on my dad's face was unmistakable.

"Looks like you could use some practice." He tried for a joke. It failed.

"Maybe later," I said, attempting to sound casual as I opened the fridge. I took out a carton of eggs, milk, and every vegetable I could find. I didn't know what I was going to do with it all—make the world's most loaded omelet?— but I needed somewhere to point my gaze. I needed something to do with my hands.

Thankfully, my dad did what we Cartwrights do best: he avoided the issue altogether. He placed the football down on the counter and walked out of the room. After his footsteps retreated, I closed the fridge and stared at the ball.

It said more just by sitting there than my dad ever could.

Thankfully, he got called back to the mainland for some business and left this morning.

I down the rest of my beer and crush the cup. "Want another?" I ask Mike.

He seems distracted by something—thinking about Harper, no doubt—but he nods. "Sure. Thanks."

I dash up to the bar just as someone turns around with two full cups in their hand and nearly dumps both of them down the front of my shirt. I jump back just in time to avoid the beer bath and look up to see Harper trying to recover her drinks.

Shit.

I feel a flash of anger at the sight of her standing there,

dressed in an as-sexy-as-hell sundress, her lips stained bright pink. Why is she here? She had to know Mike would be here. Is she trying to mess with his head by flaunting her perfect little body at him? And who is that other beer for? Most likely some rebound guy she brought along. This girl is a real piece of work.

"Hey," she murmurs softly, refusing to meet my eye. For some reason she looks embarrassed, obviously at having been caught lurking around this party. She knows I hate it when she plays these kinds of games.

"Hey," I mumble dismissively as I step around her to the bar. When I glance back again, I don't see her. Hopefully, she's scurried off somewhere. Hopefully, to the other side of the island.

As I carry the beers back, I silently debate whether or not I should tell Mike that Harper is here. Or should I just try to discreetly lead him away and suggest we go hang out somewhere else?

But I soon realize it's a moot point, because when I reach Mike, I find him staring intently at something on the other side of the pool. His eyes are narrowed and his stance is rigid. I follow his gaze to see Harper sitting on a chair in one of the cabanas, sipping her beer and chatting with Bree Olsen, another local girl who went to school with Mike and Harper.

Well, at least it's not a guy.

I hand Mike his drink. He chugs half of it.

"She had no right coming here," I grumble, trying to be helpful.

Mike scoffs. "She had every right coming here. It's a public party."

"Yeah, but you know what I mean. It's an unspoken rule."

Mike's face is inscrutable, like he's mentally chewing on something. Then he says, "I'm going to talk to her."

I launch my good arm out to stop him. "No way. I can't let you do that, man."

"Why not?"

"Because she ended it. It will only make you look pathetic."

Mike snorts. "She didn't end it. She only *said* she was ending it. You know she never means it."

I have a mental flash of Harper sitting on the beach last week, bawling her eyes out, babbling something about how messed up she is.

"Dude," I say sternly. "How long are you going to let her keep this shit up?"

Mike finally diverts his gaze from Harper to me. I take that as a sign to keep talking. "I mean, seriously. How many times has she pulled this on you? Twenty? Fifty? A bajillion?"

Mike looks into his half-empty cup. "I stopped counting."

I smack his shoulder with the back of my hand. "See what I mean? When is enough going to be enough? When do you finally recognize that she's insensitive and manipulative? At what point do you finally get fed up and just, I don't know, *not* be there when she comes running back to you?"

Mike sighs. He knows I'm right. I can see it in the surrendering slouch of his shoulders and the downward pull of his mouth. I hate that he's so tormented like this. It makes my anger toward Harper flare up all over again.

"*I'm* going to talk to her," I resolve.

"No," Mike says, pulling on my sleeve. "Don't. It'll only make things worse. Besides, I think I'm going to leave anyway."

"Not you, too." I hate how whiny my voice sounds.

"Sorry, man," Mike says. "I have to wake up early tomorrow. I'm starting a new job."

"Another one?" I ask, surprised.

Mike looks uncomfortable as he finishes off his beer. "Yeah." He swallows. "I'm trying to save up this summer."

For some reason I get the distinct impression that Mike is lying. He's never been very good at it. But I'm not going to pressure him. If there's something he doesn't want to tell me, then there's a reason. And I certainly can't argue with him having to leave early because of a second job. I mean, without sounding like a spoiled, rich asshole.

"Okay." I finally give up. "But are you still coming by to watch *Crusade of Kings* tomorrow? Rumor has it douchey King Kleo is finally getting whacked."

He shrugs. "I don't know. I guess I'll see how I feel."

Mike holds out his fist to me, and I smile. My hand moves instinctively, running through the steps of our secret handshake: fist bump, then two taps on the top, two taps on the bottom, finishing off with a palm-to-palm finger wiggle. The three of us made it up when we were eight years old, thinking it was the coolest thing in the world. We still break it out from time to time.

When we smoothly slide our hands away from each other, Mike laughs. This time it actually sounds genuine. Then he pats me on the back and disappears in the direction of the club's main building. I turn my gaze to Harper. She's watching him leave, a pained expression on her face.

Don't go after him, I silently warn her. *Don't you dare go after him.*

Thankfully, she doesn't. She refocuses back on Bree. But just as she's turning her head, her eyes find mine. I expect her to look away. I expect *me* to look away. But, for some reason, neither of us does.

That is, until another face appears right in front of me.

"Hi!" says a bouncy, high-pitched voice.

It takes me a moment to recognize the girl. Nicole. Non-Leggy Seashell Barrette from the last party. The one who stormed off my boat only twenty minutes after she stepped onto it.

What is she so giddy about? I thought she hated me.

"Hi," I reply cautiously. I lean left to steal another peek at Harper over the girl's shoulder, but Harper has already gone back to her conversation.

"How have you been?" Nicole says, and I immediately smell the booze on her breath. She's tipsy.

"I didn't think you'd ever want to talk to me again." I'm surprised by my own bluntness, but I'm just not in the mood to play games tonight.

She bites her lip thoughtfully. "Yeah, about that. I've been thinking. I'm sorry about everything. It was totally my fault."

Say what?

"I was drunk and came on way too strong," she continues. "And there you were trying to be a gentleman about it and not rush things. It was sweet. And I totally overreacted. So I'm sorry."

I'm 170 percent sure that's *not* how it happened. She was half-naked in the bed, grinding on top of me, and I pushed her off and said I wasn't feeling it.

"I'm willing to give it another shot, if you are."

I look into the girl's hopeful (half-glazed) eyes, and I feel a tug of something familiar deep inside. I could do it. I could take her somewhere right now and we could hook up and I could be the same old Grayson Cartwright I came to this island to be.

But then, out of the corner of my eye, I see Harper

Jennings stand up from her chair and start walking around the pool, toward the clubhouse. I automatically search for Bree and find her in a conversation with Noah, one of Mike's friends from school. This means Harper is alone.

She's going after him! The nerve of that girl.

"So," Nicole says, bringing me back to the conversation. "What do you think?"

I place my hands tenderly on her shoulders and say in the gentlest voice that I have, "I just don't think it's going to happen with us. I'm sorry, Nicole."

Then I take off after Harper. I may not be the same Grayson Cartwright who sleeps with random tourists anymore, but I'm still the same Grayson Cartwright who looks out for his friends. And I'll be damned if I let Harper ruin another one of Mike's summers.

CHAPTER 11

As soon as I'm away from the pool, I feel the knot in my chest start to unravel. There was something about that party. It was suffocating. Not just because Harper was there. And not just because we had our first kiss in the deep end of that very pool. It was something else.

It was Grayson.

He's always been a pretty wound-up kind of guy. He has his dad to thank for that. But tonight it was different. There was a desperation about him. An uneasiness. It was circling around us like flies around a carcass.

Or maybe Ian's situation was just making him uncomfortable. I know it has been making me uncomfortable. The guy has been through so much, but I don't know how to talk to him about it. I keep hoping he'll bring it up first so I don't have to pry, but he never does.

At first I was kind of bummed that I'd have to work all summer, but now, after tonight, I'm almost feeling relieved.

The shortest route to the other side of the beach club's main building is through the kitchen. When I get there, something is burning in the oven.

I lunge for the controls and turn off the heat. When I

open the oven door, the smell of burned bread stings my nostrils. I wave away the smoke, grab a pot holder, and remove a tray of charred biscuits from the rack.

I look around for Mamma V, the beach club's head chef, and finally find her asleep in a nearby chair. It's not like her to let things burn. I think about waking her, but she looks so peaceful. So instead I head into the supply closet, grab an oversize chef's coat, and drape it gently over her like a blanket. I'm not sure why Joey, the owner of the joint, insists on ordering these chef coats from the uniform company when Mamma V refuses to wear them. She says only amateurs wear chef jackets. The real chefs—people like her—don't need to prove themselves with fancy getups.

She startles and snorts when the fabric brushes against her skin, but then quickly settles back into her nap.

Mamma V is like a second mother to me. To Ian, Grayson, and me, really. She's lived and worked on this island for longer than I can remember. Sometimes when I was a kid and my parents had overlapping shifts at their jobs, they would bring me here so Mamma V could babysit. I would hang out in the kitchen while she cooked. She would stand me up on a chair and let me put vegetables into the food processor or stir cake batter. Then, when I turned thirteen, she got me my first job washing dishes. Legally you're not allowed to work in this state until you're sixteen, but no one seemed to care. And definitely no one argued with Mamma V.

She also has never told anyone her real name. She insists that everyone call her Mamma V, even though she has no children. I always wondered what the *V* stood for. I asked several times growing up, but she'd always just wink or tweak my nose and then make up some obviously ludicrous answer like, "'Mamma Velociraptor' if you don't scrub those pots hard enough." Or "'Mamma Vengeance' if you get on my bad side." Or "'Mamma Very Pleased to Meet You,' if I like the look of you."

I'm almost to the back door when she snorts awake, looking confused and disoriented. Her face softens when she sees me. "Mikey!" she croaks in her usual smoker voice (even though she swears she's never touched the stuff). She tries to stand, but it's clearly difficult. I run over to help her up and feel a pang of concern.

How old *is* Mamma V?

I remember her seeming like an old lady even back when I was a kid. But I never recall her having trouble getting around the kitchen.

"What happened?" she asks, glancing around like she doesn't recognize her surroundings. "Where's my biscuits?"

I cringe. "I think they're toast."

"Not toast. Biscuits."

"I mean they're burned."

She waves this away and hobbles over to the tray. I can see the distress etched into her face. And I can also see the moment she decides to conceal it. "Don't be ridiculous. They're supposed to be like this. I'm trying out a new recipe."

I stare, dumbfounded, at the as-black-as-night biscuits, then back at Mamma V. "Are you feeling okay?" I ask.

"Of course, Mikey. I'm feeling fine. You go on home. I'm going to butter these biscuits."

I'm anxious about leaving her alone, but when I linger in the doorway, she shoos me again. "Go!"

So I do.

It isn't until I'm halfway through the grounds that I remember I left my phone in the employee break room this afternoon, and have to turn around. Normally I would just leave it and come back for it in the morning—I've never been overly attached to my phone—but my dad's friend Dave is supposed to text me first thing tomorrow morning with the address of the roofing job.

I went to see him about it earlier in the week, just as I promised my dad I would. Dave was worried about the fact that I've never worked on a roof by myself before, but I assured him I would be fine. I've helped my dad on enough of his jobs that I'm confident I can hold my own.

I jog into the break room and yank open the door of my locker. My phone is waiting for me on the top shelf. I pocket it, slam the door, and spin around, coming face-to-face with a girl covered head to toe in every color of paint imaginable.

It's that cute girl who tried to rescue me from not drowning last week, although it takes me a second to recognize her without the wet duck pajamas . . . and with the green paint in her hair.

"Hey!" I say, suddenly realizing I never actually got her name.

"Julie," she says, reading my mind. "Kind of hard to believe that of all the words that came out of my mouth that night, my name wasn't one of them."

I chuckle. "That's okay. I'm Mike."

"I know."

"You do?"

"Your name came up the other day when I was talking to one of my coworkers. Apparently you're a legend around this place. Have you really been working here since you were twelve?"

"Thirteen, actually."

She shakes her head in disbelief. "Amazing."

"Not really. It just means I haven't had a life since I hit puberty."

She laughs so hard, she actually snorts. It's kind of adorable.

I glance down at her outfit. It's the usual club employee getup: khaki shorts and a white polo shirt. Except hers looks like a badly replicated Monet. "Well, you apparently had an interesting day."

She sighs. "Yeah. Remind me to never do craft hour after Popsicle time. Sugar rushes and wet paint *don't* mix."

I take a step back, admiring the artwork on her uniform. "I don't know. I think you might have something here. Maybe impressionist."

"Oh, no," she deadpans. "It's cubism all the way. When that five-year-old is dead, this polo shirt is going to be worth a fortune."

I laugh. "It looks good on you."

It isn't until her face flushes with color that I realize what I've said. Was I flirting? I certainly didn't mean to. I've never been very good at the flirting thing. I've never really had to get good at it. Harper and I have been dating since we were twelve.

I try to backpedal. "I mean, the *art* looks good. Not the polo shirt. It's hard to look good in those stupid club uniforms. Not that you look *bad* in it. It's just, you know, a polo shirt."

And now I'm rambling.

She giggles. "Well, I better go finish cleaning up the room. If you think my shirt looks good, you should see the walls."

"Do you need help?" My mouth says the words even though my body screams in protest. I'm so tired, and I have such a long day tomorrow.

Thankfully, she says, "Oh gosh, no. I'll be fine. I put on cheesy pop music and make a dance out of it. It's probably not your type of music."

The image of Julie dancing around the kids' camp, scrubbing paint off the walls, makes me smile. "You're probably right." I start for the door.

"Mike?" she says, and her voice reveals just the slightest flicker of hesitation.

I turn around. "Yeah?"

She fidgets with the hem of her painted shirt. "I'm new to Winlock Harbor, like I said, and I was just wondering, since you seem to be a pro, if maybe you could give me a tour tomorrow. Show me around a little?"

My heart lifts, and then immediately plummets back down again.

Is she asking me as a date? Or just as friends? Are we friends?

"Oh," I falter, feeling stupid. "I . . . I actually have to work tomorrow."

"Right," she says hastily. "Of course. Right. You work a lot. I get that. Totally. Okay, well, see ya." She turns toward her locker and swings the door open.

I stand there like an idiot, my mind whirling. Suddenly all I can see is Harper in that amazing sundress tonight, laughing and drinking with Bree like nothing ever happened between us. And then suddenly all I can hear are Grayson's words to me before I left.

"At what point do you finally get fed up and just, I don't know, not be there when she comes running back to you?"

"Maybe some other time?" I blurt out to Julie before I can stop myself.

She beams back at me. "Sure. Whenever you're ready, I'm around."

And as I walk out of the employee break room, I can't help but wonder if I'll ever be ready.

CHAPTER 12

The first time I ever threw a punch was the day we received the medal from the army.

It had been a week since we'd gotten the phone call politely informing us that my father was dead, and my mother's screams were still constantly echoing in my ears.

I didn't know what to do. I tried to comfort her, but there was no room for that. All of her brothers and sisters were so tightly crammed around, it was almost impossible to get to her. Like they'd built a fortress of bodies and I didn't know the password.

The first few days I was numb. I couldn't play guitar. I couldn't speak. I couldn't feel. I could sense the emotions on standby, leaning impatiently against the door, waiting until I turned the knob and they all came tumbling into my life.

I was able to keep them at bay for almost a week. Then the medal came. My mother opened the package and fell apart all over again. It dropped to the floor and spilled out of its little box. My eyes tracked it as it bounced twice in slow motion before coming to rest near the foot of the coatrack, where my dad's winter coat was still hanging, reminding me that he would forever be cold, from that moment on.

All I could focus on was how gold the medal was. So bright and shiny that it hurt my eyes. Like looking directly at the sun. I knew my dad had received it because he'd been courageous. Because he'd sacrificed his own life for the lives of his men. Somewhere out there people were living because of him. Somewhere out there people were eating, drinking, breathing, running, jumping, sleeping, waking, laughing, crying, while all we had was this shiny piece of shit on the floor of our crappy apartment.

I turned, right then and there, and rammed my fist into the door.

It hurt like hell. I sprained three fingers. I couldn't play guitar for a month. And yet I didn't even cry out. I didn't feel a thing.

My dad had tried to teach me to fight my entire life, and I would never partake. He signed me up for karate when I was seven; I quit after one class. He installed a punching bag in my room when I was twelve; I used it to hang clothes on. When we would come to Winlock Harbor in the summers, Grayson and Mike were the ones he would wrestle with and play army base with on the beach, while I sat in a nearby chair and read. When I turned eighteen, he tried to get me to enlist, but I had no interest.

Even though he would never say it, I think he was always disappointed that I hadn't inherited his competitive streak. His need for physicality. I always thought it was stupid. Punching something to release your anger.

I guess I had just never been angry enough.

Despite my one-hit-wonder punching match with the apartment door, I've never actually been in a *real* fight before. Something I might have been wise to remember before I dove through the window of Whitney's bedroom like a wannabe action star.

But I wasn't fueled by wisdom at that moment. I was fueled by something else. Something I hadn't felt since that day they delivered my father's medal.

I catch them both by surprise when I tumble onto the hardwood floor. They're on the bed. He's on top of her, pinning her down with his hands. Her tank top is pushed up, revealing her bra underneath, and her jeans are unbuttoned.

Something animalistic comes over me and I lunge forward, grab the guy by the shoulders, and rip him off her. He's on his feet in a second, throwing the first punch. I dodge that one easily and feel pretty good about myself. Until the second punch hits me in the side of the face and knocks me right off my feet. Even though I've never fought before, I know that being on the floor this early is a bad thing.

I scramble to my knees just as his foot makes contact with my stomach. I let out a groan. I suddenly wish I had paid more attention in that one karate class.

I can write a ballad that will sweep a girl right off her feet, but when it comes to actually saving her, it turns out I'm pretty useless.

The guy gets in two more blows to the stomach before I collapse again. I cough, and blood trickles out of my mouth.

I can hear my dad's voice in my head. *Get up, Ian! Fight back!*

But I've already given up. The guy has already won. I'm just going to have to live with the fact that I tried to rescue Whitney and I failed. If Grayson were here, this would be another story. He'd have the guy pinned and pleading for mercy by now. Even Mike would have thrown a stupid punch. I just stood there and let myself be taken down.

I cover my head and brace myself for more blows. He'll

want to finish me off. He'll want to make sure I'm really down.

I try to disappear. I try to escape this moment by retreating into my head, so I don't have to be here. So I don't have to acknowledge the fact that I'm a big fat failure. That I let my dad down in more ways than one.

I think about my mom dancing the Macarena on the beach. I think about my grandparents cooking breakfast together in the kitchen the way they do every morning. I think about fishing with my father. I think about Whitney beating me with a straightening iron.

Then suddenly my thoughts are interrupted by a loud, girly shriek.

Panicked, I lift my head and pop to my feet, discovering an untapped well of strength.

But what I see stops me cold.

The guy is on his knees, hunched over, his forehead resting on the ground. He's moaning in agony. I recognize the sound of that agony. It's a pain only another man can fully understand.

Whitney stands next to him, breathing heavily.

"What did you do?" I ask dazedly.

"What do you think I did? I kicked him in the nads."

My eyes widen. That was *him* who screamed like that? I stare back and forth between Whitney and her attacker — who has now become the attackee — and I can't seem to find the right words. Or any words, for that matter.

Whitney, however, doesn't seem to have that problem. "You're welcome."

An hour later I'm holding a cold compress to the side of my head while Whitney is frantically cleaning her bedroom, trying to erase all signs of the struggle. Apparently I didn't even realize I crashed into a lamp when I fell to the ground in my champion prize fight.

"Are you sure you don't want to call the police?" I ask for the tenth time.

She sighs, growing impatient with me. "Yes."

"I don't get why you'd just let him walk out of here."

"Well," she says with a smile as she sweeps shattered pieces of light bulb into a dustpan, "he didn't really *walk*. It was more of a hobble."

"This is no time for jokes. He *attacked* you."

She shakes her head. "It was a misunderstanding."

"A misunderstanding?" I yell way too loudly. It echoes in my damaged brain, causing the room to spin a little. "C'mon, Whitney. I know you're not that stupid."

She freezes, her body hunched over the dustpan. I can't see her face, so I can't read her expression, but it doesn't seem to matter, because a second later she resumes sweeping. "I gave off the wrong signal. Apparently that's what I do. *Apparently* what I think is a profound, meaningful conversation is actually just foreplay."

For the first time since this whole ordeal began—maybe even for the first time ever—I hear the fragility in her voice. I catch a peek at the vulnerability under her tough exterior. And it stabs me in the chest.

"You have to tell your dad," I say quietly. "Or at least Grayson."

She points the full dustpan at me. "And you need to keep pressing those frozen peas to your head. Maybe it'll freeze your brain so you'll stop coming up with boneheaded ideas."

"I don't think you get how serious this is," I go on. "If I hadn't come in, he would've . . . he could've . . ." But I can't even bring myself to say the words.

Whitney laughs. "If you hadn't come in and kicked the shit out of him?"

I scowl. "You know what I mean."

She dumps the glass pieces into a trash bag. "Look. I'll make you a deal. You won't tell anyone what happened here tonight, and I won't tell anyone that you got your ass saved by a girl."

"But if we tell the police—" I begin.

Whitney cuts me off, all the playfulness drained from her voice. "If we tell the police, the whole island is going to know what went down here, and then the whole island is going to be thinking, 'Well, it's Whitney Cartwright. What did you expect?'"

I fall silent.

Does she really think that?

"Whitney," I begin hesitantly, "why did you stop coming to Winlock Harbor?"

She doesn't answer. She just goes to work spritzing the hardwood floor with cleaner and wiping up my blood with a paper towel.

"Whit . . . ," I implore, using Grayson's nickname for her.

"You, of all people, Ian, should know what it's like to have things said behind your back."

I recoil. "What's that supposed to mean?"

She rolls her eyes. "Don't play dumb."

"I'm not. What are people saying?"

"Only the truth!" she cries. "That your father is dead. That your mother is drinking. That you aren't handling it well at all."

"How the fuck am I supposed to handle it?" I roar, tears springing to my eyes. I swat them away. "What am I supposed to do? Erect a park bench? Join a grief support group? Here's a news flash for you, Whitney. There is no way to handle it well. And what my mother drinks or does not drink is no one's goddamn business."

I storm out of Whitney's room, stomp down the hallway to the guest room, and slam the door. It takes me a few minutes and several deep breaths to calm down, but once I do, that's when I finally realize what just happened.

She manipulated me.

That sneaky girl.

I shake my head in disbelief and yank the door back open. I march back down the hallway, ready to give her an earful. Ready to let her know, quite forcefully if I have to, that I'm onto her games. She can't just turn the conversation around because she doesn't want to face what happened. She can't just name drop my dead dad and borderline alcoholic mother to avoid dealing with her own crap.

I'm not falling for it.

Her door is closed. I try the handle but it's locked. I rap hard and wait. There's a long pause before she says, "Go away."

"I know what you just did, Whitney. You can't turn this around on me. This is not about me."

Another really long pause. It feels like hours before she responds again. "I said GO AWAY, Ian."

I let out a huff and plod back to the guest room. I pace the length of the room for a good five minutes, trying to work off the steam that's rapidly rising inside me.

Why is that girl so infuriating?

And the better question, why do I even let her get to me?

I flip on the TV and navigate the DVR to the recorded episode of *Crusade of Kings*. Even though five people die in the first five minutes, I can't sit still long enough to keep watching.

My fingers twitch. I try to shake them out. I make a fist

and release it over and over again, but nothing works.

I know exactly what this feeling is. And I know there's only one way to get rid of it.

I yank open my door again and practically run into Grayson's room. I search every drawer until I finally find what I'm looking for—the key.

I open the hall closet, grab my guitar and legal pad, and carry them back to the guest room, then slam the door behind me and lock myself inside.

I sit cross-legged on the bed, press record on my phone, and start playing. Words and melodies and chords pour out of me so fast, I can barely keep up.

I don't even hear them. I live inside them. I become them and they become me.

I don't stop until the song is finished.

By then it's four in the morning.

CHAPTER 13

I find Harper in the beach club's deserted kids' camp. She's sitting on the edge of the small kiddie pool with her bare feet in the water. She's inched up her sundress so the tops of her thighs are visible. Her lean, tan legs look incredible in the pool lights. I force myself to look elsewhere.

It's not the first time I've noticed Harper. After all, we grew up together. I remember the summer when my family came back to the island and she magically had breasts. Mike caught me staring at them once and got really upset. But can you honestly blame me? I was thirteen. And Harper is a knockout. She always has been. But from that day on I trained myself to keep my eyes above the neckline. Out of respect for Mike.

"You thought I was going after him, didn't you?" Harper says as I approach. She barely even looks up from the water. I wonder how she knew it was me.

I shrug and sit down next to her, kicking off my flip-flops and dipping my feet into the warm water.

"I thought about it," she admits.

"What made you change your mind?"

"That." She nods to a garden shed designed to look like a small cottage just outside the pool's gate.

I smile at the memory. It was six summers ago. We were twelve and decided to play Spin the Bottle. It was Harper's idea. She'd seen it in a movie or something. She gathered Bree and Riley, two of her friends from school, and Mike gathered me and Ian, and the six of us sat in a circle inside the shed where they keep the lawn mowers and weed whackers and bags of mulch.

We didn't have a bottle, so we used a flashlight we'd found.

Mike and Harper weren't exactly an official item yet, but it was only a matter of time. They spent nearly every waking moment together. Their chemistry was palpable even back then.

Harper was the first to spin, and the flashlight landed on me. There was no room for interpretation. It was pointed directly at me. If the thing had been on, it would have been a spotlight. Instinctively I looked to Mike, but he was unreadable. His eyes were cast to the ground.

Harper started to crawl toward me, her lips pursed.

I knew, from her previous lengthy explanation of the rules, how this was supposed to work. I was supposed to meet her halfway. We were supposed to kiss in the middle. But suddenly I couldn't move.

I remember how scared I was. This was going to be my first kiss. And it was going to be with the girl I knew Mike was in love with, even if he didn't quite know it yet himself.

It didn't feel right.

In fact, it felt so wrong, I thought I might throw up. I may not have been experienced with girls yet, but I *did* know that vomiting into a girl's mouth was not the right move.

Bree nudged me with her knee. "That's you," she whispered. "Go kiss her."

My mouth went bone-dry as I started to lean forward, as I started the slow crawl toward the center of the circle.

Time stood still.

I could feel Harper's breath as her mouth neared mine. I could see her eyes close, because mine were still wide open. I could smell her cherry-flavored lip gloss.

But I never tasted it.

Because before our lips could touch, Mike jumped up from the circle. "I have a stomachache," he proclaimed, like he was making an official statement to the press. Then he ran out of the shed. We all watched him in shock, none of us quite knowing what to do. Were we supposed to chase after him? Were we supposed to continue on with the game? Was I still supposed to kiss Harper?

Thankfully, she answered that question for me when she sat back down, a glum look on her face.

We all stared at each other for a few seconds, and then the game just kind of fizzled out and the group disbanded. I didn't see Mike for the rest of the day.

"I didn't go after him then," Harper says to me, bringing me back to the present moment. The kiddie pool. Her hiked-up sundress. The lights shining on her gorgeous legs. "Even though I knew he wanted me to. I was only twelve years old, and I knew that was what I was supposed to do. But I was too scared."

"We all were," I say.

"Tonight it was like the other way around. I knew he didn't want me to follow him, and suddenly that was all I wanted to do. Then I saw the shed, and I don't know, my feet just stopped moving."

I nod but don't say anything.

"Do you remember what happened after that? After he ran away?" Harper asks with a tinge of playfulness in her voice. She splashes water at me with her feet.

I feel my cheeks warm, and I lower my head to avoid her gaze. "Of course I do. How could I forget?"

We fall silent, letting the memory sit there between us like a third person.

"You're a good friend," Harper says after a while. "To Mike. You've always been good to him, even when I've been shitty to him."

"Hey, you said it. I didn't."

She laughs. It lifts the mood a bit.

"I know what you think of me. You think I string him along. You think I play games with his head."

I open my mouth to protest, even though I'm not sure why.

She holds up a hand to stop me. "And you're right. I have strung him along. But don't think for a minute that I haven't felt awful about it. Don't think for a minute that I haven't hated myself for it. I'm not like you, Grayson. I don't make the right decisions all the time. I don't have successful footsteps to follow in. I'm running blind here, trying to figure it out as I go."

I chew on the inside of my cheek for a second before finally mumbling, "I don't make the right decisions all the time."

She guffaws. "Yeah, right. What was your last big mistake? Choosing a Beemer over a Benz?"

"No," I reply blankly. "It was crashing that Beemer into a tree after my mom walked out on us."

I can't believe I just said that. I can't believe I just admitted all the things I promised I would never admit. And to Harper Jennings, of all people. I feel incredibly stupid as soon as I do. And yet, at the same time, I feel like a huge weight has been lifted.

Plus, the look on her face is pretty priceless.

She slowly puts the pieces together. "Your arm."

"It wasn't a football injury. And yet I'm not sure I'll ever be able to play football again. I'm not even sure I want to."

Harper is completely silent.

But for some reason, I suddenly can't stop talking. "I'm not who you think I am. I'm not who anybody thinks I am. I mean, maybe I was at some point. Maybe I used to be. But that guy died in that car accident. And I'm his fucked-up replacement."

Then suddenly Harper's lips are on mine. There's no buildup, there's no slow crawl to the center of the circle. It just happens. One minute I'm babbling incoherently, and the next she's kissing me. And I'm kissing her back. And it feels amazing. And I hate myself for even thinking that.

I pull away, and her hand instinctively goes to her mouth. Like she could possibly erase the last ten seconds from existence.

My gaze lifts, and there she is. So close. Her eyes staring back into mine. Her expression mirroring the same conflict that's ripping me apart inside.

That shouldn't have happened.

That shouldn't have felt so good.

"I'm sorr—" she tries to say, but I cut her off. I kiss her so hard, we nearly tumble right into the pool.

I don't know why I do it. Maybe to stop her apology from coming out. Maybe to keep my mind from getting tangled up in the implications of the first kiss.

Maybe to prove to her once and for all that I'm not the guy who's incapable of making mistakes. Because this might be the biggest one I've ever made.

She reaches up and tangles her fingers into my hair. I press one hand against her lower back, the other resting on her thigh. It's just as smooth and soft and perfect as I always imagined.

This time it's Harper who pulls away. And this time her eyes don't linger on mine, searching for something that will make it all okay. This time she stands up, grabs her sandals, and runs off without another word.

I sit there, motionless and numb, for a good sixty seconds, trying to keep the enemy emotions at bay. Trying to ward off an army.

But it's no use. The fight has already begun. My thoughts are already at war. It's going to be a bloody battle.

I push myself off the edge of the pool and slide under the shallow water with all my clothes on. I lie on the bottom of the pool, counting the seconds until I run out of air and have to resurface.

It's the only place in the world where I can't hear my mind screaming.

CHAPTER 14

The next morning I awake to a cacophony of suspicious sounds coming from the kitchen. When I burst in a few seconds later, I expect to find one of the twins dead in a pile of cereal. But instead I find a poorly constructed barricade of pots and pans on the floor, with Jake and Jasper positioned behind it. My mom, dressed in her work uniform with her dark hair pinned back, stands at the stove, stirring oatmeal with a familiar look of frustration on her face. It's one we all wear far too often in this house.

"What's going on here?" I say, stepping forward to give my mom a kiss on the cheek. I can't help noticing how tired she looks. There are lines on her face that I swear weren't there last week.

"We're staging a coop!" Jasper yells like a battle cry. Jake raises a wooden spoon in the air and waves it wildly.

I look to Mom.

"They don't want oatmeal," she translates. "We were out of cereal, and I couldn't make it to Coconut's last night before they closed. My shift ran late."

"I'll try to go tonight," I tell her, then turn to Jasper. "Where did you even learn that phrase?"

"*Crusade of Kings*," Jasper says.

Mom and I share a look, mutually calculating the level of childhood innocence that has just been flushed down the toilet.

"I thought Dad was supposed to put a password on the DVR," I say.

"His leg's been bothering him," she explains. "He's still asleep."

"I'll wake him up," I say. "I'm supposed to start the roofing job today. He'll need to watch the boys."

I scurry down the hall to my parents' bedroom. My dad is completely passed out, one arm hanging off the bed, the other flung over his face. I notice a bottle of prescription painkillers on the nightstand. He must have been in a lot of pain. I can barely convince him to take Advil when he has a headache.

That means his leg is not healing the way he keeps insisting it is.

That means it's going to be even longer before he's back at work.

And that also means I can't leave the boys here. My dad is dead to the world, and the villains are in rare form this morning. They're already staging coups over oatmeal. It can only go downhill from here.

I close my eyes, pushing down a swell of frustration that threatens to rise up. How much longer can we keep going like this?

"I want Apple Jacks!" I hear Jasper scream from the kitchen.

"No!" Jake screams back. "I want the Apple Jacks!"

Great. Now they're arguing over phantom cereal.

I hurry back to the scene of the crime. My mom is pouring oatmeal into bowls. She sets them on the table. I pick

Jasper up from the floor and deposit him into a chair, then do the same with Jake.

They cross their arms simultaneously, glaring stubbornly at the oatmeal. They really are a unified front.

Mom sighs. "I can't do this today," she whispers under her breath, her voice breaking.

I put my arm around her. "Mom. Go to work. I'll handle this. And don't worry. I'm sure it's just a phase."

Her face breaks into a grateful smile. She gently touches my cheek, then slips out the front door without putting up a fight.

"Okay," I say, clapping my hands. "How about I buy a big box of Apple Jacks tonight and for now everyone eats oatmeal?" I glance around the kitchen. "Wait, where's the dog?"

"We locked him in the pantry," Jasper explains. "He was being naughty."

Shit.

I yank open the pantry door, already knowing what I'll find. And yup, there he is, covered head to toe in flour, chocolate syrup, and about a thousand other random ingredients. The pantry is trashed. The mutt has gotten into just about everything within reach.

The dog runs into the kitchen, flour following in his wake like a storm cloud. Jake and Jasper think this is the funniest thing ever. They squeal in delight.

"Walter!" I call after the dog as he makes a bee line for the sofa.

"His name is Phil now!" Jasper calls after me.

"I don't give a crap what his name is!" I yell back, trapping the dog just before he dusts the couch with a layer of flour.

"Ooh!" Jake scolds. "You said the *C* word."

"Trust me," I grumble as I grab the dog by the collar and guide him out the back door. "That's *not* the *C* word."

"Yeah," Jasper says knowingly. "Everyone knows the *C* word is 'cow plop.'"

This cracks both of them up. "Cow plop! Cow plop! Cow plop!"

I tie Phil to the long line, turn on the hose, and give him a quick rinse. He shakes violently, drenching me with water. I suck in a deep breath. I'm about this close to losing it.

"All right!" I say sternly as I step back into the kitchen. "I want everyone to get dressed and meet me back in this kitchen in *ten* minutes."

"But we didn't get breakfast," Jasper protests.

"This is not a negotiation. Either you do it or I give the dog away."

They both look to each other, silently deliberating whether or not my threat is credible. And you know what? At this point it is.

Fortunately, they believe me. After a chorus of grunting and grousing, the twins begrudgingly rise out of their seats and shuffle to their bedroom.

"Ten minutes!" I call after them.

I dress in my work clothes, run some cold water over my face, brush my teeth, and grab my cell phone from the charging cable. I look at the screen. The text I've been waiting for hasn't arrived yet. Dave is supposed to send me the address for the roofing job.

Fortunately, I was able to convince my boss at the beach club to let me set my own hours. "As long as that grass doesn't cover my toes and I don't spot a single weed, you can come at two in the morning, for all I care," were his exact words to me.

I promised him I wouldn't let him down.

With a little luck I just *might* be able to pull this off.

Miraculously, when I get back to the kitchen, the twins are waiting there fully dressed and ready to go. They've even eaten some of the oatmeal. They're wearing mismatched socks and their hair is a mess, but you pick your battles.

"Where are we going?" Jasper asks as I hustle them out the door and into my dad's truck.

"I'm dropping you off somewhere for the day. You'll have fun."

They give me identical suspicious looks as they buckle themselves into the cab. "Where?" Jake asks.

I sigh. "You'll see."

When we arrive at the outdoor playground of the beach club's kids' camp a few minutes later, Julie greets me with a huge smile. She's wearing the same khaki shorts and white polo—this time minus the paint—and I can't help but notice how good she looks. Obviously, she's a gorgeous girl. That was obvious from the moment I met her. But today, I don't know, something is different. Seeing her just immediately puts me in a good mood. Which is a welcome change from the shitty morning I've been having.

"And who are these handsome gentlemen?" she asks, bending down to make eye contact with the boys before glancing up at me through her dark eyelashes.

Jasper, normally the bold and courageous one, turns beet red and hides behind my leg.

"Jasper and Jake, my brothers. I'm really sorry to ask this, but I'm in a bit of a jam. I'm starting a new job today and, well . . . Do you think I might be able to leave them here for a few hours?"

"Of course!" She stands up. "I'd be delighted to have them."

I cringe. "I wouldn't speak too soon. They're a bit of a handful."

She laughs like I'm joking.

"I'm not joking," I assure her.

"You forget I'm a professional."

"That you might be, but they're professional monsters, so . . ."

Before I can finish, she squats down, and Jasper retreats further behind my leg. "I bet you can't guess what number I'm thinking of," she says to him.

Jasper contemplates this challenge for a minute. "What do I get if I do?"

I chuckle. "Always the negotiator."

Julie pretends to think long and hard. "You get to play with the very special toys."

He twists his mouth in deep concentration.

"What are the special toys?" Jake butts in.

She shrugs. "I can't tell you until you guess the number. But unfortunately, I don't think you'll get to play with them. No one has *ever* guessed the right number."

"Seven!" Jasper blurts out, taking a brave step out from behind the safety of my leg.

Julie's jaw drops open. "What! How did you do that?"

Jasper takes another step forward, smiling broadly at his victory. "Mom says we're psychic 'cause we're twins."

"Hmm," Julie says thoughtfully. "I don't know. I think that was just a fluke." She turns to Jake. "If you two really *are* psychic, then you'll be able to guess the next number."

"Nine!" Jake shouts without delay.

Julie giggles. "Hold on. I haven't even thought of it yet!"

I watch this whole spectacle with great fascination. Within seconds she's got the two of them practically eating out of her hand.

"Okay," she prompts Jake. "I'm ready."

Jasper watches him, biting his lip in anticipation. Julie has a smug look on her face, certain that she'll win this time.

"Um . . ." Jake hesitates.

"Think hard," Jasper commands him.

Jake closes his eyes tight and scrunches up his face. Julie looks up at me again, and we share a smile.

Jake's eyes flash open decisively. "Eighteen!"

The reaction on Julie's face is priceless. Her eyes spread wide, and she falls back onto her butt in the sand. "W-w-what?" she stammers. "H-h-how? I don't understand! That's impossible!"

Jake and Jasper squeal in delight and jump up and down.

"How did you do that?" she asks them in shock.

They're giggling so hard, they can't even respond. Even I find myself chuckling a little at the charade.

"That's Mike's age!" Jake gives away his secret. "Eighteen!"

Julie slaps her head. "It is? That's my age too! I guess I shouldn't have picked such an easy number, huh?"

"Now we get to play with the special toys?" Jasper confirms.

Julie pushes herself to her feet, wiping sand from the back of her khaki shorts. "I guess I have no choice but to let you."

She looks at me. "What time will you be back to get them?"

I wince. "Is five o'clock too late?"

She waves her hand. "Of course not. I'll be here until six, so that's fine."

I shift nervously from foot to foot, feeling super-uncomfortable for even asking, but I know I have to.

"About the tuition," I begin, scratching at the stubble on my face. With all the commotion this morning, I totally forgot to shave.

She holds up a hand. "Don't worry about it." Then she leans in close to me, and I can smell her citrusy shampoo. "No one has to know."

I still feel weird about the whole thing. I hate asking people for charity. But I admit that I'm totally relieved to hear her say that. Even with the discount for locals, the kids' camp tuition is pretty ridiculous this year. And there's no way we could leave these two with Mamma V like my parents used to do with me. Every guest in the restaurant would end up with earthworms in their spaghetti.

"Thanks," I say appreciatively. "I owe you big-time."

Jasper tugs at Julie's shirt. "Special toys. Special toys."

Julie laughs and takes each of them by the hand. "Go," she tells me as she begins to lead them away. "I've got this."

"If you have any trouble," I call after her, "I've found that threats work really well."

I watch in utter disbelief as Julie brings Jasper and Jake over to a group of kids their age and whispers something into each of their ears. They both nod and start playing quietly with the other children.

I'm beginning to think the girl is pure magic.

I wave good bye to Julie and start to walk back to the parking lot, just as my phone vibrates in my pocket. I pull it out and glance at the screen. It's a text from Dave. He's finally sent me the address for the roofing job.

321 Sea Star Lane. Be there by 9.

I stop dead in my tracks. I know that house. I practically grew up at that house. But I've never had to actually *work* in that house. In all the summers the guys and I have been friends, money has never divided us. It's never even been an issue. At least not for me, and I'm the poorest of the group.

But we've also never been in a situation like this.

There's no way I can turn the job down now, though. Not after Dave pulled so many strings to get it for me, and we *really* need the money.

Nope, this is happening.

I'm just going to have to find a way to come to terms with the fact that for the next two months I will be fixing the roof over Grayson Cartwright's head.

CHAPTER 15

I wake up with a fog around my head. My vision is swimming and my temples throb.

It feels like the University of Pennsylvania marching band is practicing right inside my brain.

Emotional hangovers. That's what my therapist calls them. It feels like you've consumed all the booze in a twenty-mile radius even if you haven't had a drop to drink.

I've had one every single morning since my dad died.

"Grief can be just as intoxicating as alcohol," my therapist told me.

I made a joke that I'd rather just have beer. At least then you have a fun night to blame the headache on. He did not appreciate my humor.

It also doesn't help that I got my face smashed in last night and then I barely got any sleep. I spent nearly the whole night working on my song, tweaking some of the lyrics and chord progressions and practicing it over and over again. For the first time in months, I felt inspired by something, felt like I was actually creating something worthwhile. It might just be the best thing I've ever written.

Too bad it's about someone I can't stand.

Never in a million years did I ever think Whitney

Cartwright would serve as my muse. But apparently the girl infuriated me to the point where I became a decent songwriter.

I push myself out of bed and pad into the bathroom, my usual morning queasiness following me like a shadow. I check my reflection in the mirror, cringing when I see the aftermath of my one-sided fight with douche pants. I admit it's bad, but it's not *that* bad. It could have been way worse. If Whitney hadn't stepped in. Or rather, *kicked* in. My lip is busted, my cheek is bruised, and my left eye looks like it's been crying red food coloring all night, but hopefully my face will be healed in a few days.

I pull on swim trunks and a T-shirt and wander to the kitchen, passing Whitney's door on the way. I consider knocking to see if she's awake, but then I think better of it. She'll come out of there soon enough. And then maybe I can actually talk some sense into her and convince her to call the police about what happened.

I head into the kitchen to make some coffee. I pour the grinds into the filter, fill the reservoir with water, and flip the switch. I watch the slow drip, drip, drip of the coffeemaker as it fills the pot. It starts to lull me into a trance, until the spell is shattered by the sound of the landline phone ringing. I look around for someone to answer it. Even though I've been living here for more than a week, it's not really my place to answer the phone.

It stops ringing. Then immediately starts again.

With a sigh I pick it up. "Hello? Cartwright residence."

"Ian."

My whole body freezes as all of the light and energy immediately gets sucked out of the house.

I consider hanging up. I consider throwing the phone into the pool. But I know I can't do that.

"Mom," I reply through gritted teeth.

"Good morning, my love. How are you?"

I search her voice for signs of intoxication. Would she really start drinking this early? Who knows? Thankfully, she sounds relatively sober.

"Why are you calling here?" I ask, keeping my tone formal and impervious.

"Because you haven't been answering your cell. Or returning any of my texts."

I feel my hand grip tighter around the receiver. She's right. I haven't. And for a very good reason. I've been trying to avoid this very conversation and this very feeling that's knotting up my stomach.

"How's Grayson's?" she asks cheerfully, and I know exactly what she's doing. She's trying to butter me up before she drops the bomb. Before she starts talking about *him*. "Are you having a good time?"

"Yes," I reply tightly.

"Your grandparents and I miss you." She lets out a laugh. "They've started watching some horrific show. *Battle of Kings* or something. It's so violent. I can hear the bloody battles from my room! But they seem to enjoy it. It's all they can talk about."

A faint smile spreads across my lips at the thought of Nana and Papa sitting through one of those episodes. Can their hearts even survive all that brutality?

"It's *Crusade of Kings*, Mom."

"What?"

"Never mind. Did you need something?"

She sighs. "Yes, actually. I could really use your help with something."

I plop down onto one of the stools at the kitchen counter and run my finger over the flawless marble countertop. "With what?"

"I was hoping you could come by today and help me clean out some boxes in the garage."

My spine stiffens.

Clean out boxes.

That's code for "dig up the past and reminisce about better days," when my father was alive and we were a real family. Not these broken pieces that once made up something whole.

It feels like my family used to travel the world on this happy, colorful merry-go-round, bobbing up and down on beautifully painted porcelain horses, throwing our heads back in laughter. But then my dad's death cranked the lever up to full speed, spinning us faster and faster until we could no longer hold on. Until we were both flung off the ride in different directions. My mom landed in a bottle of chardonnay. And I landed here. At Grayson's house. With nothing to keep me company but my guitar and a collection of *Crusade of Kings* reruns on demand.

"Your grandparents are too old to be moving all of that stuff, and—"

"I can't," I tell her hastily. "I'm busy today."

"What about tomorrow?"

"I'm busy tomorrow, too."

She falls quiet. I hope that means she got the message. I'm not interested in going down memory lane with my sobbing three-sheets-to-the-wind mother. I'm not interested in unpacking the past. The past is better off staying sealed in boxes.

"Fine," comes her terse response a few seconds later. "I'll do it myself."

I grip the phone more tightly, feeling the familiar guilt and tension settle atop my shoulders, weighing me down like a ton of bricks.

I should help her.

I shouldn't be so hard on her.

She lost someone too.

But just as I'm about to change my mind and tell her I'll stop by, she says, "You know, Ian, you shouldn't be avoiding your feelings like this. It's not healthy."

And then I remember why I left. Why I'm staying here. It's to avoid statements like that.

I have a burning desire to fling the accusation back at her, asking if I should just get smashed off my face every night like she does. Is *that* the best way to own up to my feelings? And she thinks I'm the unhealthy one? At least I'm not making a fool of myself in front of the entire island every night. At least I'm dealing with my pain in an artistic, creative way.

She's just a walking cliché.

But I know I can't say any of that. No matter how angry I am, she's still my mother. And I know she's in mourning. But that doesn't mean I have to sit in the front row and watch as she self-destructs.

"Okay," I say into the phone. "Well, thanks for the call. This has been pleasant, as always. Good-bye."

Frustrated, I hang up and slam the phone back into the charger.

Just then Whitney comes striding into the kitchen wearing shorts and a tank top. She freezes when she sees me, and then turns her back to pour herself a cup of coffee from the pot I just made. She suddenly becomes super-interested in a pile of mail on the counter.

I roll my eyes and push past her, grab a mug from the cabinet, and fill it.

"You're still here," she intones, flipping open a clothing catalog.

I sneer and take a sip from my mug, but it's way too hot,

and the damn coffee burns a hole in my tongue. "Shit!" I swear, and spit it out into the sink.

Whitney does little to hide her smirk. "That's the thing about coffee," she says breezily. "It's best served hot."

I fight back a bitter retort and stick my mouth under the faucet, letting the cold water run over my tongue. Whitney watches me with a disturbed expression. "Oh, Ian. When did you get to be so classy?"

I shut off the faucet and try my coffee again, this time making sure to blow on it first.

My phone dings in my pocket, and I pull it out to find a text message from my mom. I delete it without reading it and stuff the phone back into my pocket with a huff.

Whitney cocks an eyebrow at me as she flips another page of her catalog. "Girl trouble?" she asks.

I snort. "You wouldn't understand."

She grabs her coffee and takes a sip. "Why don't you try me?"

"Why don't we talk about last night instead?"

She flips another page. "You mean your face? It looks pretty bad. Did you fall out of bed?"

"Don't do that."

"Do what?"

"That!" I say, growing impatient. "Don't pretend like nothing happened."

"Nothing *did* happen," she snaps, shutting the catalog. "Not to mention the fact that it's none of your goddamn business, so just stay out of it."

"Fine," I agree tightly. "I'll stay out of yours if you stay out of mine."

"Gladly." She pours her untouched coffee down the drain, drops the mug into the sink with a *clank*, and storms down the hallway to her room.

Agitated and all riled up, I trudge out the back door to the patio and stare at the magnificent view, hoping it will help steady my erratic breathing. The crystal-blue water of the infinity pool sparkling in the morning sun. The ocean glistening just a few feet beyond. The sound of seagulls fishing for breakfast echoing in the breeze.

And yet I can't bring myself to see it. All I see is a pool that will no longer feel soothing to swim in. An ocean that will never again wash away my troubles as easily as it once did. A beach that my dad will never set foot on again.

My father's death has ruined this island. Ruined everything that I used to love.

The wind picks up, and I hear a bizarre slapping sound. Curious, I walk around the side of the house. Whitney's bedroom window is wide open, and the curtains are blowing wildly, smacking against the wall.

I feel my teeth gnash together as I lean into the open window and glance around the empty bedroom. The bed is unmade, there are heaps of clothes on the floor, and Whitney is nowhere to be found.

As someone who's made a habit of sneaking in and out of windows, I immediately recognize the signs of a hasty exit.

CHAPTER 16

I dream about the accident. It's been a common dream lately. Except instead of stumbling dazedly out of the wrecked car, holding my shattered, throbbing arm in my hand, the door is stuck. I can't open it. Then the car catches fire. It flares up all around me, stinging my eyes and burning my skin.

I wake up sweaty and breathless, with an ache in my arm that feels like my flesh really is on fire.

I get up and scrounge around in the bathroom for some Advil. The bottle says to take two. I pop six into my mouth and swallow them dry. They burn going down. Like a lump in my throat that will never go away. A mistake that I'll never be able to forget.

My head hasn't stopped pounding since last night. It started shortly after Harper stuck her tongue in my mouth. I've tried to tell myself that it was all *her* fault. That she's completely to blame. That this is the very reason I've never liked Harper Jennings—because she sticks her tongue in other guys' mouths while her on-again, off-again boyfriend (my best friend!) nurses a broken heart less than a mile away.

I continually try to delude myself into thinking I'm blameless in this whole thing.

But then, without fail, the full memory—the truth—comes barreling into my mind like a high-definition freight train.

I kissed her back.

Then I just kissed her.

Who does that? Who kisses their best friend's ex-girlfriend? Who is that shitty a person?

Unfortunately, the answer is obvious.

I'm on a real roll this year.

I hear my phone vibrate, and it takes me a good five minutes to locate it in my room. It's buried under a pile of clothes. I check the screen to see I missed a call from my mother.

Good, I think bitterly. *I wouldn't have answered anyway.*

Then I notice I have four unread text messages. All from Harper. My pulse kicks it up a notch as I open the app and read them one by one.

I think we should talk.

I'm kind of freaking out.

Grayson! Text me back!

Fine. I'm coming over.

My gaze darts to the time stamps. The last one was sent more than fifteen minutes ago. I start to panic. She can't come over. She can't be in this house. Ian is still crashing in the guest room. What if he sees her? What if she starts yelling at me and he overhears? What if he pieces it together and tells Mike?

I hastily tap out a reply.

Don't come over. I'll meet you somewhere.

A few seconds later, she texts back.

Too late. I'm already here.

The doorbell rings, and I nearly jump out of my boxers. I scramble to throw on a T-shirt and shorts and run for the door, just barely managing to beat Ian, who, for some reason, looks like he's been in the boxing ring with a rabid kangaroo.

I stop just short of the door, momentarily forgetting about the disaster that's waiting outside. "Dude, what happened to your face?"

He reaches up to touch his purple cheek, and winces, his gaze darting irritably in the direction of the bedrooms and then back to me. "I fell out of bed," he mutters.

I scowl. "Were you sleeping on the roof? Jeez, that looks bad."

"It's no big deal." He ducks his head and reaches for the doorknob.

"I've got it!" I say, gently nudging him aside. I try to sound cheery and not at all as frantic as I feel, but Ian gives me a strange look, letting me know how miserably I've failed.

"Fine," he says, holding his hands up like a caught criminal. "What is *with* everyone today?" He backs away, mumbling something about going to watch TV.

I open the door a sliver, slip through the crack, and yank the door closed behind me.

Much to my dismay, Harper looks incredible. Again. She's wearing cutoff shorts and some sort of strapless tube top thing. Her golden hair is loose, falling around her shoulders in glossy waves. If she's going to just show up here with barely any notice, the least she could do is look like crap.

"What are you doing here?" I hiss. I take her by the hand and lead her around to the pool in the back of the house.

"We need to talk," she says, looking down. That's when I notice I'm still holding her hand.

I quickly release it.

"Ian's here," I tell her sharply.

"So?"

I glance over her shoulder and immediately realize that the pool was a mistake. The windows in the living room look right out at us. I can see Ian carrying a bowl of cereal from the kitchen to the couch. He flips on the TV and sits down, propping his feet on the coffee table.

I grab her hand again and lead her around to the other side of the house, behind one of the landscaped hedges. "*So*," I repeat, flustered. "It's Ian. If he sees us together, he might suspect things."

"You're acting kind of crazy," she points out.

"You *think*? I kissed my best friend's girlfriend. Of course I'm acting crazy!"

"*Ex*-girlfriend."

I throw my hands up in exasperation. "That doesn't matter."

"So you agree it was wrong?"

"Uh, yeah, it was wrong."

She sighs in relief. "Good. Me too. I was up all night thinking about it. I feel horrible. I wanted to come by and tell you that it can't happen again."

"Yes. I mean, no. Never again. Absolutely."

She nods. "Good. And also, we can't tell Mike."

Just his name on her lips makes my stomach convulse. "Agreed."

She sighs again. This time her breath hits my face, and I smell cherries. It immediately brings me back to that garden shed, when Harper's flashlight landed on me. Does she wear the same lip gloss she wore when she was twelve?

"I'm so glad we're on the same page about this," she says.

"Me too." I feel the knot in my chest start to unwind. Maybe this doesn't spell complete disaster. Maybe this was just a simple mistake that both of us can own up to and agree to never repeat. Then we can move on with our lives.

"Hug?" Harper asks, already stepping toward me with her arms outstretched.

I'm not sure it's such a good idea—being that close to her—but I don't really have time to react. Harper's arms are suddenly around me. Her body is suddenly pressed into me. She's not wearing a bra.

And that smell. What is that? It's like she bottled everything I love about summer and rolled in it.

But I can't just stand here with my arms hanging down like a chump. I have to hug her back.

She moves her head ever so slightly, and I can feel her breath on my ear. It's having a serious effect on me. The kind of effect a girl can feel when she's pressed this tightly against you.

I need to pull away. This needs to not be happening.

"Oh shit," Harper says, her body tensing.

Damn it. It's too late. She's already felt it. She already knows.

"Mike," she whispers into my ear, which totally confuses me, not to mention, completely solves the little problem I was having.

I pull back and hold her by the shoulders. "Okay, whispering his name into my ear is not making this any less awkward."

"No," she says quietly through clenched teeth. "I mean *Mike*. He's here."

CHAPTER 17

During the whole drive to Grayson's house, I tried to figure out what to say once I arrived.

Surprise! I'm going to be hanging out here every day.

Surprise! I'm now just another hired hand at the Cartwright house.

Surprise! I need your dad's money to pay my dad's mortgage.

I assured myself repeatedly that Grayson won't mind. He's never let money be an issue with us. One summer a few years back, the cleaning service that my mother works for assigned her to clean the Cartwrights' house. Grayson never let it get weird, though. He was always extra polite and respectful. He treated my mom like his own mom.

I was grateful, however, when the house got assigned to another employee the next summer.

By the time I park my dad's truck in the driveway, I decide it would be best to clear the air with Grayson first. Before I climb up a ladder and start banging around on his roof.

I stand nervously on the front porch and ring the doorbell. Then I stuff my hands into my pockets. Ian answers a few seconds later with a hell of a shiner. He looks genuinely confused to see me.

"I thought you were Grayson," he says.

"What the hell happened to you? Did you stumble into a bar fight on your way home from the party or something?"

"Or something," he mumbles.

I take a step closer to examine his face. "Did you put ice on it?"

"Yes," he says dismissively, moving away from me. Whatever happened, he clearly doesn't want to talk about it, so I let it drop. "So, Grayson's not here?"

I admit I feel somewhat relieved. Maybe it would be easier to just start working and explain myself later.

"Dunno," Ian says. "Someone rang the bell, and before I could answer it, he disappeared out the front door and hasn't come back since."

"Probably another random girl he hooked up with," I say with a laugh, hoping it will raise Ian's spirits a bit. He's obviously in a miserable mood.

He barely cracks a smile. "Probably. Although he was acting really cagey. It was weird. So, are you coming to hang out?" His spirits seem to lift at the question, which makes mine shatter into a million pieces. "I haven't watched the newest *Crusade of Kings* yet. I mean, I only watched the first five minutes of it. We could put it on."

I feel a stab of guilt in my chest. *Crusade of Kings* has been one of our summertime staples for the past three years. The new season always starts in mid-June and goes through the end of August, ceremoniously marking the start and end of each summer. We always used to watch the new episodes together when they aired Sunday nights or first thing Monday mornings, commiserating over the loss of our favorite characters, cringing at the gratuitously violent battle scenes, and drinking at every single appearance of female genitalia. Needless to say, we were always pretty wasted by the end of the sixty minutes. It's hard to imagine a summer in the Locks without that tradition. But things happen and things change.

"Actually," I say remorsefully, "I can't. I'm starting a new job today."

Baffled, Ian looks around the outside of the house. "What? Here?"

I point up. "There. I'm replacing the roof."

Ian peers behind me at the truck in the driveway with the Metzler Roofing logo on the side, and a flash of comprehension comes over his face. He must know why I'm so uncomfortable right now. If anyone gets what it's like to be an outsider on your own island, it's him. Even though he's not technically a local, he's not really a tourist, either. His grandparents have a house on the beach, but they certainly aren't dripping with cash like all of their neighbors. Ian and I have always had a kind of kinship that way. The two "poorer" friends of Grayson Cartwright.

"Is that gonna be weird?" he asks.

I shrug. "I hope not. But I'm gonna talk to Grayson about it, just to make sure."

"Good idea. Maybe check around by the pool?"

"Thanks. I'll see you around?"

"Sure," he mumbles, and it's like I can see the cloud of heaviness drift back over him again. I feel the urge to question him about it, but what do I say? How do I even bring it up?

"You doing okay?" I ask lamely.

He seems to perk up a little at the question. "As good as can be expected, I guess."

And then he just watches me, like he's waiting for me to dish out some Yoda-like wisdom about life and death and the great, unexplained mysteries of the universe. But I don't have any of that. I don't know any of that wisdom. So I just say, "Good. Well, I better get to work."

"Yeah," Ian mutters. "See ya."

"Maybe we can watch the episode when I'm done?"

Ian nods. "Okay." And then he closes the door.

I walk around the side of the house to the pool but am stopped halfway when Grayson suddenly comes spilling out of the bushes, looking incredibly flustered.

"Mike!" he says, his voice way too high and squeaky for a six-foot-two football player.

"Hi," I say hesitantly. "What are you doing out here?"

He brushes a few stray leaves from his shirt. "Me? Oh, you know, just trimming some edges."

"You mean 'hedges'?"

He seems completely distracted, like he can't quite focus on my face. "Yeah. That."

I have to laugh at the idea of Grayson doing yard work. Or any work at all, for that matter. "Since when do you garden?"

"Uh," he says haltingly. "Since recently. I just got into it."

I look back to the bush he just tumbled out of. For a second I swear I see it move, but it's probably only the breeze. I point to an overgrown bulge on the side and start walking toward it. "Looks like you missed a spot."

Grayson lets out a strange yelping sound and runs to step in front of me. "Let's not talk about gardening. That's so boring. What's up? Why are you here?"

I almost forgot the real reason I came. For just a second it was every other summer, and I simply stopped by to hang out at Grayson's pool or play football on the beach.

Then the second is over and the reality of *this* summer comes rushing back to me.

I take a deep breath and steel myself for what I'm about to say. "Actually, there's something I want to talk to you about. It's a little . . . um, awkward."

Grayson looks like he just swallowed a spider. He glances uneasily over his shoulder. "Sure. What is it?"

"I didn't really want to bring it up because it's kind of, I don't know, embarrassing, but now I think I have to."

Grayson looks confused. His brow furrows tightly, and he rubs at the stubble on his chin. "Okaaay," he says slowly, like he's convinced I'm going to say something horrible next.

"A few months ago my dad had an accident on a roofing job. He hurt his leg. It's not healing the way the doctors want, so he hasn't been able to work for a while. That's why I've had to pick up some of the slack this summer to help with the bills, and my dad got word of a new roofing job and . . ." I let my voice trail off, hoping Grayson will pick up on the implication and I won't actually have to spell it out, but he still looks like he hasn't followed anything I've said.

"I didn't know it was here until after I agreed to take it," I tell him. "I just hope it won't be, you know, weird."

"Wait," he says, after an awfully long pause. "You're going to be working *here*? On *this* roof? All summer?"

Finally. Jeez, that took long enough.

"If it's too weird, I understand," I rush to say, looking anxiously down at my feet and praying he won't tell me that it is. "It's just that we could really use the money. And if Harper and I leave for New York in the fall—"

"Harper?" he blurts out. "You and Harper? Are you back together?"

God, he really is acting crazy. Maybe the idea of me working for his family *is* too much.

"I mean, not yet. But you know how it is. How *she* is."

"No, I don't," he snaps, startling me. "I don't know how she is. Why would I know how she is?"

"Because you told me," I say, convinced I've missed something. "We talked about this, last night at the party when you said she was insensitive and manipulative."

Grayson flinches and once again casts his eyes hastily over his shoulder.

Is he on something?

"I mean, I know you said I should move on," I continue, trying to ignore this strange behavior. "But I guess I just haven't quite given up hope yet. We've been planning this move since we were fourteen."

Grayson doesn't say anything. But he looks like he's trying to do complicated mathematics in his head.

"So, I could really use the extra cash, you know?"

His gaze darts to me. "Huh?"

"Extra cash. The roofing job. What's going on with you, man? Did you take something last night at the party?"

"What? No," he says hastily.

"So, it's okay then?"

"What's okay?"

I just have to laugh now. This is the most pointless conversation I've ever had. "Me taking this roofing job. Working here all summer. Stomping around on your roof, peering into your windows, watching your every move."

Of course I'm totally kidding with that last part, but Grayson kind of flinches when I say it.

"Oh, um, sure. Totally okay. I've got nothing to hide."

I shake my head. "Great. Well, I better get to it. I guess I'll see you around."

"Yeah, okay," he mumbles.

I walk back to the truck, pull the ladder from the bed,

and lean it against the side of the house. I climb up, then cringe as I gaze across the mansion's massive roof. I can see why they hired someone. These shingles are one storm away from total disaster.

I hear hushed voices coming from the side of the house where I just left Grayson, and I think about what Ian said a few minutes ago. How Grayson has been acting kind of cagey. I wonder what that's about. Curious, I step off the ladder onto the roof and make my way in the direction of the voices. I carefully scoot to the edge of the house and peer into the hedges below, but no one is there.

Grayson has mysteriously vanished.

CHAPTER 18

and me another box of screws," Mike calls down from the roof. I search the worktable until I find the plastic container of metal screws, then climb up the ladder to hand it to him. For the past two weeks I've been hanging out more and more with Mike while he works on Grayson's roof, because there's really not much else to do around here.

Normally we'd all pass our summer days swimming in the pool or catching footballs on the beach or watching episodes of *Crusade of Kings* until our souls couldn't take the pain anymore, but it's already Fourth of July tomorrow, and we haven't done any of those things. It's like our group is drifting apart. Mike is always either working here or mowing lawns at the beach club, and Grayson has turned into a regular Houdini. He disappears for hours on end and doesn't tell anyone where he's going.

And Whitney?

I don't even want to think about her. She's been completely avoiding me. If she's not in her room with the door locked and the music blasting, then she's off traipsing around the island somewhere. We haven't really talked since that morning after the pool party, after she nailed that douche bucket in the balls, who, come to think of it, I haven't seen around the island since. Not that I've left this house much in two weeks. Which is probably a good thing. I'm not sure what I'd do if I did see him.

Probably get my ass handed to me again.

"Are there any more boot vents down there?" Mike's face appears over the edge of the roof again.

I scan the worktable, pushing aside tools and scraps of material. "What do those look like again?"

"Tubey-looking thing with a flat base. They fit around the plumbing pipes."

I don't see anything matching that description. "I don't think so."

He climbs back down the ladder. "I'll have to swing by the hardware store to get some. Wanna come?"

I shrug. "Sure." Because, really, what else do I have to do today?

We climb into the truck and rumble out of the driveway.

"How much longer do you think the job is going to take?" I ask as he turns onto the main road.

"Probably at least another month. The roof is in terrible shape."

He rolls down the window and sticks his arm out, letting the breeze lift his hand up and down, like the ocean under his surfboard. I wonder if he even gets a chance to surf anymore. Or is he too tired at the end of the day?

"It's exhausting," he continues. "But it keeps my mind off things."

He doesn't have to say what exactly he's trying to keep his mind off. I already know. It's been almost a month since Harper ended things, and I don't think they've spoken once. Or if they have, Mike certainly hasn't said anything.

This is how we are now. We don't talk about things. At least not about anything real. We just avoid.

It's like we've settled into this comfortable little bubble of delusion.

"How's the job at the beach club?" I ask, searching for a topic to fill the silence.

"It's good," he replies. "The same." He's quiet for a second before he adds, "There's some new people working there this summer, which makes things kind of interesting."

I swear I see the hint of a smile light up his face as he says this, and I'm about to question him about it when he suddenly, out of the blue, asks, "Have you talked to Grayson recently?"

"Not really. Why?"

"Have you noticed he's been acting strange lately?"

I think about how many times Grayson has been gone before I've gotten up, and how many times he has come home after I've gone to bed. And come to think of it, whenever he is around the house, he doesn't really say much. Sure, we chitchat and joke around like usual, but he's been sort of distant. Cutting conversations short for no reason, constantly distracted by his phone.

"I guess, a little."

"He's barely said a word to me since I started the roofing job."

"That's weird," I agree.

"Do you think it bothers him? Me working at the house?"

"That doesn't seem like Grayson."

"Yeah. I know. That's why I was wondering."

"He probably just has some pop tart in town that he hasn't told us about yet. You know how Grayson gets when he finds a hot new distraction. He goes all AWOL."

"Maybe," Mike admits. "But then why ignore me for two weeks?"

"He's probably so distracted that he doesn't even realize he's doing it."

"Yeah," Mike says, but I can tell he doesn't buy it. And truthfully, I'm not sure I buy it myself.

When we get to town, Mike runs into the hardware store while I wait outside by the truck. I lean against the door and survey the little downtown area of Winlock Harbor. I always used to love it down here. All of the little shops where you can buy the most random things. Antique telephones, jams made from berries you've never heard of, and monogrammed food bowls for your dog.

My dad and I used to walk to the candy store, and we'd pick out mix-and-match saltwater taffy and eat it the entire way home. When we'd get back, our stomachs would be hurting and we'd be trying to pick all the leftovers out of our teeth for hours. My mom would yell at me for eating too much sugar and then yell at my dad for letting me.

My dad would nod and say things like, "You're absolutely right, Jackie. That was irresponsible of me." And then he would give me a wink, and two days later we'd be right back at that store.

I let my eyes drift to near the candy store, but I'm too afraid to look directly at it. Like how you're not supposed to stare right into the sun. So I let my gaze settle on Barnacle Books instead. It's a safer option. My dad was never a big reader. I remember one time when my mom took me in there to buy a birthday present for Whitney when she turned twelve. I complained the whole time, asking why I had to buy a present for someone who wasn't even my friend.

"Because she's Grayson's sister and Grayson is your friend, and she invited you to her birthday party," my mom said.

"But I'm not going," I told her.

She acted like I had just told her I'd spanked the pope. "Of course you're going. Don't be ridiculous."

"But it'll just be a bunch of girls," I said, feeling disgusted at the very thought of it. I was thirteen but had always been a little behind in the maturity department, especially when it came to the opposite sex. While Grayson had already started noticing girls and making embarrassing comments about their changing bodies, and Mike and Harper had already purportedly made out twice in some little secret alcove on the beach, I had absolutely zero experience with girls and even less interest in changing that.

I sulked the entire time my mom and I were in the bookstore. She picked out a copy of whatever popular book preteen girls were reading at the time, had it wrapped in pink heart wrapping paper, and handed it to me to deliver to Whitney.

When I got to the party, Whitney unwrapped the present right away. She took one glance at the book, and her mouth fell into a pout. She turned to one of her annoying little friends—a girl with glasses and braided pigtails—and said, "Here, Carly. Ian got you a present."

Now, while I wait for Mike to come out of the hardware store, I watch a group of older women—probably a tourist book club—enter Barnacle Books. I'm just about to turn my attention to the next store on the block when the last of the book club ladies holds the door open for a customer coming out.

My eyes nearly fall out of their sockets when I see the familiar dark skin, wavy black hair, and long, lean legs.

It's Whitney. Coming out of a bookstore. She may as well have been coming out of Diagon Alley.

She's dressed in shorts and a loose-fitting T-shirt, and

she's carrying a giant shopping bag with the Barnacle Books logo on it.

Whitney Cartwright doesn't read books.

Whitney Cartwright doesn't even want to be seen *carrying* books.

Unless that bag is full of fashion magazines, then I've definitely fallen through a wormhole and landed on the wrong planet.

I watch in awe as she carries the bag to the curb, but instead of getting into her Mercedes convertible—which, come to think of it, I haven't seen at all this summer—she places the shopping bag in a wicker basket secured to the back of a red bike that's parked nearby, and swings her leg over the seat.

Whitney is riding a bike?

The thought is just so ludicrous that I almost laugh. But in reality I'm too intrigued to laugh. She starts to pedal away, and I get this insane urge to follow her.

For no other reason than to try to solve this strange, alternate-universe mystery.

Maybe she has a secret twin who I never knew about.

A twin who reads books and wears glasses and rides bikes.

I check the hardware store again—still no sign of Mike—and decide I'm just going to steal a peek at which direction she's heading. Maybe then I can deduce where she might be going. But as soon as I cross the street, something else snags my attention.

It's the other Cartwright. Grayson. He's walking down a small alley toward the beach, and he's not alone. He's with someone. A girl.

The elusive pop tart, I presume.

Grayson stops and backs the girl up against the side of the building. He puts a hand on either side of her shoulders and leans in to kiss her.

She giggles and ducks playfully out of his reach, then runs ahead of him toward the entrance to the beach.

Well, there's one mystery solved. At least Grayson seems to be having a normal summer. I guess one of us should.

It isn't until she turns around to make sure he's chasing her—which he most certainly is—that I recognize her.

And I feel the ground tremble beneath my feet.

This is far more shocking than a bicycle-riding, book-reading, T-shirt-wearing Whitney Cartwright.

This is downright disturbing.

I always knew Grayson could be self-centered and a little arrogant, but that's usually just part of his charm. This, however, seems excessive. And just plain *wrong*.

Suddenly that haunting premonition I had at the pool party two weeks ago comes rushing back to me, crashing over me like a massive tsunami.

I had a feeling something catastrophic was coming. Something that would strike a fire and set our little friendship boat ablaze until it burned down to nothing more than a pile of rubble at the bottom of the ocean.

I just had no idea that Harper Jennings would be the match.

CHAPTER 19

The beach is packed full of people. The Fourth of July weekend visitors are already congregating, arriving by the ferry load. Harper is still running ahead of me, continuously looking back to make sure I'm following her.

Of course I'm following her.

I've spent the past sixteen days chasing after her. Up and down and back and forth and hot and cold and off and on. First she kisses me by the pool. Then the next day she tells me it was a mistake. Then that very same night she texts me and lures me out to the beach, where she proceeds to kiss me again, only to pull away and insist that it's the last time. I'm already losing count of how many "last times" we've had in the past two weeks.

And I can't just blame *her*. I know that. I'm just as desperate for her as she seems to be for me. What is that about? I can hook up with any girl on this island, and yet all I want is Harper. *Mike's* Harper! It makes me sick.

I don't want any of these beachgoers to see us together and assume something, so I stay several paces behind her, keeping her in my view the entire time. She leads me further and further away from the main beach, the population growing thinner as we go, until I realize where she's heading.

The marina.

My father's boat.

We've already hooked up twice on it in the past two weeks. It's one of the few places on the island where we don't have to worry about being spotted.

She runs ahead of me and jumps onto the bow. She looks back to flash me a seductive smile before ducking down the hatch.

I chase after her, checking the marina for nosy onlookers before hopping aboard and following her down the stairs. She grabs me and pulls me to her. We kiss so hard, we stumble over each other's feet and go toppling onto the long, upholstered bench. She climbs on top of me, straddles me, her mouth hungering for mine.

Then, just like every other time, without warning she simply stops. She stands up and wipes her mouth, leaving me lying there, breathless and totally turned on.

She starts to pace the length of the boat's small living room, running her fingers through her gorgeous blond hair. "What's wrong with us?" she cries.

I sit up but don't answer. We've had this conversation at least five times already, and it never changes.

"You're Mike's best friend."

"You don't need to remind me," I grumble.

"This is so wrong. This is *so* wrong." She collapses down next to me and starts to cry. I put an arm around her shoulders.

"Hey, hey," I soothe. "It's okay."

"It's not okay! I lie in bed at night thinking about how *not* okay it is. I promise myself it's over. It's not going to happen again. And then I see you, and, I don't know, my resolve goes out the window."

"I know," I say softly.

"Do you?" She says it like a challenge. Like she doesn't believe me. Like she thinks she's in this alone.

"Yes," I say a little too forcefully. "Do you think I like this? Do you think I want to betray my best friend? That night on the beach, when I tripped over you, I felt like my life was spinning out of control. I still do. But when we're together, suddenly it's like everything makes sense. Until my brain catches up to my body and I realize how fucked up it is, and then it all spins out of control again."

Harper gets very quiet. "You think we make sense?" she asks, her voice so broken.

I close my eyes. "I think . . ."

I don't know what I think. I don't know how I feel. I just know that when Harper is around, I want to kiss her. I want to be with her. Like I've never wanted anything else.

I just know that I've hooked up with countless girls on this island, and no one has made me feel like this.

I sigh. "Yes. I think we make so much sense that it's killing me."

She sniffles, drying her eyes. "Do you remember the first time?"

I sigh. "By the kiddie pool? Yeah. It was only a couple of weeks ago."

"No. The *first* time."

I press my lips together, feeling another cocktail of guilt and nostalgia mix dangerously in my stomach. "Yes."

I only let myself think about that night a few times a year. The rest of the time I keep it locked in a closet in the back of my mind. Like an old Halloween costume that you store in the attic. You don't need to wear it, or try it on; you just need to know it's there.

It was the night we played Spin the Flashlight in the garden shed—after Mike ran off, and the rest of us decided to go swimming in the beach club pool. It got late, and people started to go home. One by one our little group dwindled until it was just Harper and me left. We were having so much fun, I barely even noticed that we were alone until the night lights came on and I glanced around to find the rest of the pool empty.

We both started to shiver from being in the water for too long, and I noticed that my fingertips were wrinkly and Harper's lips were almost blue. She suggested we get out, and I didn't argue.

Silently we wrapped ourselves in towels and just kind of stood there on the cement, staring at each other, wondering who would speak next.

Maybe it was just me, but I felt like our "almost kiss" in the garden shed earlier was still lingering in the air, waiting to be acknowledged. Waiting to be finished.

Maybe that's why I didn't question her when she asked me to follow her. When she told me she wanted to show me something. When she led me right back into that garden shed.

When she pressed her cold, bluish lips to mine.

There was no lead-in. There was no talk. There was no time to prepare.

One moment I was following behind her, and the next she was kissing me.

It didn't last long. Maybe a few seconds. The whole thing felt kind of impersonal. Perfunctory. Like a task you check off your to-do list. There was no tongue. No open mouths. No touching. In fact, my fingers never stopped holding the towel that was draped around me like a cape.

Our lips just came together, and then they came apart.

And it was over.

"Did you ever tell anyone?" Harper asks me quietly as I fidget with a seam in the fabric of the bench seat.

I shake my head. "Never."

She laughs weakly. "Me neither."

"So Mike still thinks . . ." I start the sentence, but I'm not sure if I can finish it. My thoughts and emotions and libido and conscience are all tangled up, and no matter what I do, no matter how many nights I lie awake searching for a solution, searching for a way to make this all okay, I can't seem to untangle them.

"That he was my first kiss?" Harper finishes. "Yeah."

I let my head hang forward. "This is so messed up."

Harper is quiet for a moment before she asks, "Do you ever wonder what it would have been like if you and I had gotten together? Instead of me and Mike?"

I bite my lip, wondering if I should tell the truth, wondering how damaging it will be in the long run.

Of course I've thought about it. How could I not? Harper is beautiful and vivacious and impulsive. And that first kiss, way back when, set some tiny flame ablaze in me that I don't think ever fully went out. Despite how I've felt about the way she's treated Mike over the years, I've always found her attractive and, I suppose, even enticing in some way. But she was never an option. She was always off-limits. She was always Mike's. Her future was already decided.

Just like mine.

Until they both weren't anymore.

"Yes," I finally admit. "More than I should."

She sighs. "Me too. A lot more recently, though."

I smile. "Oh, really? My rugged good looks never did it for you before?"

She playfully slaps my arm. "Your rugged good looks

always did it for me. It was that perfect tough-guy exterior that turned me off."

The smile instantly vanishes from my face.

She must notice, because she rushes to explain. "You always seemed like you had it all figured out. You were Grayson Cartwright. Rich, talented, going places. It was impressive yet so intimidating. I always thought I could never be with someone like that. Someone who knows exactly where they're going. Because I knew I'd always feel lost in comparison. And then when you tripped over me on the beach that day, I don't know, it was like I finally saw the cracks. And I started to realize that we had more in common than I ever thought possible."

A lump forms in my throat. It's the worst thing she could have ever said to me. And the best.

She shakes her head, letting out a nervous laugh. "Anyway, ever since then I can't help thinking about what it would have been like all those years. If that first kiss between us had led to . . . something more."

"It never would have worked," I say with confidence.

She looks slightly offended. "Why not?"

"We were never right for each other," I tell her, letting it linger in the air for ten long, tense seconds, until I add the two words that I know I won't be able to take back. "Until now."

Her gaze snaps to me, her eyes full of questions. So many questions. Between the two of us there are enough unknowns to fill every boat in this marina.

Where do we go from here?

What happens now?

In what implausible scenario does this ever work out well for anyone?

I lean back into the bench with a sigh. Harper rests

her head against my chest. "I mean, I feel bad about it and everything," I admit, stroking her hair. "Obviously I do. But I also . . ." My voice trails off.

Can I say it out loud? Or is it just too horrible?

"What?" she asks, lifting her chin to look at me.

"I also haven't felt this happy in a long time," I whisper. And there it is.

However awful it is. However inappropriate it is. However shitty it makes me as a person. It's still the truth.

"What if . . . ," Harper begins pensively, and then falls silent, like she's lost her nerve.

"What if what?" I prompt her. If she has a suggestion on how to fix this whole mess, then I'm all ears.

"What if we just, I don't know, tell him?"

I sit up straight and gently push against her shoulders until she's looking at me. "About the garden shed?"

"No. About *this*." She gestures between us. "About us."

"No," I say automatically. "Bad idea. Absolutely not."

"Why? Mike and I aren't together anymore. I broke it off with him. He's probably moved on by now."

"Probably moved on?" I spit back at her. "You clearly don't know him very well. Only two weeks ago he was still talking about moving to New York with you."

She bites her lip, clearly having forgotten that part of the conversation she overheard from behind the hedge in my yard.

"And even if he *had* moved on," I continue, "it would still be a horrible idea. You're not a guy. You don't understand. There's a code. You don't date a friend's sister, and you definitely don't date a friend's ex."

She rolls her eyes. "Guys and their stupid codes."

"They're not stupid."

"They're too broad and inflexible. They don't allow for exceptions."

"That's because there are no exceptions."

"What if you fall in love with someone?" she asks, and then suddenly her body goes rigid beside me, and I feel like a stone has just lodged itself in my throat.

When did love enter the conversation? Is that what she's thinking about? Does she think I might be falling in love with her? Is she falling in love with me?

My mind clamors for something to say. A change in topic. A baseball stat. Anything. But I'm drawing blanks.

Harper has fallen silent beside me, and I wonder if she's trying just as hard to come up with something. But she must fail too, because the next thing I know she's kissing me again. Kissing me to change the subject. Kissing me to erase the very words from her mouth. Kissing me because it's about the only thing that seems to make sense between us.

And this time I don't think either one of us is going to be pulling away anytime soon.

CHAPTER 20

When I walk out of the hardware store, Ian looks like he's just seen a ghost. He's so visibly shaken up, I actually scan the street, fully expecting to see some horrific car accident or bike crash or downed pedestrian. But Ocean Avenue, the main shopping street of Winlock Harbor, looks the way it always looks in the summer: bustling with charm, and tourists with cash to spare.

"What's wrong?" I ask, and he startles at the sound of my voice, even though I could swear he was looking right at me.

"Nothing," he says quickly, glancing down the small alley that leads to the beach. "Did you get what you need?"

I shake my head. "They don't keep boot vents in stock. They have to order them from the warehouse. It'll take a week."

"A week!" he practically shouts, as if I just told him I had only that long to live.

I give him a strange look. "Everything's on a delay because of Fourth of July tomorrow."

"But what about the roofing job?"

"I just left a message on Mr. Cartwright's cell. I'm going to have to shut down until the parts come in. It's actually a good thing. Now I'll have some time to catch a few waves during the day and hang out with you guys. Maybe we can go to the beach."

Ian's gaze flickers again in the direction of the alley.

"Do you want to head down there now?" I ask, locking the truck. "I can leave the car here."

"No!" Once again his reaction is totally over-the-top.

"Okaaay," I say with a chuckle.

"Sorry. I just really, really need to get back to the house. I, uh, promised Grayson's dad I'd check the mail while he was gone."

Great. Now he's acting weird too. First Grayson, now Ian. What have these two been smoking?

"And the mail won't still be there later?" I ask.

Ian looks flustered. "It's just that he's waiting for a really important document, and I have to alert him as soon as it arrives."

I shrug and unlock the door again. "Okay."

Ian hops into the cab faster than a golden retriever who's just been told he's going to the dog park. I get in behind the wheel and shoot him another strange look.

"What's gotten into you?" I ask once we're less than a half mile from the Cartwright house.

He glances at me out of the corner of his eye. For a second I get the feeling that he's going to confess something to me. Something big. Maybe he finally wants to talk about his dad. I admit, the thought makes me feel terrified and relieved at the same time.

"It's just . . . ," he begins hesitantly.

"Yeah?"

"It's just . . . ," he starts again, and I'm convinced he's going to trail off once more, but then he suddenly blurts out, "It's Grayson!"

I pull into the driveway of the house, shut off the car, and look at him. "What about Grayson?"

He rubs at his eyebrow, just above the fading purple bruise that you can barely even see anymore. Whatever he's about to tell me is obviously incredibly difficult for him.

"It's his sister," he finally says, his voice shifting ever so slightly.

"Whitney?" I ask in surprise. This was definitely *not* what I expected him to say.

"Yeah." He clears his throat. "She's driving me crazy."

I let out a laugh. "What else is new?"

"No," he goes on, opening the door and hopping out of the truck. "I mean, she's really driving me crazy. I can't figure the girl out. Remember how she used to be so materialistic and stuck up?"

I hop out too. "*Used* to be?"

"That's the thing. It's like she's undergone some strange transformation. She dresses in completely different clothes now. She wears glasses. Glasses! Whitney! And just a few minutes ago while we were in town, I saw her buying books."

"Books," I repeat, certain I must have misheard.

He throws his hands into the air. "Yeah! Books!"

"Like, real books?"

He chuckles. "Right? I'm so confused."

"Aha!" I say, with sudden realization. "Now I get it."

"Get what?"

"You," I tell him. "When I came out of the hardware store, you looked, I don't know, traumatized or something. Now I understand why."

I swear I see Ian flinch, but before I can be sure, he's smiling and nodding. "Exactly. I mean, Whitney Cartwright buying books? What could be more traumatizing than that?"

He starts toward the house, walking briskly, like something is chasing him.

"Wait," I call out, and Ian turns around. "Didn't you need to check the mail?"

It's obvious from his expression that he completely forgot about that. He runs over to the box, pulls down the little metal door, and peers inside. "Nope. Not here yet," he announces, and then he bounds up the front steps of the house, leaving me alone to figure out what I'm going to do with my unexpected day off.

I wonder what time Julie gets off work.

CHAPTER 21

I am a coward.

A big, fucking coward.

I'm spineless. I'm weak. I'm wasted space.

If my best friend was cheating with *my* ex-girlfriend, I would want Mike to tell me. And Mike is the kind of guy who *would* tell me! Because he's a good person. Because he doesn't deserve any of this. Because *he's* not a coward like me.

I retreat to my room and pick up my guitar, strum a few bars of the song I wrote a few weeks ago. I've been tinkering with some of the chords and melodies, trying to get it just right. The sound of it now settles my roiling stomach somewhat, so I keep going, softly humming along with the melody.

The more I play, the more I start to wonder if maybe telling Mike *isn't* the right thing to do. If maybe keeping what I saw a secret is the smart decision. Maybe even the *kind* decision.

This is Grayson we're talking about. Odds are he'll be over this fling in a matter of days. And it's Harper. She has a reputation for pulling stunts like this all the time. She does this nearly every single summer. She breaks up with Mike, she flirts with the tourists, she comes back to him. That's her MO. That's *both* of their patterns. It just so happens that this summer their patterns overlapped.

Harper and Grayson together is just a catastrophe waiting to happen. I wouldn't be surprised if this whole thing blew over in less than a week. Then everything will go back to normal.

Grayson will go back to hitting on girls at beach parties. Harper will go back to Mike. And I can go back to moping around the house while trying to avoid another infuriating confrontation with Whitney.

But if I told Mike about Grayson and Harper, all hell would break loose. I'd basically be bringing about the end of our friendship. It's not worth destroying what we have for a stupid summer fling, is it?

No, definitely not.

I'll just lie low and pretend I never saw anything. And really, what *did* I see? A harmless little chase game on the street? An *almost* kiss? It could be nothing. It probably *was* nothing.

I'm staying out of it.

Besides, I'm not sure I can handle the emotional burden right now. Not with my mother still texting me nonstop trying to get me to come over to watch home movies or browse through photo albums, or take a tour of all the places on the island my dad loved to visit. I don't know how many times I have to turn her down before she finally gets it. I have no interest in skipping merrily down memory lane with her.

I hear a strange scraping sound outside my window. I assume it's Mike packing up his truck, but I pull back the curtain to check anyway.

Outside by the pool Whitney is rearranging lounge chairs. She's wearing a one-piece bathing suit, an oversize sun hat, and a sarong. The way the sarong is cut, every time she takes a step, the fabric inches up her thigh, revealing one of her long, lean legs.

She finally positions the chair to her liking and plops down, propping her knees up so that the sarong falls down around her hips, giving me a perfect view of both legs.

My stomach does a series of crazy acrobatic moves.

When did Whitney become so sexy? I mean, she's always *dressed* sexy, but it was like a little girl who had raided her mother's closet and makeup drawer. It always looked like she was trying too hard. And she used to have these scrawny little legs that were way too skinny, and puny arms that I probably could have wrapped my hand around twice.

But now it's evident that sometime in the past two years, she acquired a few curves. And in all the right places too.

I soon realize how creepy and pervy I am, just sitting here, staring at her through the window. I'm about to let the curtain fall back down, when Whitney pulls a giant hardcover out of her bag, flips it open to a marked page, and starts reading.

So I wasn't hallucinating when I saw her come out of that bookstore. Whitney Cartwright is sitting by the pool reading a *book*.

Hell has officially frozen over.

I have to get to the bottom of this.

I drop the curtain, letting it swish back into place, and walk out to the pool. She doesn't look up from her book, but she must notice my presence because she says, "About time you stopped being a total perv and came out here."

So she saw me. Great.

I plop down onto the next chair, angling my body so I can face her. She stays focused on her book.

I flick my finger at one of the pages. "So what's this all about? Trying to impress a college guy?"

She sneers. "Did you have to wait for your boner to go down before you came out here to talk to me, or are you just hiding it between your legs?"

I feel a flicker of exhilaration pass through me. The thrill of arguing with Whitney, of desperately grasping for the better comeback, is starting to become an all-too-familiar sensation. One that I'm afraid might actually turn into a full-on addiction.

"Let me know if you come across any big words that you don't understand."

"I will," she immediately retorts, still not looking at me, "so I can send you to fetch a dictionary."

I tilt my head so I can see the title of the book. "*Sense and Sensibility*," I read aloud. "Two things that you severely lack. Is this a self-help book?"

"Actually, yes." She stretches out her legs, crossing them at the ankles. "I'm learning lots of useful things, like how to stay away from Willoughbys like you."

I assume this is a reference to something in the book and I grudgingly admit that I've never read it. I hate that she has the upper hand here and can get in jabs that I don't even understand.

"Seriously," I say, trying not to stare at her body. "What is this about? The glasses? The books? Did you join a cult or something?"

"I didn't realize reading was a crime."

"For you, it might as well be."

She sets the book down on her stomach, and I see the flash of anger in her eyes. "Why do you even care?"

She's totally stumped me there. Why *do* I even care?

"I—I," I stammer. "I'm living in this house now, and

you're my best friend's little sister. I care about what goes on around here."

She breaks into a sarcastic laugh. "You're so full of shit, Ian. All you care about is your stupid guitar and playing your stupid sappy love ballads until four in the morning." She smirks at my reaction. "Oh, yeah. I hear things. The walls are not that thick."

I feel frustration boil up inside me. She heard me singing? Did she hear the lyrics? Does she know they're about her?

"At least I'm doing something with my life," I shoot back, even though it's a pitiful argument and I'm running out of steam. I'm like a pitcher who's pitched eight and a half innings and all I've got left is a pathetic excuse for a fastball, with no oomph. "At least I'm not spending every waking hour of my day shopping and texting and being vapid."

She sits bolt upright, glaring at me from behind those admittedly sexy-as-hell tortoiseshell glasses. "If I'm so vapid and useless, why are you even out here with me? Why aren't you in your room saving the world with your super-important music?"

I shoot to my feet and yell, "I came out here to . . . to . . ." But I can't think of a single thing to say. My witty comebacks are gone, and now all I'm left with is the truth. A truth I don't even realize until it comes tumbling out of my mouth.

"To ask you out!" I finish, my voice still loud and full of angst.

"You came out here to ask me out?" she screams. "Like on a date?"

"Yes!" I fire back.

"Fine!" she roars. "Eight o'clock tonight. Don't be late. And don't wear those stupid shorts."

"Fine!" I yell, and stalk back into the house, then slam the glass door behind me. I stomp all the way to the guest room. The first thing I do when I get there is stare in the mirror at the shorts I'm wearing.

What's wrong with these? I think huffily.

I turn to the small overnight bag I packed when I snuck out of my grandparents' house. There's nothing in there but T-shirts and swim trunks and more shorts that look pretty much identical to these.

Which means that sometime between now and eight o'clock tonight, I'm going to have to do the one thing I hate doing more than anything else in the world.

Shop.

CHAPTER 22

When my phone vibrates in my pocket, Harper and I are still kissing. I pull it out to ignore the call, assuming it's probably my mother again, but freeze when I see Mike's name on the screen.

My vision clouds over, and the inside of the boat starts to spin.

Does he know?

Did he see us?

Did someone else *see us and tell him?*

I knew it was a mistake to walk down Ocean Avenue with her. This town is far too tiny to make stupid mistakes like that.

I jump up from the bench seat. Harper looks insulted by my hasty retreat. That is, until she hears me answer the phone.

"Mike!" I say, too chirpy, too squeaky. I clear my throat. "What's up, man?"

I'm a terrible, terrible, shitty, shitty person.

"Hey," he says. "I just wanted to let you know that we had to delay the job for a few days while we wait for the hardware store to get a part in."

The roof? He called to talk to me about the roof?

Relief floods through me, followed by a quick chaser of wretchedness. "Oh, right. Cool. That's totally fine. Take as much time as you need."

"Thanks, man. We should be back up and running by Friday. I taped the first invoice to your front door, if you want to just have your dad write me a check or whatever."

"Of course," I say uncomfortably. Mike and I have never actually had to talk about money before. It's admittedly weird.

There's an awkward pause on his end. It makes me squirm. "Where are you, anyway? Ian says you've been in and out all week."

"He did?" I croak, feeling like there's a huge seashell lodged in my throat. "Right. Yeah. I'm just hanging out."

I can almost hear Mike smile into the phone. "What's her name?"

My gaze whips to Harper, who opens her eyes wide.

I force out a laugh. "You know me too well, my friend. Her name is . . . is . . ."

Harper starts mouthing something that I can't understand. It almost looks like she's saying . . .

"Ebba," I say into the phone. "Her name is Ebba."

Harper rolls her eyes and shakes her head at me.

"Ebba?" Mike repeats. "What kind of name is that?"

"It's . . . French, I think."

Harper throws up her hands in defeat. I need to shut this thing down.

"So, what's up with you?" I ask him, trying to make my voice light and airy.

"Nothing much. We just haven't seen you around here a lot. I guess now I know why." There's a trace of mocking in his tone, and it feels like a punch in the stomach.

"Yeah, sorry about that. Hey, why don't we hang out

tonight? Just the three of us. We can catch up on *Crusade of Kings*, play our usual nipple drinking game."

Mike hesitates. "Actually, I think Ian has a date tonight."

This is a surprise. I haven't seen him leave the house in two weeks. How the hell did he meet someone? "With who?"

"Dunno," Mike replies. "But he seems really into it. He just left to go shopping for something to wear."

Ian, shop?

I laugh. "Must be some girl."

"I know, right?" Mike chuckles too, and for just a moment we feel like ourselves again. Making jokes at each other's expense. Messing around. Laughing. For just a moment I'm able to fool myself into thinking that this is any other summer. When my mom isn't gone and my arm isn't killing me all the time and Ian isn't moping around and I'm not hooking up with my best friend's ex-girlfriend.

But then I peer around the inside of my father's boat and see Harper standing just a few feet away, her hair mussed from my hands, her clothes rumpled, and I'm back to feeling like shit.

"Well, anyway," Mike goes on, "we should all hang out tomorrow for the Fourth. I'm off all day."

"Great!" I say, but even I can hear how fake my enthusiasm is. "Let's meet at my house. I'll fire up the grill."

"Great."

"Great," I say again, feeling like an idiot. "Okay, then. Bye." I quickly hang up the phone, before my guilt literally makes me keel over.

"I said 'Emma'!" Harper immediately attacks me. "Not 'Ebba.' What kind of name is Ebba?"

"I don't know! I couldn't understand you. It looked like you were saying 'Ebba.'"

"I chose Emma because it's a popular name so it's harder to narrow down. I figured there's gotta be, like, ten of them on the island. There were two in my graduating class alone." She stops ranting when she sees my tortured expression. "What? What happened? What did he say?"

I shake my head, running my fingers through my hair. "Nothing. But I think I should go home."

"Why?" she asks, and I don't miss the hurt in her voice.

But I can't deal with that right now. I can't deal with anybody else's emotions. Not when mine are running so rampant.

I just lied to my best friend.

I lied like it was nothing.

I can't stand myself right now. And I definitely can't stand being here with Harper. But it's not like I can tell her that.

It's not like I can tell anyone anything. All of these secrets I've promised to keep. All of these things I've sworn to hide. They're all snowballing in my brain. I can't even keep them straight. I can't remember who or what or why I'm not supposed to tell.

The truth about my mom.

The truth about my arm.

The truth about my uncertain future.

The truth about Harper.

I suddenly feel anxious and alone and desperately in need of something I fear I may never find. And worse, something I may never even identify.

"I don't know," I mumble miserably as I stuff my phone back into my pocket and hurry to the stairs of the hatch. "I just . . . can't be here right now."

I don't wait around for Harper's response. I know she's not happy with me right now. She can join the club. I pound up the stairs, leap onto the dock, and start running.

Always, always running.

From what?

I can't even keep track anymore.

For how long?

I wish I knew.

To where?

Well, there's the biggest question of them all.

CHAPTER 23

When I arrive at the outdoor playground of the kids' camp, I'm attacked by two simultaneous human darts. Bam! Bam! Jake is hanging from my left arm while Jasper is attached to my waist.

"Mike! Mike!" they scream in unison. I've been bringing them here every day for the past two weeks. The doctor told my dad that if he wants any chance of going back to work by the end of the summer, then he has to completely stay off his leg during the day. And that means that chasing a pair of six-year-old monsters around the house is out. Julie swore it was no big deal for the twins to be here, so now my dad is holed up on the couch watching cooking-competition shows all day.

"Come see my tie-dye shirt!" Jake begs, swinging back and forth.

"No! That's stupid and hippie!" Jasper says, tugging on my shirt. "Come see the bottle rocket I made."

"Bottle rocket?" I ask, trying to walk with my extra "limbs."

Julie appears from behind a tree, laughing at my attempts. "Don't worry. It's fake," she whispers behind her hand. "Full of sand."

I quickly get to work detaching each child.

"It is not fake!" Jasper insists, frowning at her. "It really works."

"He didn't want to do any of the normal arts and crafts," she tells me.

"Why am I not surprised?"

Once I'm free of dangling children, I'm able to get a good look at Julie. She's wearing her usual khaki shorts, but her polo shirt is gone. Instead she has a simple black one-piece bathing suit on, which, admittedly, she looks incredibly sexy in.

"Oh," she says, glancing down at her top. "Right. I had to take off the polo. It got covered in tie-dye."

My gaze rockets back up. I feel like a total idiot for blatantly staring at her chest. Not to mention, my face is probably bright red right now. The twins, having evidently grown bored of this conversation, wander off to the swing set, where they immediately start fighting over which swing goes higher.

"I wasn't . . . ," I try to say, but stop myself. It's a lost cause. She clearly knows I was checking her out. "Sorry to hear about the shirt. You seem to be having a hard time wearing clothes lately."

She tilts her head, confused. And then I hear my words repeated in my head. "No, no," I amend quickly. "I mean, because every time I see you, you're covered in seawater, paint, or . . . You know what? Never mind. Can I start over?"

I walk out of the gate and then back in. When I do, Julie is grinning from ear to ear.

"Hi!" I say, overly bubbly. "How's it going? Long time no see!"

She laughs. "You're pretty adorable, you know that?"

"What? This old thing?" I ask, pointing to my face.

She giggles again. The sound of her laugh is kind of awesome. So openmouthed and uninhibited. Like she doesn't care who hears or what they think.

"Are you here to pick the boys up early?" she asks.

"Actually, no." I hesitate, feeling my throat constrict. "I came by to see you."

Her grin broadens. If that's even possible. "Here I am."

"Yes," I say, breathing out. "Here you are."

I can feel my heart start to thud in my chest.

The truth is, I've been trying to work up the nerve to ask her out for the past week, but the timing never seems to be right. I'm always working or running home to make dinner for the twins. But now I guess I have no more excuses. I have absolutely nowhere to be for the next twenty-four hours.

But can I really do this? Can I really just *ask* her out? I've never asked a girl out in my life. With Harper it was always assumed. We were just together, from the moment we shared our first kiss at the bottom of the beach club pool. After that there were no questions. No date requests. We were just Harper and Mike for the next six years.

I try to remind myself that I'm not really asking Julie out. She already did that part when she asked me to give her a tour of the island. I'm just finally committing to a time, which technically should be easier. After all, I already know she wants to go. That much has been established.

So then why are my palms sweating?

I rub my hands on my jeans.

"Didn't you say you're working a roofing job?" she asks, and I immediately wonder how much time has passed since I last spoke. Was it a normal amount of time? Or have I just been standing here staring at her like a moron?

"Yes. Right. The roofing job." That puts me back on track. "There's been a delay while we wait for some parts to be delivered. Which means I'm free this afternoon, and so I was wondering if maybe you want to do that island tour? Or not. I mean, if you're busy, I completely—"

"Oh, that's perfect!" she exclaims. "The boss just told me that a bunch of kids are leaving early today because of the holiday, so I'm off this afternoon too. Can we go to the basket museum? I've been hearing such amazing things about it."

"Oh, um," I begin awkwardly. The basket museum really wasn't what I had in mind. It's so cheesy and packed with tourists, but looking into her big round eyes, there's really nothing else I can say but "Sure, sounds fun!"

She does another one of her cute little bounces and claps her hands. "Awesome. I get off in about an hour. Do you want to come back, or do you want to wait?"

I look over to the grassy area where a day care staffer is organizing the entire group of children into a circle.

"We're about to play Simon Says," Julie informs me. "So I totally understand if you wanna just come back later and—"

"Are you kidding?" I interrupt. "I'm the reigning champion of Simon Says."

She giggles and gestures to the circle. "Well, then, champ. Let's see what you got."

CHAPTER 24

've never felt more ridiculous in all my life. A skinny, overly chatty salesgirl named Molly is pulling at my shirt and adjusting my pant leg while telling me how handsome I look, and all I want to do is crawl back into that dressing room and die.

"This looks amazeballs," she gushes, standing behind me so we can both look at my reflection in the three-way mirror. But I'm not too sure about her assessment. She's dressed me in this dark blue suit with shoes I can literally see my reflection in. And a tie.

I don't do ties.

The last time I wore a tie was at my father's funeral, and that's the last thing I want a reminder of tonight.

The salesgirl reaches around my waist to pull down the suit jacket. "Your girlfriend is a lucky girl."

"It's not like that," I say uncertainly.

She cocks an eyebrow. "First date?"

I shrug. "I guess."

Hearing that aloud makes it sound so corny and Hollywood and like such a bigger deal than it really is. A first date with Whitney Cartwright? I almost laugh aloud. What was I thinking asking out Whitney Cartwright?

But she's so different. She's changed so much. And when I think about being alone with her, I get this strange flutter in my stomach. Which is totally bizarre, given that I've known the girl since she was five years old and swimming around with floaties in the Cartwright pool.

And now I'm going on a date with her?

"Aha!" the salesgirl says as if this changes everything. "If it's a first date, then you definitely need a hat."

"Um," I falter, but she's already off, presumably to add another ridiculous item to this monstrosity. When she returns and places the hat on my head, I take one look in the mirror and know it's *all* wrong. I look like a Cuban mob boss roaming the streets of Miami.

"Actually," I say, taking off the hat and shrugging out of the jacket, "I think I want to go in a different direction."

Her face visibly falls, like she's a parade balloon that someone let all the helium out of. "But this is so amazing."

"Sorry. It's just really not me."

Her expression grows serious again, and she snaps back into go-mode. "Got it. Say no more. I know exactly what you want."

I highly doubt that, I think as I watch her scurry away to assemble the ingredients of Ian 3.0.

God, I hate shopping.

Two hours later we've finally settled on a look that is guaranteed to "sweep her off her feet" (Molly's words, not mine) but also doesn't cost every last dollar I have. It was a rough negotiation. Molly kept trying to put me in outfits that I was sure would make Whitney crack up laughing, while I kept trying to pick out clothes that Molly assured me would send Whitney running for the next ferry back to the mainland.

She rings me up at the register and places each new item carefully into a brown paper bag. One white linen button-up shirt, one pair of brown boat shoes, and one pair of jeans that is just a little too tight for my comfort but that Molly swears makes my butt look scrumptious (again, her word).

"Now, you have the whole night planned, right?" Molly asks, dropping my receipt into the bag and giving it a pat.

I shrug and take the bag by the handles. "Sure. I guess."

She grabs the bag back from me. "Hold up just a sec. You *guess*?"

"I don't know. I was just gonna, like, wing it. I'm a spontaneous kinda guy."

Molly immediately starts shaking her head. "Oh, no. No, no, no, no, no, no, NO. If this girl is as sophisticated and special as you say—"

"I didn't say anything about her," I interrupt.

She ignores me and continues. "Then you need to step it up a notch. You need to plan something she'll never forget. You need to *woo* her."

"Woo her?" I repeat, the skepticism dripping from my tone. "Is this the twenty-first century or the nineteenth?"

She waves this away with her hand. "That doesn't matter. Even the most progressive girls like to be wooed. It shows you care. It shows you're not just trying to get into her pants." She narrows her eyes and shoots me a glare. "You're not just trying to get into her pants, are you?"

My face flushes with heat. "What? No. I mean, she's like a little sister to me."

Okay, that came out totally wrong. Molly now looks horrified.

"Not like that," I clarify. "She's a little sister of a friend. I've known her almost all my life. I'm not just trying to . . ."

But I can't even say the words. "I'm not trying to do that."

Molly pins me with another stare. "So what are your intentions with this young lady?"

Okay, what is going on here?

"I—I," I stammer. "I don't know."

Molly is growing frustrated with me. "Okay. What *do* you know?"

"I like her," I say without thinking, and suddenly realize that it's true. I do like her. I like Whitney Cartwright. I never thought I'd ever think those words, let alone say them aloud. But there they are. Out in the open.

"She's pretty, isn't she?"

I shrug. "Yeah. I mean, she's gorgeous, but that's not it."

Molly leans forward on the counter, suddenly very interested in what I have to say next. And I become hyper-aware of how awkward this situation is. Why am I confessing my feelings for Whitney to a complete stranger?

Maybe because I can't say them to anyone I actually know.

Molly blinks, her large eyes staring expectantly at me.

"She . . . ," I begin, trying to put into words exactly what it is about Whitney that has gotten to me over the past month. "She challenges me. At a time when I guess I need to be challenged."

As soon as I say it, I know it's exactly how I feel. Just like with that song I wrote, Whitney seems to bring out a side of me that I didn't know I had.

Molly lets out a wistful sigh. I glance down at the shopping bag still in her clutches.

"Can I have my clothes now?" I ask.

She seems to snap out of a trance. "Oh! Right. Of course."

I grab the bag just as my phone rings. I pull it out of my pocket and instantly deflate when I see my mother's name on the caller ID. It's incredible how quickly she can erase my good mood. Like water washing away a beautiful chalk drawing on the sidewalk. One sight of her name on my screen, and my mood is a messy blur of inscrutable shapes and muddy colors.

I hastily press ignore and stuff the phone back into my pocket.

I yank the shopping bag from the counter. Just feeling its weight in my hands and knowing what it represents, I start to calm down. I don't have time to think about my mother and her incessant need to make cleaning out the garage a family affair. I have a date to think about. And according to Molly, the salesgirl, I'm highly underprepared.

"Thanks for your help," I say, trying to keep my voice as upbeat as possible as I head for the door.

"You're welcome!" Molly calls after me. "Good luck tonight! Woo her pants off!" She stops and thinks about that. "But not literally!"

CHAPTER 25

When I get back to the house, I'm an agitated mess. I can't sit still. I pace the length of the living room. I dribble a tennis ball around and around the pool. I put in a video game, only to get impatient with the amount of time it takes to load, and flip off the TV.

I eat. I drink. I even look for the emergency pack of cigarettes that my dad always keeps stashed somewhere, but I can't find them.

Nothing seems to calm my ragged nerves.

I feel like bugs are crawling all over me. I feel like my skin is itching. I feel like a crazy person.

I start organizing the clutter of mail and paperwork on the counter. I've never been much of an organizer. If anything, I'm more of a *de*-organizer. Just like in life. I make messes of things. My friendships. My future. My life.

But there's something about arranging this pile of envelopes into a tight little stack that makes me feel just the slightest bit better. So I keep going.

"What's your problem?" Whitney appears from the back patio, carrying her cell phone.

I shake my head and go back to my stack. "Nothing."

"You're cleaning," she says blankly.

"No. I'm organizing. It's different." I look at her again, this time taking a moment to study her. Something's different about her, but I can't put my finger on what it is.

"I just got off the phone with Mom," she says.

My hands freeze around a pile of catalogs and magazines. I whip my gaze to her.

"She asked me why you haven't returned any of her calls or texts," she goes on, unfazed by my look of utter disbelief.

"You talk to her?"

She shrugs and takes a bottle of sparkling water from the fridge. "Yeah."

Like it's no big deal. Like our mother didn't just walk out of our lives and leave this family in ruins.

"Why?"

She unscrews the top of the bottle and takes a sip. "Because she's my mother. And I miss her."

"But . . ." I falter.

"But she walked out on us?" Whitney finishes. I don't like her tone. It's too blasé. It's too forgiving.

"Yeah!" The word comes out sloppily. A fine mist of saliva accompanies it and lands on the Pottery Barn catalog in my hand.

"She feels bad about that," Whitney says. "That's what we were just talking about. She wants to apologize to you. She wants you to forgive her."

My grip on the catalogs tightens. I can hear some of the pages ripping. "Forgive her?" I snap. "For destroying our family? For ruining my life?"

"You crashed that car yourself, Grayson," Whitney heartlessly reminds me. "She had nothing to do with that."

"But she . . ." I trail off, quickly realizing that I don't

know where this argument is going. It doesn't even sound like a real argument. But I have to finish what I started. I can't just let it linger there. So I grasp for the first thing I can think of. "She ran out! Without any explanation."

"If you'd just give her a chance, she'll *give* you an explanation."

"She doesn't deserve a chance."

"We all make mistakes," Whitney says. "And we all deserve a chance to fix them. Don't you think?"

I stare at my little sister in astonishment. What are these words coming out of her mouth? When did she become the wise Zen master of the family? Does this have something to do with how different she seems?

Why have I not noticed it until now? Have I been *that* preoccupied with my own stupid problems?

She holds my gaze, challenging me to speak. To refute her statement.

"Some mistakes are too big to fix," I mumble.

Whitney shrugs, like she really doesn't care one way or the other. "Fine."

She walks over to me, dislodges a magazine from my death grip, and disappears back out the sliding glass door with her water.

I stand clutching the stack of mail in my hand, watching the supple white couch on the cover of the Pottery Barn catalog wrinkle and tear beneath my sweaty fingers.

She talked to Mom.

She took her call.

How could she do that? How could she just *forgive* so easily like that?

I don't care what Whitney says. Yes, I may have crashed that car myself. Yes, I may have overreacted. I may have jeopardized my own future. But what our mother did was worse. She broke our family apart. She walked out on her responsibilities.

She quit.

Cartwrights don't quit. My father has been drilling that into my mind since the day I was born. Maybe even before that. Perseverance is baked right into my DNA.

And yet my mother just gave up. She just left.

We all make mistakes.

I shake my head and keep organizing. Stacking and restacking and arranging and rearranging.

Just when I think there's absolutely nothing else I can do, I catch sight of an envelope poking out from one of my meticulous stacks. I pull it out and read the handwritten note my father has scribbled on the front.

For Mike.

I open the envelope and withdraw a check. It's all made out. Pay-to line, date, signature. Only the amount is left blank.

My father must have wanted me to fill it in once we got the first invoice.

Then I remember what Mike told me on the phone today, and I scurry over to the front door. I open it to find, just as Mike promised, an envelope taped to the wood, with an invoice inside.

I study the number at the bottom of the invoice. The amount due for the first two weeks of work.

Eighteen hundred dollars.

I look at the check again. At the big empty box next to the dollar sign. It suddenly feels like a void. But unlike all the other voids in my life right now, this is one I can fill.

One I can fix.

Before I have a chance to change my mind, I grab a pen from the drawer in the kitchen and fill in the blank space.

Three thousand dollars.

I tell myself this has nothing to do with Harper. It has nothing to do with my own stupid mistakes. Mike said his dad was injured and they need extra cash. That's all this is. A friend helping out another friend.

Nothing more.

But as I slip the check into the envelope and secure it back to the outside of the door, I can't help but feel the weight on my chest lift just the slightest bit.

CHAPTER 26

S imon says spin in a circle. Simon says jump up and down. Pull out your ears and make a fish face."

I immediately tug at my ears and fashion my lips into a perfect trout pout. Twenty kids squeal and jump and dance and point at me. Like a chorus of adorable little chirping insects.

"What?" I ask them, feigning innocence as I continue to suck air in through my puckered lips.

"Simon didn't say!" they all shout in unison.

"He didn't?"

They shake their heads, and I let my fish face fall into a scowl. "You mean I lost *again*?"

Another fit of giggles.

"This game is too hard!" I grumble, giving Julie a wink. She beams back at me. Over the past hour we've managed to keep these kids thoroughly entertained through a strategy we developed without saying a single word to each other. She calls out the most embarrassing actions for me to possibly do, and I lose on purpose. We quickly discovered that a grown-up—or whatever I am—losing at Simon Says is funnier to these kids than anything Disney could animate.

"Okay, kids!" she calls, clapping her hands together once. "Let's all go inside for the Silent Movie game!"

They squeal again, until Julie puts a finger to her lips, and the entire group falls quiet. One of the other staffers leads the kids back into the clubhouse, and I watch in awe as they pretend to talk to each other without sound, moving their lips and pantomiming. I'm shocked to see Jasper and Jake playing along with the other kids. I didn't realize they even understood the word "silent."

"What's the Silent Movie game?" I ask as I help Julie pick up the trash around the grass and deposit it into the bin.

"It's just a little game I invented to calm them down a bit. I showed them clips from a bunch of old silent movies and told them that the first person who talks loses the game. We play music just like in the films, and they all go around pantomiming."

She picks up an ice chest that was once full of Popsicles and begins to carry it inside.

"Here," I say, taking the chest from her. "I got this."

"Thanks."

I follow behind her into the day camp's main room, and nearly drop the ice chest on my feet when I see what has transpired inside. Soft piano music is streaming from a pair of speakers, and every single child that was, just five minutes ago, bouncing around and giggling like they were high on something is now either sitting quietly on the floor with a book or sleeping on one of the cots.

I search the room for Jasper and Jake, certain that they must be the only two rug rats still running around and kung-fu-ing the air like the maniacs that they are. But my mouth literally falls open when I find them curled up on the same cot together, sleeping soundly.

"You're a genius," I whisper.

She giggles and directs me to put the ice chest in the small kitchen.

"Please tell me you drugged them."

"I'm pretty sure I'd go to jail for that." She grabs a bottle of cleaner from the cabinet above the sink and begins wiping the Popsicle residue from the inside of the chest. "Kids are a constant learning curve. I discovered really quickly that"— she lowers her voice to a mere whisper—"'nap' is a dirty word. So I started to brainstorm other ways to get them quiet for a few minutes a day. And then I found that once they were quiet, most of them would just fall asleep."

She tosses the used paper towel into the trash and slides the ice chest onto the top of the fridge.

"I am in awe of you," I say, bowing slightly. "Teach me all of your secrets, wise master."

Julie shoots me a coy look. "Learn them yourself, you must," she says in the most perfect Yoda voice I've ever heard.

A smile bigger than the state of Texas spreads across my face.

Two hours later I've completely relinquished the role of tour guide. Julie has dragged me to every single tourist hot spot that I swore I would never step foot in as long as I live. At the Seashell Shack we eat overpriced burgers that are surprisingly good. We take the guided tour of the lighthouse, a building I've admittedly only seen from the outside. We even visit the tiny Winlock Harbor Basket Museum just like she wanted, which I haven't been to since our second-grade class took a field trip there. (When you grow up on an island the size of the Locks, your field trip options are extremely limited.) I remember the museum being incredibly boring and tedious, but with Julie it's actually fun. She somehow manages to make a joke out of everything.

By the time we start heading back to the club so that I can take the boys home, I've laughed so much that my stomach muscles are sore. But I don't want to say good-bye to her yet. Everything about her—her personality, her smile, the way she sometimes hums to herself even when I'm walking right next to her—is infectious.

"So," I begin anxiously, shoving my hands into my pockets. "I just have to take the twins home. Do you want to go for a walk on the beach or something later?"

As soon as the words are out of my mouth, I realize how nervous they make me. Even more so than I was earlier today.

"Actually, no," she says with a frown.

My heart sinks to the pit of my stomach. "Oh. That's okay. Do you have plans or something?"

Of course she would have plans. I don't know how I could possibly be the only person on this island to recognize how awesome she is. I imagine she has a whole slew of dates lined up, one for every night of the week. How could she not?

"No, no plans. I just really had a horrible time with you today, so . . ."

My gaze darts to her face, and I immediately wilt in relief when I see the teasing smirk there. I let out a chuckle and try not to let show that I actually, for a split second, believed she was telling the truth. "Right. Of course. Me too. Terrible time. You are just the worst company."

"Oh my gosh!" she exclaims. "You too? I'm so happy to hear you say that. I thought it was just me."

I continue to play along even though I'm completely

unable to keep a straight face. "No. It definitely wasn't just you. I hated every single second of it."

"I know. Totally," she agrees wholeheartedly. "I spent the entire afternoon just thinking about things I'd rather be doing. Like getting teeth pulled. Pouring lemon juice into paper cuts."

"Rubbing sandpaper on my sunburn."

Now she breaks character and starts giggling. "You're just so . . . I don't know . . . boorish and impolite."

"And you smell," I put in.

She sniffs her armpits. "Yeah, sorry about that. I have a gland malfunction disease."

"That's unfortunate."

She's laughing really hard now. "Very unfortunate."

We reach the front entrance of the beach club, and I pause next to the door. "So then, I guess I'll see you . . . what? Never?"

She pretends to contemplate the question. "Well, I mean, I don't really have any lemon juice in the house. Or sandpaper."

"And the only dentist on the island is probably closed for the Fourth of July tomorrow."

"Probably," she agrees, screwing her mouth to the side and tilting her head from side to side. "So, if I promise to wear deodorant and you promise to stop acting like a brute, maybe we could keep hanging out?"

Despite my efforts I can't stop the ear-to-ear grin that covers my face. "I think I can manage that. So I'll meet you by the cottages in an hour?"

She looks at me like that's the most ludicrous idea I've had all day. "Don't be silly," she says, pulling open the door and holding it for me. "I'll walk you boys home."

CHAPTER 27

This was a huge mistake.

I've spent the past hour on the beach behind the Cartwrights' house, wrestling with uncooperative wooden poles and wrinkled cotton sheets and pesky tea candles, erecting what the Romance Guru blog calls "The Ultimate Beach Love Hut."

That stupid salesgirl made me completely paranoid that I wasn't doing enough to "woo" Whitney, so I spent the whole afternoon getting sucked into a Google spiral of dating advice. Now Whitney is scheduled to arrive any minute, and this tent is about to collapse into the tea candles and set fire to the whole damn thing.

Why didn't I just opt for a romantic dinner at one of the island's nicest restaurants?

Oh right, because I can't afford any of the island's nicest restaurants.

What made me think I could possibly impress Whitney Cartwright? The girl who grew up with everything. She's probably dated a hundred guys who can afford much better than a lousy makeshift love hut on the beach.

No, I try to reassure myself. *This will work.*

I try once again to insert the supporting pole into the

sand, wedging it down far enough that I'm sure the people in China are wondering why there's a freaking pole sticking out of the ground. It seems to take, but just in case I keep one hand firmly wrapped around it, holding it in place, while I bend at an embarrassingly awkward angle to grab the bedsheet.

The blog post entitled "Summer Lovin' Ideas" that I found on the Romance Guru website didn't say anything about what *kind* of sheet, so I just grabbed a clean cotton one from the linen closet at the Cartwright house. But now I'm thinking that this one might be too heavy. The support pole looks like it's about to buckle under the weight of it.

I find two large rocks nearby, pull the sheet taught, and secure the ends down with the weight of the rocks. That seems to keep the whole contraption stable.

For now.

I spread the blanket down underneath the tent, rearrange the throw pillows I stole from the guest bedroom, position the tea candles so they form a circle around the perimeter, and go to work arranging the food. Nothing fancy. The article said wine, fruit, and cheese would suffice, but once again it didn't specify what kind. I spent twenty minutes at Coconut's Market deliberating over the cheese selection. What kind of cheese do rich people eat? Brie? Gouda? Some other French kind I can't pronounce? What if Whitney is lactose intolerant? How come after all these years I can't summon a single memory of her consuming dairy?

I eventually opted for a Welsh cheddar. It seemed like a safe compromise. A cheese I recognize from a country I probably can't locate on a map.

Despite my efforts, Old Man Finn at Coconut's refused to sell me any wine, so I bought sparkling grape juice instead, figuring it counts for the wine *and* the fruit. But now that I look at my pathetic spread, I fear it's severely lacking.

This is supposed to woo her?

A bottle of fizzy juice and some cut-up chunks of cheddar cheese?

Ugh. This is totally hopeless.

I should have asked Mamma V at the beach club for help. She knows everything about food, and she's always eager to help us out, especially when it comes to girls. One summer she actually helped Grayson bake cookies for a hot new tourist he was trying to impress. It went over so well, they dated for two whole weeks. Basically a record for Grayson. But asking for help would require actually *telling* someone about this date, and I still haven't even wrapped my own head around the idea.

Maybe I just need some crackers or something. I wonder what the Cartwrights have lying around in their pantry.

I check the clock on my phone. Two minutes until eight. I can make it if I run.

I sprint up the beach and across the plank walkway to the Cartwrights' backyard. I opt for the back door so I won't have to accidentally bump into Whitney on the way in. I don't want her to see that I'm still scrambling around at the last minute. I want her to think this was all part of my plan.

Suave, smooth, sweep-her-off-her-feet-with-crackers Ian.

I rifle around the pantry but can only scrounge up a half-empty sleeve of Ritz. I guess it's better than nothing. I grab them and hurry back out the door.

Whitney and I must have just missed each other, because when I arrive back at the "love hut," she's already there. Her back is turned to me, but I can tell she looks incredible. She's wearing a black off-the-shoulder dress that hangs, loose and flowy, around her slender frame. Her dark skin practically sparkles in the moonlight. And her as-black-as-night hair is tied back in a bun at the nape of her neck.

She's staring at my construction, and I pause to watch, hoping to glean a reaction, but it's impossible because I can't see her face.

Is it just me, or does it seem like she's been staring at it for an awfully long time?

It's the cheese. It's not fancy enough. I knew I should have gone with the Brie.

I take a single step toward her, hoping she'll hear the footfall, but it's muffled by the sand and the sound of the waves in the distance. I should say something slick and charming and Casanova-like, but all I can come up with is, "Hi."

She startles and turns around, wiping hastily at her eyes.

Was she crying?

Panicked, I look at the tent. It's not *that* bad, is it?

"Sorry," I rush to say. "It looked better in the pictures online. I think I used the wrong sheet or something. But it didn't say what kind of sheet, and—"

She stalks toward me, her steps heavy and purposeful. I'm pretty sure she's going to walk right off the beach. I'm pretty sure I royally fucked up this whole wooing thing. That's the last time I listen to random salesladies when it comes to dating advice.

But Whitney doesn't walk off the beach. She walks right to me.

She smashes into me.

She collides with me.

She kisses me.

Hard.

Her lips are searching for something. Her mouth moves eagerly against mine. I drop the crackers and wrap my arms around her waist, pulling her to me. Her body feels amazing pressed against mine.

We stumble backward, falling onto the pillows inside the makeshift tent. She never pulls away. She kisses me like she's trying to save my life. Or hers. Or both.

I'm going to have to write the Romance Guru a very passionate fan letter tomorrow morning.

We lie on our sides, our bodies facing each other. Our lips still moving, exploring, dancing.

I place a hand on her hip and pull her closer. She rolls on top of me, and I can feel every inch of her. Every gorgeous curve.

But her foot must accidentally knock into the support beam in the process, because a second later the entire contraption comes collapsing down on top of us.

Thankfully the wind must have already blown out all the tea candles, because we don't instantly catch fire. We just lie there, staring at each other, unsure what to do next. I say the first thing that pops into my mind.

"Do you want some cheese?"

CHAPTER 28

The Fourth of July is a big deal on Winlock Harbor. Visitors come by the boatload from all over the East Coast to watch the parade, visit the shops downtown, eat ice cream at Scoops, swim in the ocean, and take over our beaches like an invasion.

Traditionally Ian, Mike, and I don't do anything special. We hang out at my house, drink by the pool, swim, chat, eat, and watch the fireworks at the end of the night. Anything to avoid dealing with the mob. And I'm actually looking forward to these little acts of normalcy.

I'm looking forward to the three of us hanging out like old times.

No girlfriends. No dates. No drama.

I haven't spoken to Harper since I left her on my father's boat yesterday. She's texted me twice, but I haven't responded. I don't know what to say to her. I don't know what to do. If I see her, I'll kiss her. If I kiss her, I'll feel wretched.

And yet all I want to do is see her.

Being with her feels safe. It feels right. Even though I know it's not.

The whole thing is just messed up.

The guys and I have the house to ourselves today. My father is on the mainland for work, and Whitney left about an hour ago, looking as giddy as a schoolgirl. No doubt she's found some hunky tourist to keep her company for a few days.

I turn on the barbecue and go inside to get the steaks from the fridge. On the way back out I grab the chips and salsa, and set them on the table next to the cooler.

I'm just putting the first filet on the grill and taking a sip of beer when the doorbell rings.

"I'll get it!" Ian calls, emerging from his room and sprinting toward the door. It's the first I've seen of him all day. Sometimes I get the sense that he's avoiding me, although I don't have the faintest idea why.

A few seconds later Ian steps onto the patio with Mike. We exchange fist bumps, and then for a minute we all kind of just stand there, staring at each other, wondering what comes next.

No, I think. I will not let this become another one of those awkward conversations where none of us can find anything to say to each other. I will not endure that torture again.

Yes, we're all going through some shit, but we're best friends. There has to be *something* we can talk about.

"So, Ian," I say, trying to sound casual, which, of course, makes it sound just the opposite. "Mike told me you had a date yesterday. How'd that go?

Girls. Girls are always a good topic.

"Oh," Ian says, sounding flustered. "That. Yeah, it wasn't really a date. It was no big deal. Just a casual thing." I try to give him a knowing look, but he refuses to meet my eye. He plunges his hand into the cooler and grabs two beers, then hands one to Mike and unscrews the other to take a long gulp. "What about you?" He lobs the question back at me. "Mike says you have a new lady friend you've been sneaking off to meet."

My gaze darts quickly to Mike, then back to the grill.

Okay, maybe girls was a bad topic.

I shake my head, clearing my throat. "Yeah. Well, you know me."

"We sure do," Mike says with a chuckle. I know he means it in jest. Making fun of my continual rotating door of hookups has always been a harmless joke between us. But today, I don't know, there's something about the way he says it that strikes a nerve.

Or maybe I just need to chill the fuck out.

I press down on one of the filets and listen to the satis-fying sizzle.

The guys must sense my unease, because Mike changes the subject. "I saw a football on the kitchen table. Wanna toss a few while those steaks cook?"

I press down harder on the steak, until my arm starts to throb. "Maybe later," I grumble, and out of the corner of my eye, I just manage to catch the look Mike and Ian exchange.

"So," Ian says, bouncing on his toes a little. At least someone seems to be in a good mood. "How long do you think those steaks will take, anyway?"

I shoot him a look. Does he have somewhere else to be?

"The normal time," I tell him. "Unless you want yours rare."

He shrugs. "I could do rare."

"You *are* rare," Mike jokes.

"Yeah, rare form," Ian counters, striking a ridiculous pose.

Mike guffaws, pointing to Ian's beer. "How many of those have you had?"

"This is my first one!" Ian swears. "I'm just high on

life." He breaks into an awkward dance move that is *way* too advanced for him and spills his beer in the process. "C'mon, Grayson," he coaxes in a falsetto sexy voice. "Give it to me *rare*."

Mike breaks out laughing.

"We're not eating rare steak," I snap, and immediately wish I could take it back. Ian stops dancing, and Mike's laughter screeches to a halt. They're both staring at me like I've completely lost it.

And who knows? Maybe I have. Maybe I really am going insane.

I rack my brain for something to say. A safe topic. "Hey, did anyone watch *Crusade of Kings* yet?"

Ian and Mike both take long sips of beer, shaking their heads in unison.

"Me neither," I say, sounding *way* too chipper. "Maybe we can watch it later."

"Yeah, maybe," Mike says, but I can tell he doesn't mean it.

Fifteen minutes later the steaks are done. I shovel them onto plates and hand them out to Mike and Ian, who head over to the patio table in silence. I go inside to grab some steak sauce from the fridge. By the time I get to the table, Ian has already consumed half his steak.

"Hungry?" I ask with a chuckle.

He looks down at his nearly empty plate and belches. "Yeah. I guess so." He cuts another huge piece, shoves it into his mouth, and chews obnoxiously.

"So, who do you think will die in this episode?" I ask, pouring sauce onto my plate.

"I really hope it's LaMestra," Mike says with his mouth full. "She's such a manipulative bitch."

I shake my head. "You know she's gonna be there until the bitter end. Just to mess with us."

Mike groans. "I know. And it kills me."

I hear a scraping sound and look over to see that Ian has cleaned his plate and is now wiping his mouth with a napkin. "Well, I've gotta run."

I blink at him in confusion. "Huh? But we just started hanging out."

He rubs anxiously at his chin. "Yeah, but I actually have other plans. I'll catch you guys later, okay?"

Before I can argue, he's scooting his chair back and carrying his empty plate inside.

Mike leans back in his chair and stretches his arms above his head. "Yeah, I should probably get going too."

I stare at him, openmouthed. "What? Why?"

What is happening right now?

He crumples his napkin and places it down on his half-finished steak. "I promised I'd help out a little at the club."

I'm pretty sure he's lying, because he won't meet my eye. I'm itching to call him on it. To demand a better explanation. A *real* explanation. But then I think of Harper and me on that boat. Her body sprawled out on the bench seat, her shirt unbuttoned, the soft moans that escaped her lips as I kissed her.

And my mouth feels clamped shut.

"Thanks for the steak, man," he says, picking up his plate. "It was delicious."

I sit in stunned silence as Mike disappears into the house, and a few seconds later I hear the front door opening and closing.

Cursing, I push my chair back and stand up, then grab my plate and dump the huge hunk of untouched meat into the trash. Just like that, in the span of less than a half hour, my perfect Fourth of July went right out the window.

Why does it feel like the more I fight for just one last normal summer, the farther it slips away from me? Why does it feel like our little group—the one that tossed footballs on the beach and snuck beers from the fridge and got drunk watching *Crusade of Kings*—is a thing of the past?

And why do I have this nagging suspicion that everything I came here for, everything I chased all the way to this island, is gone forever?

I lean over to grab another beer from the cooler and raise it up in a lonely, single-person toast.

Then I wait ten full minutes before texting Harper.

CHAPTER 29

The rest of July is a blur of lawn mowers and roofing tiles and weed whackers and trimming shears and late nights walking on the beach with Julie. I spend most of the hot days on Grayson's roof and then have to stay late at the beach club to work on the grounds. Julie always waits for me, staying extra hours in the kids' camp with the boys until I'm finished, before she walks us all home. Then I turn around and walk *her* home.

I feel guilty that she stays so late so often, but she swears she doesn't mind. I offered to pay her once, but she wouldn't have it. She knows we need to save every cent that we have. She knows that even with the extra money Grayson's dad has so generously been giving me for my hard work on the job, we're still struggling to keep our heads above water.

She knows because I've told her. Because that's all we do on those long walks to my house and then back to her rental cottage, purposefully weaving through town or taking longer routes around the marshland to prolong the night. We tell each other things.

She tells me about her friends back on the mainland, her family, her experiences being homeschooled for the past two years because of girls bullying her at school. I tell her about the twins, how my parents weren't even planning to get pregnant again and then two popped out. I tell her about how that started us on a downward spiral with money and I had to help out, taking shifts in the kitchen with Mamma V. I tell her about Mamma V and the time she got Grayson, Ian, and me out of a jam by telling Officer Walton that she had *ordered* us to let those crickets loose in the beach club spa. I tell her how weird it is to grow up as a local on a tourists' island. Like home only belongs to you in the off-season.

The only thing I don't tell her about is Harper.

It's as though I've sectioned off all of those memories with DO NOT CROSS police tape and have somehow managed to steer clear of them. She doesn't ask about ex-girlfriends, and I avoid the same kind of questions with her.

I've come to look forward to our walks. They've become the highlight of my long, strenuous days. Julie is so easy to talk to. And it's nice, for two hours a day, to live in a world where Harper doesn't exist. Where she isn't a permanent tattoo on my past. Where my identity isn't completely intertwined with hers.

Avoiding her in my stories is like getting to rewrite my history. I get to have a version of my life in which I made different choices. Wandered down different avenues. Kissed different girls.

Maybe even a version of my life in which I never took her back that first time.

I don't see Harper around the island that much. We've both done an excellent job of avoiding each other. Either out of respect for the other, or for the sake of our own sanities. But it doesn't mean I don't think about her. It doesn't mean her face doesn't occupy the other twenty-two hours of my day.

In fact, I haven't seen much of anyone this summer, apart from Julie and the twins and Mamma V, who always keeps a plate warm for me in the kitchen for after I finish landscaping the grounds.

It seems like everything has kind of shifted since the Fourth of July. A slight turn of the kaleidoscope, and the island is a totally different place.

Even though I'm at Grayson's for more than five hours a day, the house is eerily quiet. His father has been on the mainland for work a lot. Whitney is always off gallivanting around the island the way Whitney does. Grayson has been mysteriously MIA. And even Ian has kind of vanished into the ether. I occasionally see him on his way out in the morning, but he never tells me where he's going or what he's doing. And I don't ask, because whatever (or whoever) it is seems to have finally dragged him out of his funk. He seems almost happy again, and I don't want to mess with that.

We all know how fragile Ian's happiness can be.

Tonight I'm working especially late. The beach club had Movies under the Stars at the pool, where they project a film onto a large screen near the deep end. People gather around in lawn chairs and on floating rafts, drinking and eating popcorn and basically making a huge mess.

One of the regular janitors called in sick, and I got stuck on cleanup duty. And let me tell you, that popcorn? It gets *everywhere*.

When I finally finish pulling kernels out of the pool drain, it's nearly ten o'clock. I check my phone and immediately feel the familiar pang of guilt for making Julie wait so long for me.

I carry the final tray of dirty dishes to the kitchen, where Mamma V is struggling to scrub out a soup pot that's probably half her size.

"Why are you doing that?" I ask, setting the tray down and rushing over to help her. "What happened to Jason?"

"The new dishwasher?" Mamma V lets out one of her signature harrumphs. "I sent him home. He's terrible. He left residue in all my pots."

I gently push her out of the way and take over the scrubbing.

Mamma V collapses noisily into a nearby chair. She watches me with a half smile. "You were my very best dishwasher, you know that?"

I roll my eyes. "Something to be proud of, I suppose."

"It is!" she insists grumpily. "You should always be proud of doing something well. No matter how menial the task may seem. These new boys, they have no sense of pride in their work. They think they're above it all. They're going to run off and put on their white collars and work in an office one day. They think this job is just a bridge to get them where they want to go, so they don't even try. Don't you become one of those boys, Mikey!"

I chuckle. "I'll try not to."

She grunts. "You say that, but that ungrateful girlfriend of yours has sunk her poisonous claws into you. She wants to take you away from here and turn you into some snooty New Yorker. Don't you forget where you're from, mister. There's no shame in working hard. No matter what color your collar is."

I frown into the sudsy pot. I haven't told Mamma V about the breakup. I never tell her about *any* of the breakups. She has always been fairly vocal about her dislike of Harper. And I've always been afraid that if I told her we were broken up, she'd get so excited, it would be too hard to explain it to her when we got back together.

I look over at Mamma V. She's grabbed a pot holder

from a hook by the stove and is fanning herself with it. For some reason I get this burning desire to talk to her. About everything. About Harper. About New York. About how this treasure map that I've been holding on to my entire life, thinking it will lead to the future I want, might turn out to be a fake.

But before I can get a single word out, my phone chimes with an incoming text message, shattering the moment. I quickly set the pot aside and dry my hands before checking my phone.

Shit.

It's from Julie asking if I'm almost done.

"I gotta go," I tell Mamma V, and bend down to kiss her on the cheek.

"Off to meet the boys?" A frown suddenly tugs at her mouth. "I haven't seen them around here much. Are you three getting along?"

I bite my lip. I hate lying to Mamma V, but I know that I don't have time to explain everything that's been happening this summer. Especially when I'm barely able to explain it to myself.

"Sure," I tell her. "We're getting along fine."

She gives me a conspiratorial smile. "What kind of trouble have you been getting into these days?"

"Only the best kind of trouble," I assure her with a wink.

She swats me on the butt with her pot holder as I leave.

The boys are both asleep in cots when I get to the kids' camp, and Julie is sitting in a nearby chair reading a book. She grins when she sees me, depositing the book into her bag and standing up.

"I'm so sorry," I tell her. "It was movie night. A janitor called in sick. And there was popcorn. Everywhere."

She laughs. "Don't worry about it."

"But I do," I tell her honestly. "I worry about it. All the time."

Julie's expression shifts. Her radiant smile fades ever so slightly, and she looks at me with an intensity that until this moment I didn't even know she had. "Mike," she says with a quiet gravity, "out of all the things you have to worry about, I'm not one of them. Okay?"

I grab her hand and give it a quick, grateful squeeze. "Okay."

Without another word we turn toward the sleeping boys. I pick up Jasper because he's the most difficult to carry, and Julie bends down to scoop little Jake into her arms. I feel this peculiar warmth in my gut as I watch Jake wrap his arms and legs around her like a baby monkey.

She catches my eye and flashes me another smile, her radiance returning in full force.

When we get to the house, my dad is yelling at the TV. "No! You can't *cook* the toro! It's a fatty tuna. It needs to be raw!"

"Sorry," I whisper to Julie. "He's gotten really into these cooking-competition shows lately. This is the one where they have to make a meal out of mystery ingredients."

"Hi, Mr. M.," Julie says as we slip by him to the boys' bedroom.

He barely looks away from the screen as he calls out, "Hi, Julie." Then he goes back to yelling at the TV. "Citrus marinade? Amateur!"

"He really needs to get back to work," I whisper as I deposit Jasper onto the top bunk. Julie lays Jake down on the bottom, and I kiss them both good night. We retreat toward the hallway, but a tiny groggy voice stops me just short of the door.

"Mikey?"

It's Jake. I step back toward the bunk bed. "Yeah?"

"Where are you going?"

"Julie and I are going to take a walk on the beach. But don't worry. Dad's here if you get scared."

Between the two of them, Jake is the one who gets the worst nightmares. He's also the one who still occasionally wets the bed, which is the reason he's on the bottom.

"I like Julie," Jasper murmurs from the top bunk. His face must be smashed against the pillow, because the words come out garbled and nearly incomprehensible.

"Me too," Jake agrees.

I turn and flash Julie a smile. "You have a fan club," I whisper.

"She's so much better than Harper," Jasper murmurs.

I freeze on the spot, my stomach instantly clenching. It's a good thing the bedroom is dark, because I'm pretty sure my face is as white as a sheet right now.

"Okay, good night." I quickly shut the door.

I hurry Julie back through the house and out to the front porch. "I'll be back in a bit," I tell my dad, but he's too absorbed in his show to hear me.

"Sorry about that," I say once we're outside. I take a deep breath, unsure how to proceed. I knew it was only a matter of time before her name came up, before I was forced to talk about her. I guess now is as good a time as ever.

"About what Jasper said," I begin anxiously.

But Julie stops me with a tender hand on my arm. "I know," she admits softly.

I blink at her in surprise. "You do?"

"The twins talk about her sometimes. At the club."

"Oh." I try to make my voice sound completely neutral

and unaffected, even though my mind is reeling. I want so badly to ask what they've said about her, what kind of secrets they've unknowingly revealed about this part of my life that I've worked so hard to keep hidden.

Fortunately, or unfortunately, Julie tells me anyway.

"They said she's the girl who used to climb through your window at night."

I bark out a laugh. "I didn't know they knew about that."

"And that she hates Ned."

"Who's Ned?"

Julie shoots me a confused, almost worried look. "Your dog."

"Oh! Right. The dog. Sorry. He's had a few name changes."

A cool breeze blows between us, and I immediately notice the tiny goose bumps that appear on Julie's arm. I run back inside to fetch her one of my hoodies. She slips it on gratefully, zips it all the way up, and pulls the hood over her head.

I have to admit it's difficult to see her in it. Harper used to love wearing my sweaters. She was always stealing the softest ones and refusing to give them back, until I had nothing left in my closet but the hard, crunchy old stuff that the twins had spilled stuff on a hundred times.

"How do I look?" Julie asks, posing like a model.

How does she look?

She looks incredible.

She looks adorable.

She looks like everything I'm not sure I'm ready for her to look like.

"Comfy," I finally respond, and she giggles.

"I *am* comfy!"

"Well, there you go."

We start walking back toward the beach. Julie chatters incessantly about some of the kids at the camp, particularly the crazy ones, but I'm only half listening while I attempt to build up the courage to continue our previous conversation.

It isn't until we reach the sand that I'm finally able to say, "Hey, I'm sorry about the boys. About what they told you."

Confusion flashes over her face.

"About . . . ," I continue, but I can't even bring myself to say her name. Why am I here with this beautiful, amazing, vivacious girl if I can't even say her name?

"Harper?" Julie says it for me, and it's even stranger coming from her lips.

"Yeah." My voice sounds like someone has been hacking at my throat with razor blades.

"You don't need to apologize," Julie says sympathetically. "We all have a past."

I nearly trip over my own two stupid feet. That word. It's like a dagger in my chest.

Past.

We all have a past.

Is Harper really my past now? But how can that be, when she has always been my future? The thought of Harper being just a fading spot in my rearview mirror is making it hard to breathe. Sure, she told me this time it was over for good. Sure, we've managed to avoid each other for weeks. But that's just what we do. That's what *she* does.

Eventually she'll come back, right?

But is that even what I want anymore?

The last few weeks, hanging out with Julie, have been amazing. They've been refreshing. They've been *fun*. Harper can be fun too, but mostly Harper is just complicated.

That's the thing about Julie. She's so very *un*complicated. And yet here I am, walking the beach with her, thinking about Harper.

Thinking about the past.

I guess I've always just assumed that Harper would become my future again. That she'd never *stay* buried in the past. It's always been a given with us. But now it seems the likelihood of us actually getting back together is getting smaller with each passing day.

This is definitely the longest we've ever been split up. Harper's little "breathers" have never lasted more than a week, two at most. But it's been nearly two months since she stood in the Cove, our special spot, and told me it was over.

And for the first time all summer, I think I might be starting to believe that she meant it.

"Ooh!" Julie squeals, running ahead. She bends down and digs something out of the sand. "This could be it!" She unburies a small white seashell and holds it in her palm. Then she reaches into the pocket of her khaki shorts and pulls out another white seashell that looks almost identical. She compares the two, side by side, and her face falls. "Nope. Not it."

She drops the newly uncovered shell back to the ground and dusts off her hand.

"What was that?" I ask, catching up with her.

She holds out her open palm. "This is the first shell I found when I got to the island. I've been searching for its other half."

"Its other half?" I ask, intrigued.

She continues walking. "Yeah. You know, all clamshells come in a pair. They were once complete before they broke apart and scattered along the beach. I've heard it's good luck if you can find two halves that are a perfect match. It's my goal to find the match to this one before the end of the summer."

She looks at me and smiles. "What?" she asks, and I realize my expression must be inscrutable.

"Nothing," I reply, shaking my head. "I've just never heard anyone talk about shells that way before."

"Well, that's because you've never met anyone like me before." She does a little twirl, and I have to laugh.

"That's very true. You are the only person I've ever met who says good night to the ocean."

She frowns. "That makes me sad. The poor ocean. Nobody says good night to it."

I'm not sure what comes over me right then. Maybe it's because of what Mamma V said to me in the kitchen. Maybe it's because of what Jasper said to me in the boys' bedroom. Maybe it's because Julie just shared a tiny piece of herself with me. But I suddenly feel this intense desire to share a piece of *me* with her.

A piece she's never seen.

A piece I've been purposefully avoiding on every single walk we've taken.

"Do you want to see something?" I blurt out before I can stop myself.

She tilts her head, a playful smile lighting up her eyes. "I don't know. Do I?"

I grab her by the hand and start leading her down the beach. Toward the place that has been forever linked with my past. A secret that I haven't shared with anyone since I first took Harper there when we were thirteen years old.

It's been a long time since I've even been to the Cove

myself. I was afraid of its memories. Afraid of the ghosts that might still be lurking there.

But I'm too old to believe in ghosts. I'm too old to be haunted by nightmares.

I think it might finally be time to chase those demons into the past, where they belong.

CHAPTER 30

pace the sidewalk outside of Coconut's Market, fairly certain this night is going to end with both of us in jail. Then, just when I'm about to dash inside and run some kind of interference, Whitney prances breezily out of the store, with a bottle of wine and a smile.

My mouth falls open. "How did you do that? Old Man Finn laughed in my face when I tried to buy a bottle."

She shrugs. "Easy. I gave him a blow job."

All the blood drains from my face.

Whitney bursts out laughing. "Relax. Jeez. What kind of girl do you think I am?"

I'm still too speechless to answer. Whitney must interpret it horribly, because her smile vanishes and she snaps, "I was kidding, Ian. But thanks for the vote of confidence."

She struts past me, making sure to ram me with her elbow as she goes.

Damn it. Now she's upset.

This happens far too often. We'll be having a fantastic time, and then she'll make some kind of lewd joke like that, and I, being too boneheaded to know how to respond, ultimately end up offending her.

I run to catch up. "Whit," I say. "Wait. I'm sorry."

"For what, Ian?" she challenges, raising up the wine bottle like she's going to smash it over my head. I fight the urge to duck, knowing it will only piss her off more. "What are you sorry *for*?"

For speaking, I think, but I don't dare say that.

"I . . ." I falter. She puts her hand on her hip, waiting for me to screw up and say the wrong thing again. "I . . ." I surrender with a sigh. "I don't know, okay? I don't know what I did wrong. I don't know why you get so worked up about this stuff. But I don't know what to say. I've never been with a girl like you. I—"

Anger flashes in her eyes. "A girl like me?" she echoes. "What does that mean?

I balk, sensing that I've stepped even further into dangerous territory. "A girl as . . ." I stop, every variation of that sentence sounding ridiculous and cheesy in my head.

A girl as amazing as you.

A girl as beautiful as you.

A girl as used to guys fawning over her as you.

"A girl as easy as me?" Whitney finishes, a dagger-sharp edge to her voice.

"Wh-what?" I sputter, almost too shocked to speak.

Is that what this is about? Is that really how she thinks I perceive her? Is that why she thinks I'm with her?

I take her hand. Thankfully she lets me. I lead her over to the bench in front of Barnacle Books and sit her down. We were just in here yesterday, picking out books for each other. I'm making her read *The Outsiders*, and she's making me read *Sense and Sensibility*.

"Whit," I say softly, hoping I can make her understand. It's pathetic, really. I can form poetry into a chorus, but when it comes to everyday speech, I can never seem to get the right words out. "What is this about?"

She turns her head away from me, but I can see the misting in her eyes before she does.

"I don't want you to see me that way."

"What way?"

"The way everyone on this island sees me. People can change, you know?"

"I know," I say ardently, releasing a breath. "God, do I know."

She turns back to me, curiosity blooming in her brilliant brown eyes. "So you didn't ask me out because of my reputation for being the island superslut?"

I laugh bitterly. "Do you think I would still be here, a month later, if I had?"

That seems to stump her. She unscrews the top of the wine bottle and takes a long, hearty sip. Then she offers it to me. I decline. I need her to know exactly what I'm feeling, and I need a clear head to make that happen.

"The reason I asked you out was not because you're the same Whitney Cartwright I've known all my life, but because you're miraculously this totally different person. You . . ." I falter again, the words slipping through my mind faster than grains of sand through fingertips. "You fascinate me."

She swings her eyes to me again, and now I can see the moisture in them. Pooling on the surface, ready to spill out. "What?"

"You fascinate me," I repeat, this time with more authority. "Ever since you came back here. With your glasses and your new look and your bags of books."

She snickers. "I fascinate you because I know how to read?"

"No. You fascinate me because I feel like I've been looking at you my whole life and I've never seen you before.

And I'm just wondering what was wrong with me all that time."

"Nothing," she mumbles, taking another swig from the bottle. "It wasn't you. It was me. I was just being the girl that I thought everyone wanted me to be. The pretty Cartwright. The one who got her mother's looks and nothing else." She deepens her voice, "'You win with the hand you've been dealt,' that's what my father always says. So that's what I tried to do, my whole life. But that was never me. I mean, for the longest time I thought it was. I thought all I cared about was having the latest and greatest eye shadow palette or designer handbag or knowing who John Mayer was dating at all times. I always thought I would turn out just like my mom. I'd marry some rich banker and have this cushy life with infinity pools and big closets. And then . . ."

Her voice breaks a little. She fights to regain her composure.

"And then my mom left," she says, suddenly sounding so fragile. "And I realized it was all a sham. She wasn't happy. She didn't *want* those things. She tolerated those things. Just like I did."

She takes another sip of wine and glances up at the stars. "I remember this one day after she left. I was sitting in the backseat of my friend Willow's car. We were driving to the mall. She and Lydia were arguing over who would get to buy the latest Jimmy Choo fringe bootie. Because God forbid they *both* own a pair. I remember thinking, 'Why the fuck does it matter?' And then I answered myself. And the answer was suddenly so obvious to me: 'It doesn't.'"

It's not the first time Whitney has talked to me about her mother. She brought it up a week ago, and I was shocked to learn the real reason Mrs. Cartwright wasn't here this summer. I couldn't believe that Grayson never told me. Whitney explained that the family had agreed to keep it a secret. They didn't want the whole island gossiping about them behind their backs. And I get that, but I still wish he had confided in me.

"Why'd you stop coming back here?" I ask. It's not the first time I've asked Whitney this either. I remember posing this same question the night I dove through her window to find douche McNugget on top of her. She didn't answer me then, and after a long silence I'm afraid she's still not going to answer me now.

But then she takes a deep breath and another swig of wine and says, "I think the whole thing got away from me. It's slippery, you know? The slope from Pretty Girl to Slutty Girl. It's easy to fall down it. It's easy for you to try to hold on to one title and suddenly find yourself wearing the other. Without even realizing it until someone—or the whole damn island—points it out."

All at once every mean thing I've ever said to Whitney comes spiraling back to me, and I feel sick to my stomach.

She watches my reaction carefully, as if she can read every thought. As if every memory is being projected right across my face. "Yes," she confirms. "You did it too."

"Whitney," I begin, but she quiets me with a shake of her head.

"It's okay. You weren't the only one. But it's one of the bigger reasons I stopped coming here. I felt like my reputation was sealed. Like the label was stamped into my skin from the day I was born. There was no going back. No one on this island would ever see me as any-thing but Grayson's slutty little sister." She stops and picks at the label of the wine bottle with her fingernail. "After my mom left and I finally figured out who I really wanted to be, I decided it didn't matter anymore what people thought of me."

"You're right," I tell her. "It doesn't."

She chuckles quietly. "Yeah. I know. But sometimes that's easier to say than it is to believe."

"I was an ass," I tell Whitney. "I'm sorry."

She smiles the weakest of smiles. "It's okay. But yes, you were."

We share another laugh, but it's not the same. It's not jubilant and carefree. It's heavy and sad.

"You've changed a lot too," she says.

I cock an eyebrow. "Oh really? How so?"

She scrutinizes me like she's sizing up a horse she's thinking about buying. "You're much cuter than you used to be. Or maybe your hair is just longer."

I playfully bump her leg with mine. She glances down at my ratty swim trunks and T-shirt.

"Your choice in clothing hasn't improved much, though."

"Hey," I tease. "I'll have you know, I almost bought a suit for you."

"No, you didn't."

I sigh. "No, I didn't."

She chuckles. "You make me laugh."

I act offended. "I didn't make you laugh before?"

"No. Before you just made me want to punch things."

I can't help but chuckle too. "Likewise."

"You look at me like I'm a person." Her voice is suddenly quiet and somber. When I turn my head to look at her, she's staring back at me with such intensity, such expectation, it makes me uneasy. Like she's asking too much of me. Asking for things I don't have to give.

Things I may never be able to give again.

"Yeah," I say with a teasing snort. "A person with terrible taste in books. I mean seriously, what is with this *Sense and Sensibility* crap? Is anything *ever* going to happen? I mean, when you told me Victorian times, I thought there'd at least be *one* duel. But no. There's not even a bitch slap."

She's suddenly laughing again, and then she's fake bitch slapping me. I whip my head back and hold on to my cheek like it's on fire. "Now *that's* what I'm talking about!" I say with a wicked grin.

The breeze picks up, playing in the small hairs that have escaped her ponytail. I reach up and brush them back.

"You've grown up," she says softly after a moment. "A lot."

I let out a dark laugh and let my hand fall away from her face. "Death will do that to you."

She looks surprised by my admission. I admit, I'm probably just as surprised. If not more. It's the first time I've mentioned my father since we started hanging out. Being with Whitney these past few weeks has been heavenly. It's everything I've needed to take my mind off the worst year of my life. I'm not sure why I brought him up now. Maybe because she was so honest with me first. Maybe because pain always manages to rise to the surface, no matter how hard you try to push it down.

Maybe because it's time.

I take the bottle from her and tip it back, letting the powerful red liquid pour down my throat. Whitney bites her lip, looking hesitant. "I'm sorry, Ian. I never told you how sorry I am. Your father was a great man. I have really fond memories of—"

"Don't do that," I interrupt sharply, wiping my mouth.

She frowns, not understanding. "Do what?"

"Don't do what everyone else does. Don't tell me you're

sorry and talk about how amazing he was. I know he was amazing. I don't need people to remind me. That doesn't help."

She looks taken aback. And I know I should feel bad for lashing out, but I don't. I'm sick of it. I'm sick of everyone treating me like this fragile creature that they can't talk to. My dad is the one who died, not me. And I'm tired of everyone treating death like it's an incurable disease that's going to claim me next.

"I don't know what to say," she admits, taking the wine bottle back. "I'm bad at this."

"No one's good at this."

"What do you want me to do, Ian?"

"I want you to be Whitney."

She gives me a devilish smirk. "The new one or the old one?"

And she thought she wasn't good at this.

I match her smile. "Maybe a little of both?"

She places the bottle of wine down on the ground and leans into me, her whole body turning seductive, like only Whitney can do.

When her lips meet mine, I can taste the tartness of the wine mixed with the sweetness of her scent. It's debilitating. It's stimulating. It's so intoxicating.

As we melt together and the sour thoughts in my mind quickly ferment into something good, something drinkable, all I can think is:

With lips like those, who even needs wine?

CHAPTER 31

I sit in the sand, leaning against a sea-weathered log, while Harper lies with her head in my lap. I run my fingers absentmindedly through her hair with one hand while the other plays with my phone. She's staring silently up at the stars. She does that a lot. Stares at the sky. I think she thinks the answers are up there somewhere and if she just looks hard enough, eventually she'll find them.

This has been the majority of our summer together. Yes, we kiss. A *lot*. But we also just do this. And it's pretty freaking amazing, I have to say.

It took a while to find a spot where we could be together without the threat of all the inquisitive eyes. I never knew how hard it was to hide on Winlock Harbor until I started secretly hooking up with my best friend's ex.

Downtown is out of the question. The main beach is even worse. My house is a minefield, with Mike working on the roof and Ian camped out in the guest room. My father's boat stopped being an option after he got sick of the ferry and started taking it back and forth to the mainland for work. I don't know what he's been doing, but he's been there an awful lot. Not that I'm going to ask. The Cartwrights are a better family when you *don't* ask questions.

And then finally, a few weeks ago, Harper took me to this place. A quiet, hidden alcove tucked away from the beach that she swears no one knows exists.

I couldn't believe I had never seen it before. I've been coming to this island every summer for practically my entire life. I thought I'd combed the whole thing a dozen times. And yet I'd never seen this place.

When I asked her how *she* had found it, she got very quiet and cagey for a minute. "I don't really remember. I guess I just stumbled upon it one day," she said with a shrug.

But it doesn't really matter *how* she found it. What matters is that it's here.

It provides us with the privacy we need to be these people we've become. To live this life we've somehow constructed with each other.

To hide.

"Remember that time when we were fifteen and we all got drunk and went skinny-dipping in the ocean by your house?" Harper asks.

I feel my face growing warm at the memory. Despite my vow to be respectful to Mike and *not* constantly check out his girlfriend's body, she was *right* there. And she was completely naked.

"Yes," I say warily, unsure where she might be going with this.

"Remember how we went diving under the surface at the same time and bumped into each other?"

"Vividly," I say with a sarcastic tone.

"When we resurfaced, you yelled at me and told me to watch where the hell I was going," Harper reminds me. "You were, like, so angry at me."

"Yeah," I say slowly, setting my phone down in the sand. "That's not really why I yelled at you."

She tilts her chin up so she can question me with those bright blue eyes of hers.

I sigh. "Figure it out, Harper. You were naked! And we touched. Things *happened* to me. I needed to run interference. I couldn't let you—or Mike!—know that . . ." I let my voice trail off, hoping she can infer the rest.

She does. She starts giggling. "I always wondered about that."

I tickle her. "Oh, bullshit. You so knew. You were such a flirt. In fact, I think you bumped into me on purpose."

"I certainly did not," she vows. "Actually, I was a little afraid of you."

"Afraid of me?" I repeat dubiously.

"Yes!" she insists. "You always hated me."

I roll my eyes. "I didn't *hate* you. I highly disapproved of your life choices."

She pushes herself up and leans toward me, those irresistible pouty lips only inches from mine. "You *hated* me." She breathes the words with a delicious air of teasing and seduction.

I lunge for those perfect lips and capture them with my own. She lets out a soft moan and melts into me. I roll her onto her back and position myself on top of her, pushing my tongue further into her mouth.

I don't know how long we stay like that, our mouths moving hungrily against each other. That's the thing about Harper. It's so easy to get lost in her kisses. To let them swallow me whole and erase everything else that's happening in the world.

The pain in my arm.

Gone.

The anger I feel toward my mother.

Gone.

I pull away and gaze down at her. Harper Jennings is beautiful in every light, but this is where I love her face the most. In this quiet hideaway. With the moon reflecting in her eyes.

"Do you still hate me?" she asks, and I notice the distinct lack of teasing in her voice. There's a gravity there. A silent supplication.

I tuck a strand of her hair behind her ear. "I hate you more than I've ever hated anyone." My words are gentle. My tone is a lullaby. She understands.

She closes her eyes, and I kiss her again. This time tenderly. This time just a soft touch. On her lips. On her nose. On her cheek.

"I hate you, too," she whispers into my ear.

And then, back to her lips. She raises her hips up, pressing into me. I reach down and slide my hand under her shirt. She kisses me harder. I move my mouth to her neck. Her body shivers in response.

"How did you even find this place?"

I pull back and look at her in surprise. "What did you —" I start to ask, but I'm not able to finish because Harper's hand clamps down on my mouth. Her eyes open wide, and that's when I comprehend what's happening.

We're no longer alone.

And the voice I hear next turns my blood to ice.

"I was surfing one day when the tide was unusually high. My board actually drifted way back here."

Holy shit. It's Mike.

I scramble to my knees and peer over the small log that has thus far shielded us from view. But I know that won't last long. It's too dark to see detail, but I can definitely make out two shapes — two people — walking toward us.

"It's amazing!" the second voice says, the one I originally thought was Harper's. And that's because it's definitely female.

Mike knows about this place too? And he's brought a girl here?

Without another word between us, Harper and I scurry on all fours to the far edge of the alcove so we can try to circle around the perimeter back to the entrance.

"Hardly anyone else knows about it," Mike says.

I fight back a snort. *Yeah, except for Harper.*

"I used to come here more often," Mike goes on. "But this summer . . . I don't know. Things just got a little crazy, I guess. It's nice to be back, though. It's nice to be here with someone."

We've nearly made it back to the thick brush and tall weeds that cover the opening. But Harper, who has been crawling in front of me, stops short when she hears this. She turns and peers into the darkness, like she's trying to see what's going on.

"Thank you," the mystery girl says quietly. "For bringing me here. For showing me this piece of you."

I catch a glimpse at Harper's reaction in the glint of moonlight. She looks livid. And worse than that, she actually looks like she's about ready to jump out and start screaming at him.

She opens her mouth, and I lunge forward to tackle her. Fortunately, the sand muffles the sound. Harper squirms free and glares back at me. I shoot her a warning look and point to the opening just a few feet ahead of us. With a silent huff she resumes crawling.

Once we're through the brush and back on the beach, she stomps away from me. I run to catch up, making sure we're close enough to the surf for the waves to hide our voices.

"What is your problem?" I growl. "Do you *want* us to get caught or something?"

She ignores this question. She's too busy stewing in her own fury. "I can't *believe* he would bring someone there. To *our* place."

I blink in disbelief. "Hold up. *Your* place. That's where you've been bringing me?"

She bites her lip, looking totally conflicted, like she can't decide which issue to tackle first. Her jealousy or mine. She shakes out her hands, as though she's trying to shake off tiny, invisible bugs. "There was no other place to go!" she yells defensively.

"Harper," I begin heavily, "Mike is my best friend. And that used to be *your* place with him. Don't you realize how fucked up that is?"

"Not as fucked up as him bringing some bimbo slut bag there. It's different with you and me. We've known each other forever. He brought a total stranger there. I've never even seen that girl before."

I frown at her. "Why are you getting so upset about this? If anything, you should see this as a good thing. We both should. If he's hanging out with this girl, that means he's moving on. It takes some of the pressure off us." I stop and narrow my eyes at her. "You do want him to move on, don't you?"

She doesn't answer. She just looks at her feet.

I feel frustration boiling up inside me. "Harper," I warn.

"Yes!" she finally screams. "No! I don't know!"

"What is this?" I demand, taking a step toward her. "What are we doing here? I thought this could be something real. I thought you felt the same way. Or are you just biding your time with me? Am I just some fun little summer fling to distract you until you're ready to go back to him?"

"No," she says automatically, but there's no heart in it. She wrings her hands, looking conflicted. "It's just that Mike and I have been together forever. It's not that simple."

"It feels pretty simple to me," I snap. "You broke up with him. Which, last I checked, means you're *not* together anymore. Which leaves him free to bring whomever he wants to that place, and leaves you free to do"—I gnash my teeth together—"well, whatever the fuck this is."

Her expression softens. "Grayson," she says, and I hate the way her voice sounds. So sad and full of pity. It's the very *last* thing I want from her.

"Forget it," I spit, and turn my back on her. "Just let me know when you've figured out what you want, Harper."

I take off down the beach. Harper doesn't follow me. She just lets me leave. Which makes it all that much worse.

CHAPTER 32

When we were twelve years old, Harper and I kissed for the very first time. I remember it like it was yesterday. The four of us were swimming in the beach club pool—me, Harper, Grayson, and Ian. It was late summer. Most of the tourists had gone home so we had the pool to ourselves.

I had dived to the bottom of the pool to grab a bracelet that had slipped off Harper's wrist. I was just about to resurface, the recovered jewelry safely in hand, when suddenly she was in front of me. Her blue eyes were wide open under the water. Her hair fanned out around her like a white halo. She swam right up to me. She placed her hand securely on the back of my head. And she pressed her lips to mine.

It didn't last long. We didn't have much oxygen left. But it was amazing. It was everything I wanted it to be and more.

I had dived under that water a scared, inexperienced, scrawny twelve-year-old boy, and I resurfaced an entirely new person. There had been no time to think about the kiss. No time to agonize over what I was supposed to do or whether or not I would do it all wrong.

I felt giddy and excited and as light as air.

But above all else, there was this sense of relief. A much-needed assurance that she felt the same about me as I did about her.

Something had changed that summer. I couldn't pinpoint what it was exactly. I just knew it was different. Harper was different. I was different. I *felt* different around her.

When I looked at her, I was suddenly experiencing sensations I'd never experienced before. Things I didn't even have names for. But I hadn't been sure if I was alone in those feelings. I'd had no idea what she was thinking.

Especially after that horrible Spin the Bottle game we'd played earlier that summer. At first, when Harper had come to me with the idea, it had seemed fun. A perfect way for me to test out these new feelings I was having. I imagined her spinning the bottle and it pointing right at me. I'd be able to kiss her without all the pressure. I'd be able to see her reaction. Maybe even feel it. All under the safe guise of a silly game.

I had never even considered the possibility that the bottle, or flashlight, might not land on me.

When it slowed to a stop and I saw that it was pointing at Grayson, the whole garden shed came crashing down around me. My ears burned. My fingers twitched. And there was a knot in my stomach the size of Tennessee.

But the worst was not yet over. When the shock wore off and I finally managed to tear my gaze from the flashlight and look at Harper, I hoped her face would give away her disgust. I hoped the very thought of kissing anyone else but me would make her insides crawl.

I hoped. But that wasn't what I saw.

She didn't even glance my way to see how I was doing. She just started crawling toward Grayson, her lips already pursed, her smile already giving her excitement away.

I felt positively nauseous. And they hadn't even kissed yet. I knew I wouldn't be able to watch their lips touch. I knew I wouldn't be able to just sit there while Grayson Cartwright stole my first kiss away from me.

So I got up, mumbled something about my stomach hurting, and ran. I hid in the kitchen with Mamma V for the rest of the afternoon and well into the evening. When Mamma V asked me what was wrong, why I looked so pale, I told her I wasn't feeling well. It wasn't exactly a lie.

She made me chicken soup and let me sit in her office and watch TV on the tiny screen she kept in there.

I didn't come out until it was dark.

The next day I worked up the courage to ask Ian what had happened. I don't remember how I worded it, but I was careful not to ask the question directly. Regardless, Ian seemed to understand exactly what I was saying. His eyes showed all the empathy in the world.

He held out his fist, and we launched into our secret handshake—one front tap, two on top, two on the bottom, palm-to-palm crazy fingers—and then he patted me on the back and said, "Nothing happened."

The two most beautiful words I'd ever heard. My heart sang out in relief.

Two months later, when Harper found me under that water and pressed her lips against mine, all of that worry and anxiety and paranoia just floated away.

She liked *me*.

She kissed *me*.

She chose *me*.

I know it's wrong to think about that day now, as I'm standing in the middle of the Cove with Julie. I know it's wrong for Harper's name to be floating around in my mind, but I can't help it. She has occupied my thoughts for far too long. Like a light that's always on. That you never turn off. And eventually you simply forget where the switch is.

I've never taken anyone else to my secret spot. Ever. It was always Harper's and mine. But maybe Julie is right. Maybe Grayson is right. Maybe Harper is meant to stay in the past. Maybe I need to stop facing backward and start facing forward.

And after seeing Julie's reaction when we climbed through that brush and stepped into the clearing, I knew I had made the right decision. I knew she of all people would appreciate it.

She spins in a slow circle now, continuing to take in the quiet, secluded alcove. At first it's strange to see her here, wearing *my* sweatshirt, her bare feet buried in *this* sand. It almost feels wrong. Like putting on a brand-new pair of flip-flops that haven't yet formed to your feet. But the longer we stand there, the more acclimated I become. The more I can see how well she fits in this space. Like she was meant to be here. Like I was meant to bring her.

"It's magic," she whispers.

I've never thought of describing it that way before, but she's absolutely right. It *is* magic. With the moon glittering and the waves crashing in the distance and the wind whistling, it's the very definition of magic.

She reaches out and slips her fingers through mine. Even though I was holding her hand as I guided her here, this feels so different. That touch was functional. A means to an end. This touch is personal. A choice.

We stay like that for a long time. Not saying a word. Our fingers entwined, our gazes finding each other over and over again.

I know she wants me to kiss her. I *want* to kiss her. But

my mind just can't seem to send the message to the rest of my body. My legs and arms are frozen.

All those doubts that I never had time to think about with Harper come barreling into my mind now.

What if I mess it up?

What if I've been doing it wrong this whole time and Harper and I never knew because we never had anything else to compare it to?

What if it feels weird?

I've only kissed one girl in my entire life. How do you just kiss someone else and pretend it doesn't shatter your whole belief system to the core?

Julie takes a step toward me, blinking twice. Her face is so close to mine. Her lips are so reachable. My stomach begins to churn.

I can smell the faint scent of oranges on her skin. I wonder if she served them to the kids today. Or if she just naturally smells like oranges.

She smiles and lifts her hand, rests it on my cheek. Her eyes close.

I lean into her, but something just behind her snags my attention. Something out of place and foreign in my sacred space. A dark object near the fallen log.

I pull away, releasing her hand. I walk over to it and bend down to scoop it up.

Someone else has been here. Someone left their phone here.

I turn it on to see if I can deduce who it might belong to, and I'm bombarded by a barrage of text message notifications filling the screen. I stare in disbelief, my heart pounding in my chest.

Every single one of them is from Harper Jennings.

CHAPTER 33

D on't laugh," I warn Whitney for the fifth time.

"I'm not going to laugh!" she yells, grabbing a cherry stem from the nearby basket and throwing it at me. It's the morning after our conversation on the bench outside Barnacle Books, and we're back in the woods in the middle of the island. We've been coming here for the past month, trying to stay away from the summer crowds. And especially trying to stay away from Grayson. I don't know how he would react if he found out about Whitney and me, and honestly I don't really want to know.

It's not that I don't care what he thinks. He's my friend, after all. But Whitney is the best thing to happen to me in months, and I think I deserve a little reprieve.

"Just remember," I tell her, "I wrote it a while ago. When you were still a pain in my ass."

"I'm still a pain in your ass," she argues. "Just play already."

I take a deep breath and glance down at the placement of my fingers. All lined up. Everything ready to go. The song is ready to burst out of me. I've been waiting all summer for the right time to do this, and now there's no turning back.

I start to strum. I keep my eyes locked on the strings. I can't bear to look up at Whitney, just in case she starts laughing. After four bars I sing the first verse, feeling the emotions of those words that I wrote more than a month ago come flooding back to me.

> *"She's at an awkward age.*
> *Don't even try to make it better.*
> *Her heart's a rain-soaked page.*
> *She'll try to blame you for the weather.*
> *Like some elaborate maze*
> *You'll make it through if you remember*
> *Where you've been . . ."*

My voice is rough and scratchy, but it fits. It's a rough and scratchy kind of song. Unpolished and raw. Whitney hasn't uttered a word since I started. I plow on through the chorus, my strumming intensifying.

> *"If I'm wrong, what will she look like in the morning?*
> *If I'm strong, what will bring me to my knees?*
> *If I'm lonely in my world of make-believe,*
> *What will she be?*
> *Yeah, what will she be?"*

It's not until I finish that I brave a glance at her. But her face is a blank page scribbled with invisible ink.

"You hate it," I say, pulling my guitar off my lap. I return it to the case. I don't know what I was thinking, playing her this song, opening up this part of myself to her. It was a mistake.

She reaches out and gently touches my hand, stopping me. "No, I love it."

I narrow my eyes at her, trying to gauge whether she's being sincere or not.

"I've never had anyone write a song about me before," she goes on.

I laugh. "Sorry it's not a little more flattering."

"It's flattering."

I snort. "In what language?"

She leans in and kisses me, and I fall back with her on top of me. I wind my fingers into her hair and pull her closer. I swear I could stay here forever. I could live right here by this creek bed. Just the two of us. No other people. No friends. No alcoholic mothers waving CDs with home videos in my face.

This is where I want to be.

"Do you think anyone would come looking for us if we never went back?" she asks, propping herself on her elbows and staring down at me.

I smile, reaching up to touch her face. She's thinking the same thing that I am. Of course she is. Because this is perfect. Because we are perfect together, even if it took me twelve years to see that.

"I hope not," I tell her, catching one of her curls with my finger and letting it wrap around the tip. She stopped straightening her hair. Now she wears it down and loose, the curls flying free. It's beautiful. She's beautiful. And I try to tell her as much as possible. But she always just rolls her eyes and kisses me again.

Which is fine by me.

"Grayson will come looking for me," she says, bringing me back to reality with a thud. Just the sound of his name makes me feel a little nauseous. Not just because we haven't yet told him about us, but because I still have that horrible image of him almost kissing Harper Jennings in the alley that day. I don't know if they're still together. I don't want to know. I don't want to think about him at all.

"He'd be mad if he found out we were . . . you know," Whitney continues.

"I know," I tell her with a coy grin, falling back into our easy cadence. It's been a silent, unspoken game between us for the past month. Neither one of us will actually say aloud what this thing is between us. Is it a relationship? A fling? A summer romance? We keep trying to trick the other one into defining it first, but so far neither one of us has succeeded.

"Yes, he'd be mad," I agree, sitting up. "But you know Grayson. He always overreacts at first. He'll probably think I'm just playing you."

"And are you?" She sits up too and grabs my chin, giving it a tug. "Just playing me?"

"If anyone's being played, it's me."

She kisses my neck, lingering just long enough to make certain things stir. "Maybe you are."

"I don't mind being played." I raise my eyebrows.

She gives me a shove.

I pretend she's the strongest person in the world and fall down to the ground. When I push myself back up, Whitney is giggling.

"Do you think we should tell him?" I ask. "That we're . . . you know?"

She plays innocent. "No. I don't know. What exactly would we tell him?"

But I'm not falling for it. "Maybe we should just wait another few weeks."

Whitney cocks an eyebrow. "Another few weeks? You think I'm going to be around for another few weeks?"

"I think you are," I say confidently.

She laughs. "Well, aren't you cocky. What makes you so sure?"

"Because you can't get enough of me."

Who am I right now?

I can't even fathom the words coming out of my mouth. I'm like an entirely different person. That's what this girl does to me. She renews me. She brings out some side of me that I never knew existed.

"Or maybe *I* can't get enough of *you*," I say softly, and then I kiss her again. She climbs on top of me, putting one leg on either side of my hips, pushing herself into me. I immediately feel my body responding to hers. It's instantaneous. Just like everything else she does to me.

"So it's settled," she says, pulling away and kissing my nose. "We're not leaving here."

I nod. "Sounds good to me."

She climbs off me and stands up. "We can set up a house right over there." She points to a small embankment by the stream.

I stand too, taking a moment to readjust my shorts. "No. It should be up high." I point to one of the trees hiding our existence from the rest of the world. "Up there. We'll build a tree house."

"Yes!" she agrees giddily. "And you can wash the laundry in the creek."

"Wait, *I'm* doing the laundry?"

She puts her hands on her hips. "Well, you don't expect me to do it, do you? You've seen how I grew up."

"Fine, we'll hire someone to come do the laundry once a week. But that's it. No one else is coming to visit."

"And over here"—she pulls at my hand and guides me to a perfect clearing, canopied by trees—"you can play your guitar and write more songs about me. But no more of that angsty stuff where I frustrate the hell out of you." She winks to let me know that she's joking. "I want a love ballad."

"What *kind* of love ballad?" I clarify. "Are we talking Journey or Coldplay?"

"You're the artist. You figure that part out. But it should be about how obsessed you are with me."

"Oh ho!" I say. "Who's the cocky one now?"

I pull on her hand, pull and pull until she's wrapped around me again. Until our lips are colliding once more and I can taste her. Until my mind is filled with nothing but lyrics about her.

"And for food," she says, pulling away to continue our little game. "Ooh, I know!"

She tugs on my hand again, and I follow after her. She leads me through the trees and down a small dirt path. I can still hear the rushing of the creek somewhere to our left, but my view of it is obstructed by foliage.

"This is a pretty long walk just for food."

"Shut up," she tells me. "It's worth it."

I recognize where we are even before we reach the clearing up ahead, and my heart starts to gallop in my chest. My hand slips from Whitney's grasp. Oblivious to my reaction, she keeps walking, turning around only to call, "C'mon. It's right up here. I've heard this is the best place to fish on the entire island."

I shake my head. My lips feel numb. I will them to speak. "Let's go back."

Whitney gives me a strange look. "Don't be silly. It's right up here. The creek turns into a huge, deep ravine, and there's a wooden bridge that crosses over it. It's, like, fifty feet high. I think it's called Cherry Wood Bridge or something."

Cherry *Tree* Bridge, and I know it well.

And I don't want to see it. Ever again.

"I'm going back," I vow, and before Whitney can argue or try to stop me, I turn around and begin trampling through the forest.

Whitney catches up with me before long. "Ian, what's the matter with you? What happened?"

"Nothing. I just think we should be getting back."

I don't turn around to see her face. I know she'll be giving me that adorable pout I've come to love so much. And I know that this time I'll be able to resist it.

"Why?" she asks. "I don't understand."

But I can't explain it to her. Or rather, I don't want to. Because I know it will ruin this perfect afternoon that we've built for ourselves. This perfect . . . whatever it is that we're doing together.

Although, as I gather up the blanket and food, and stuff it into my backpack, I can feel Whitney's apprehensive gaze on me, and I have a sneaking suspicion that I've already ruined it.

CHAPTER 34

I wake up late. I can't find my phone anywhere—it must still be in my shorts from last night—so I don't even know what time it is, but judging from how much sunlight is flooding through my window, I know it has to be at least after eleven o'clock.

Groggy and still annoyed about my fight with Harper last night, I drag myself into the kitchen to make coffee. I'm in no mood to deal with anyone, least of all my father. But there he is. Standing by the counter with a scowl on his face that tells me I should have stayed in bed for the rest of the day.

When he sees me, he holds up an opened envelope. I cringe when I notice the familiar Vanderbilt logo in the top left-hand corner.

"What is this?" he asks.

"Um, a federal offense if that envelope has my name on it."

"Don't be coy with me. Tell me what this is."

I decide my best course of action is to play dumb. Fake it until you make it.

Right, Dad?

"I have no idea," I say, opening the fridge and pulling

out a beer. Screw coffee. I'm definitely going to need something stronger. I twist off the cap and start to take a swig, but my dad swipes the bottle angrily from my hand.

"This says you haven't yet registered for the football training camp. It starts in three weeks. Why would you not register? It says they've sent you numerous e-mail reminders."

I shrug, going back into the fridge. This time I pull out a carton of juice and take a long drink. "They must have gone to spam."

"What's going on with you, Grayson?"

"Nothing," I lie. "I just . . . I don't know. It slipped my mind. I'll register today if it'll make you happy."

"If it makes *me* happy? Since when is this about *me*?"

Since always, I think but would never dare say aloud.

"Is this about the accident?" he guesses. "Because your physical therapist says you've been cleared to play again."

"No, Dad. It's nothing. I'll register."

"You better," he warns. "Because if you skip training camp, there's no way they'll let you start in the fall. And if you don't start in the fall, there's a chance they'll rescind your acceptance, which, may I remind you, was contingent on you playing football. You don't have the kind of grades to get into Vanderbilt on academics alone."

"Thanks for reminding me of how stupid I am," I say bitingly, and immediately wish I hadn't.

My dad's face turns bright red. He sets the beer bottle down on the counter with a *clank*. "Don't give me that attitude, Grayson. We all have strengths in life. We have to learn to win with the hand we're dealt. Whitney got the looks just like your mom, and you got the brawn. Just like me."

"Isn't that interesting?" I muse sarcastically. "Now, is that DNA, or just selective parenting?"

My dad looks all kinds of confused. It gives me a fleeting sense of victory. "Football is your future, Grayson. Without it you have nothing left. This is not the time to dick around with your future. Ignoring something won't just make it go away."

I let out a loud, guttural laugh. "Actually, I think that's exactly what ignoring something will do. And if you don't believe me, why don't you just ask Mom?"

Pow!

I feel a throbbing in my cheek, and my skin feels like it's been lit on fire. I'm so stunned by what just happened, it takes me a moment to process it. It's been a long time since my dad hit me. The last time was when I was eleven and I said something nasty to my sister. I don't even remember what it was. I just remember how long that bruise lasted on my cheek.

I wonder how long this one will last.

"Your mother's and my relationship is complicated and private," my dad says, quietly seething.

The smart move would be to shut the hell up. But we've already established that intelligence is not my strong suit. "So private that you won't even acknowledge that she's gone?" I challenge, and immediately take a step back, afraid he's going to smack me again.

He doesn't. In fact, he doesn't do much of anything. He just stands there, fuming at me in silence.

So I keep going. Because apparently I'm on a real roll now.

"This whole summer I've been lying for you. Telling everyone that she's in Europe. Because God forbid anyone think less of us. God forbid anyone actually know the truth about us."

"This discussion isn't about me," Dad snaps. "It's about *you* and your poor choices recently. This is a precarious moment in your life, Grayson. It's not the time to be glib."

I shake my head. I've had about enough of this. I grab the beer from the counter and take a long gulp, right in front of him. Then I press the ice-cold bottle to my swollen cheek. I turn to my dad, flashing him the fakest smile I can muster. "If you need me, I'll be in my room, dicking around with my future."

I lock myself in my bedroom for the rest of the morning and well into the afternoon. I consider texting Harper, but I still can't find my phone. It wasn't in the pocket of my shorts. I figure it must be in the living room, but I'm not going back out there.

It's probably better that I don't text Harper anyway. That whole thing is a mess. Whenever I try to think about it or analyze it, I just end up confusing myself. The truth is, I like the way I feel when I'm around her. More than that, I have no idea. And I definitely don't know what she wants.

Am I just a convenient distraction for her?

Are we just convenient distractions for each other?

And if that's the case, then what's wrong with that? What's wrong with having a little distraction from your effed-up life?

I open my laptop and log in to my e-mail. There are eight unread messages in my inbox. Two are junk, five are from the head coach at Vanderbilt, and the most recent one is from my mom.

I freeze when I see her name in the from field.

Why is she e-mailing me? Why is she still trying to get ahold of me? Why can't she just leave me alone?

My arm immediately starts to throb. It's almost as though it sees her name and remembers. Like it *knows* that this is how it all started.

That my mom walked out. That I couldn't handle it. That I jumped into my car and drove like someone was chasing me. Drove and drove until I nearly crashed into a minivan, but swerved at the last minute and crashed into a tree instead.

It wasn't until later that I found out there was a one-month-old baby girl in that minivan. That I came this close to taking a life. A precious, newborn life that had barely even had a chance to begin yet.

Instead I took my future.

Three fractures in my right humerus, and a shattered elbow. Chance of being able to play football again: 5 percent. A number I never shared with anyone. A number I tried to ignore myself.

I suppose, in the end, it was a small price to pay.

My future for that little girl's.

I delete the e-mail from my mother without reading it. It doesn't matter what she wrote. I don't care what she has to say. She forfeited the right to share her feelings with me when she walked out that door.

Even though I'm sure it's only my imagination, the pain in my arm subsides ever so slightly as soon as the e-mail disappears from my inbox.

Now the most recent message is the latest one from the Vanderbilt coach.

The subject line reads:

FINAL REMINDER TO REGISTER FOR SUMMER
TRAINING

This one I do open. I skim through the text. My eyes pick up words like "extremely important" and "all freshmen required to attend" and "admission status may be affected."

I run my finger over the track pad until the pointer is hovering over the link at the bottom.

Click here to register.

For what feels like hours the pointer doesn't move. My fingertip stays poised on the button. My hand starts to shake. My arm starts to ache again.

What if it never heals?

What if I can never throw another perfect, game-saving spiral again?

What if my dad's right and this is my only future?

Whitney got the beauty, and I got the brawn. But what if I don't want the brawn anymore? What if I want to be known for something else besides football? What if I never figure out what that is?

I hear the sound of a house door closing, and a minute later, through the crack in my curtains, I see my dad's car pulling out of the garage. I wait, listening, making sure no one else is home. Then I sneak out of my bedroom.

I find the football my dad has been trying to get me to toss around with him. It's still sitting on the kitchen table, like a bizarre centerpiece. Like a constant reminder of my failure as a son. I grab it and slip out to the backyard.

The sun is high and bright in the sky. Another perfect day on Winlock Harbor.

I stand by the shallow end of the pool and position the ball in my hand, lining my fingers up perfectly with the laces. I admit, it feels good to hold it again. Like a blanket you carried around as a child suddenly rediscovered in a box of old memories.

I tap the ball against my opposite hand a few times, making sure the hold is snug. My arm is already starting to protest, as if it knows exactly what I'm warming up to do and is preempting with a healthy dose of agony.

I ignore the lightning bolts running up from my elbow, and I set up my stance so that I'm perfectly aligned with my target—the other end of the pool.

I cock my arm back, wincing as my shoulder rotates.

Then I let the ball fly.

The pain is so intense, I nearly drop to the ground. I just manage to hold myself up long enough to see the ball sputter pathetically, like a windup toy that's run out of rotations, and plummet into the center of the pool.

Even the splash it makes is pitiful.

Holding my throbbing arm, I stumble back into the house, fight to get the bottle of Advil open, and pour half the damn thing into my mouth.

I return to my computer, take one last look at the e-mail on the screen, and before I can change my mind, I click delete.

Just then there's a knock on the front door. Cradling my still-screaming arm, I hobble out into the living room and swing open the door.

Mike is standing on our front porch.

"Hey!" I say, surprised to see him here on a Sunday. It's not like we really hang out anymore. "Did I forget to leave you the last check?"

"No," he says soberly, and there's something in his voice that I can't quite identify. Accusation? Distrust? Defeat?

He holds up his right hand, and suddenly the world starts spinning way too fast. Out of control. I search for something to grab on to. But there's nothing.

Accusation.

It was definitely accusation that I heard.

I stare numbly at the phone clutched between his fingers, trying to pinpoint the exact moment when my life went so far off track.

Mike narrows his eyes at me and speaks very slowly, enunciating every word so that they echo endlessly inside my brain. "I want to know why you have twenty-two text messages from Harper on your phone."

CHAPTER 35

Grayson stares at me for a long moment, his right arm cradled awkwardly in his left. It took me all night to work up the nerve to come here. All night I stared at those text messages, reading them over and over again. Analyzing them. Dissecting them. Trying not to assume the worst.

But what else is there to assume? Especially when your ex-girlfriend is texting your best friend things like:

> I'm sorry for freaking out earlier.

> This is all uncharted territory for me. I can't figure out what to make of it yet.

> Can we meet?

That last one was time stamped at 11:02 p.m. Why did Harper want to meet him at eleven o'clock at night? Why was she freaking out? And what was uncharted territory?

These are all of the pressing questions I hoped to convey with a single look when Grayson opened the door, but I don't seem to be conveying any of it, because he just kind of stares back at me like he doesn't even know why I'm here. Like this isn't the big deal that I think it is, and I shouldn't be as stressed out as I am.

"Oh!" he says with an air of relief. "You found my phone. Thank you! I've been looking for it everywhere!"

That's the part of this he's choosing to respond to? His lost phone?

"It was at the Cove," I reply tightly. "*Our* Cove. Mine and Harper's."

Grayson narrows his eyes at me, like he's trying to keep up. "Cove?" he repeats. "What cove?"

I'm starting to lose patience. If he thinks this little game is going to deter me from the real issue here, he's sorely mistaken.

"The little alcove near the beach club. I've been going there for years."

He slaps his leg and then winces slightly, like the action caused him physical pain. "Really?" he exclaims. "I just stumbled upon it yesterday while I was walking the beach. I thought I was like Columbus, discovering some new world. Although, technically he didn't really discover it, since the Native Americans were already here and all of that. So I guess that makes us the same. Me and Columbus."

What the fuck is he talking about?

"Well," he says, easing the phone out of my grasp, "thanks for returning it."

He starts to close the door, but I stop it with my hand. "The text messages," I remind him sternly. "What are they doing on your phone? Why is Harper texting you at eleven at night."

Once again Grayson looks baffled, like he can't figure out why I'm taking this tone with him. "Because we're friends," he says, as though it's obvious.

"No, you're not."

"Uh, yes, we are. We've been friends since we were kids. Did you forget she also hung out with me and Ian all those years?"

"Is she texting with Ian too, then?" I challenge.

Grayson shrugs. "How should I know? We're not *that* good of friends."

"Why did she say she was 'freaking out' in one of her messages last night?"

He blinks rapidly, like he's trying to keep up. Then he lets out a heavy sigh. "Okay, I didn't want to tell you about it. But the truth is she's upset about the breakup and needed someone to talk to. We've been meeting up and just chatting. About relationships and life and all that girly shit. I thought if I told you, it would just upset you and make it harder for you to move on, so I didn't."

Grayson presses his lips together and moves them around, like a woman blotting lipstick. I immediately narrow my eyes in suspicion.

That's his tell.

That's what he does when he's lying. I've known him for years, and I've seen him do it a hundred times. Just never to me.

But what does it mean?

Is he lying to me?

Or are his lips just chapped?

I admit, within this new context, the text messages themselves are fairly benign. Maybe he's telling the truth. Maybe he and Harper are just friends who meet up to talk.

I just never thought Grayson and Harper had anything to talk *about*.

What could they possibly have in common?

"So that's all this is?" I confirm, staring him down. "You two have been *talking*."

"Yeah," Grayson says in the most convincingly non-chalant tone I've ever heard. "Of course that's all it is."

He gestures into the empty house. "Do you wanna come in and hang out? We can play some video games or something."

I shake my head, trying to make sense of this strange conversation. It didn't exactly go the way I thought it would. In fact, it went nothing like I thought it would.

"No," I say absentmindedly. "I actually have to work at the club in a few."

Grayson nods. "Okay. I'll see you later, then?"

"Sure," I say, and he gives me a wide smile before closing the door.

A week later I've almost managed to convince myself that Grayson was telling the truth and that I've simply turned into the kind of crazy, paranoid person I've always despised.

Of course nothing's going on with Grayson and Harper. It was a ridiculous conclusion to jump to in the first place.

Harper is my ex and Grayson is my best friend, and there's a code. A code that Grayson knows all too well. After all, he has a sister, and the same rules pretty much apply.

The guy might be known to hook up with just about anything that walks, but he wouldn't do *that*. Not with Harper. Not to me.

Julie and I are just finishing a two-hour bike tour of the island on what has to be the hottest day of the entire summer, maybe even the entire decade. When we get back to the rental shop downtown, Julie hops off her bike and wheels it up to the rack outside the shop. She unclasps her helmet and pulls it off her head, shaking out her short brown hair and rubbing sweat from the back of her neck.

"That was so much fun!" she squeals.

I squeeze the brakes and come to a stop beside her. I use the front of my shirt to wipe a layer of perspiration from my face, which must be beet red by now despite the fact that it's already after five o'clock. I can't believe Julie talked me into renting bikes. This has to be *the* most touristy thing you can do on the Locks. Every time I used to see a family pass by on the street riding those matching blue bicycles, I swore I would never do that in a million years.

Actually, I swore I would never do a lot of things on this island. But over the course of the summer, Julie has convinced me to do almost all of them.

"Wasn't that fun?" she asks, skipping over to me.

"Superfun," I say, trying to sound convincing. It's not that I didn't enjoy myself. Surprisingly, I did. It's just that my mind has been preoccupied over the past week and I'm trying not to let it show.

Julie laughs. "You know you're a terrible liar?"

I chuckle as I walk my bike up to the rack and slide it into the slot next to Julie's. I take a look around Ocean Avenue, watching the tourists come and go from shops and restaurants.

Julie stands on her tiptoes to tap my forehead. "What's going on up here?"

But I don't respond. Because my attention has been snagged by something else. Harper has just walked out of Coconut's Market and has paused on the curb to glance down at something on her phone. She's alone, which is unusual. She's almost always accompanied by a friend or a hopeful young tourist looking to score. Harper doesn't like being alone, which is ironic, given the fact that half the times she's put a pin in our relationship it has been because she said she wanted to be alone. And then the very next day I'd see her attached at the hip to Bree or Riley.

"Are you okay?" Julie says after I've been silent for I don't even know how long.

I blink and look down at her, mentally berating myself for being so distracted. Julie is amazing. She's cute and fun and laid-back, and she invited me to hang out with her today. And yet I can't help but be somewhere else.

"Sorry," I say hastily. "What did you want to do next? Go to the beach?"

Julie doesn't answer. Instead she follows my gaze across the street. "Is that her?"

I turn back and notice that Harper is still there. She's still totally absorbed in her phone, except now she's smiling and biting her lip.

My body tenses. I know that look. Sometimes she would bite her lip before she would kiss me, or when she was about to tell me something dirty. Or right before she'd slide her shirt over her head and we'd—

"Is that Harper?" Julie asks again.

I shake myself out of my funk. "Yeah," I mumble.

Julie touches my arm. "Do you want to get out of here?"

I glance back at Harper once more. She's stuffing her phone into her purse and striding purposefully down the street.

I suddenly have this insane, all-consuming need to know where she's going. To find out once and for all what's really going on here.

"Actually, I just have to do one thing," I say to Julie. "Can I meet you at the beach?"

Julie may be the bubbliest girl I've ever met, but I don't miss the flash of disappointment on her face. A flash she quickly covers up. "Oh. Okay. No problem. You do what you gotta do. I'll see you down there."

"It'll only take a second," I assure her.

Julie smiles, but there's something lacking in it. The sparkle is significantly less sparkly. "No problem."

I tell myself that I'm only doing this to put my mind at rest, so I can hang out with Julie without all these distracting thoughts spinning around in my head.

I just need to know.

"Thanks." I give her arm a squeeze, and then I take off after Harper, maintaining a safe distance behind so she won't know that I'm following her, like the stalker that I've apparently become.

CHAPTER 36

Whitney knocks on my door while I'm sitting in my room reading the last few chapters of *Sense and Sensibility*. She drapes herself over the foot of the bed with a dramatic sigh. "I'm bored. Let's go do something."

"I am *not* Mr. Willoughby," I say defensively.

She props herself up on her elbows and squints at me. "Huh?"

"Last month, by the pool, you told me you were learning to stay away from Willoughbys like me."

She laughs. "Last month you also wrote an entire song about how obnoxious I was."

I twist my lips and go back to reading. "Touché."

Whitney groans. "Seriously. Let's go do something. You've been holed up in this house for the past week."

I shrug. "I like it here."

"And I like it out there." She points to the window.

I shrug and flip the page. I can't bring myself to tell her the real reason I've barely left the house. After what happened last week in the woods, I've come to realize that the entire island is chock-full of land mines and I don't want to risk stepping on another one.

I thought as long as I didn't go back to my grandparents' house, I'd be safe. Little did I know, my father's ghost isn't just confined to the house. He can travel everywhere, which means nothing is safe.

Except this bedroom. And this house.

But even here my mind is my enemy. For the past week, despite my efforts, my thoughts keep drifting back to that bridge that Whitney and I stumbled upon in the woods. Cherry Tree Bridge.

It's kind of chilling to know that it's still there. Still standing. A landmark of my past that never changes, even as grenades fall around me, tearing the rest of my world apart.

It wasn't Whitney's fault. She didn't know. She couldn't possibly have realized that when my eyes fell upon that bridge, all I could see was him.

My father.

Casting a fishing line over the edge.

Lifting me up so I could stand on the second-highest rail and watch my lure float in the water so far below.

Helping me reel in my first catch.

A thousand perfect moments captured in a single location.

Moments that will never happen again.

Whitney starts to crawl toward me, her body slinky and catlike. She's doing that seductive thing that she does so damn well. She starts to kiss my stomach, pushing up my shirt to brush her beautiful lips against my bare skin.

A tingle shoots up my spine.

"What about Grayson?" I ask as she slowly moves her way up to my chest.

"Gone," she murmurs against me.

I tip my head back and let out a soft moan. God, those lips are magic. By the time she reaches my mouth, I'm completely turned on. She straddles me and kisses me hard.

I wrap my hands around her hips. Whitney grinds slowly against me, driving me absolutely crazy.

Then my cell phone rings, shattering the moment and bringing me back down to earth. I reach for it to silence it but inadvertently catch sight of the screen.

It's my mom.

If the mood wasn't completely spoiled a second ago, it certainly is now.

I jab my finger against the ignore button and toss the phone onto the carpet. Whitney winces at my brusqueness and quickly moves off me. "Who was that? Ex-girlfriend?"

"No one. Never mind."

But she's not having it. She leaps off the bed and reaches for the phone. In a panic I dive for it, accidentally shoving her onto her side as I scoop up the phone.

"Ow," she moans as she hits the carpet. "What the hell, Ian?"

"Sorry," I mumble, feeling anxious and guilty and completely out of control.

Whitney pushes herself to her feet. "Who was calling you? Are you hooking up with someone else?" She has her hands on her hips now, and I can tell she's about to make a much bigger deal about this than it is.

"What? No. I'm just hooking up with you."

But this response only seems to make everything worse. She scowls down at me. I push my fingertips into my eyelids, trying to regain my composure. I don't have the emotional energy to deal with this right now. "It was a wrong number," I say, hoping the iciness in my tone will put an end to this once and for all.

Of course, it doesn't.

Because it's Whitney we're talking about. Things aren't over until *she's* done.

She narrows her eyes at me. "No one reacts that way to a wrong number."

"Just drop it, Whit," I mutter through clenched teeth.

"Fine," she agrees, surprising me. I wasn't expecting her to give in so easily. Which is probably why I'm so unprepared for what she does next.

In one swift motion I feel the phone being ripped from my hand. By the time I blink again, Whitney is already on the other side of the room, scrolling through my call log.

"Whit," I warn. "Stop. Give it back."

"No," she says. "I want to know who was calling you."

"It's not what you think," I start to say, but it's too late. She's already found it. Not just the last call. But *all* of them. Two months' worth of ignored calls coming from the same number.

Her mouth drops open. "Ian," she says, but her voice has lost all the accusation it had only a moment ago. Now it just sounds sad and disheartened. Like I've let her down.

I almost wish the call *had* been from another girl. Because anything would have been better than that look.

I lower my gaze to the ground. It's the only safe place left.

"Ian," she begins again. "What is going on? Why haven't you answered any of your mother's calls?"

"Because I don't want to talk to her, okay?" I can feel myself getting riled up again. I can feel the control of my temper slipping. I need to get out of here. I need fresh air.

I open my bedroom door and walk out into the hallway. I keep going until I'm outside. Until the scorching August air is in my lungs. But it does little to calm me. Especially when Whitney appears beside me a few seconds later.

She doesn't say anything. She doesn't have to. She knows she deserves an explanation.

"She's . . . ," I try, sputtering for the right words before realizing they don't exist. "She's driving me crazy. All she wants to do is talk about my dad and reminisce about my dad and look at photos of my dad. It's exhausting. I don't want to do any of those things!"

"Why not?" she asks gently.

"Because it won't do any good!" I shout, startling her. I take a deep breath, trying to shake out my clenched fists.

This is what comes from talking about it. This is why some things are better left unsaid. When I open my mouth again, it takes all my strength to keep my voice steady. "Looking at photos or watching home videos won't bring my dad back."

Whitney is suddenly in front of me, trying to meet my averted gaze. "You have to do something," she says.

"I am," I insist, forcing a smile. "I'm hanging out with you."

She bites her lip. "That's not what I mean. If you don't talk to someone about it—"

I roll my eyes. "Oh, not you, too. Look, I don't need another therapist. I already have one. And I definitely don't need another nagging mother. So why don't you stop trying to be both and just be my girlfriend, okay?"

I don't realize what I've said until the word is already out of my mouth. Until it's zooming between us like a helium balloon that someone has let the air out of.

I've just broken our unspoken rule. I've defined the relationship. And I'm not even sure if it's a definition I agree with. It just tumbled out. Along with every other wrong thing that I've stupidly said this summer.

I cast my eyes away from her, afraid of seeing her reaction.

"Girlfriend?" she repeats tonelessly.

I take a deep breath and lift my head, braving a glance at her. To my utter disbelief she's smiling. Actually, she's trying to *hide* a smile and is failing miserably. I feel my stomach clench.

Is this what she wants?

Is this what she's been waiting for all summer?

Suddenly I'm having trouble breathing. The giant backyard of the Cartwrights' mansion is feeling claustrophobic. I can't be someone's boyfriend. I can't be someone's anyone. I can barely take responsibility for my own emotions, let alone someone else's.

This whole thing is starting to feel like a Jenga tower. For the past two months we've been so cautious. Easing the pieces out, stacking them ever so carefully on the top. Too afraid to say the words, make the promises, commit to something. Too afraid the whole thing will come crashing down around us. But like any game of Jenga, sooner or later there's not enough pieces left to support the construction. The weight is too much. The foundation is too weak.

Eventually every tower falls.

"Is that what I am?" she asks, more smile breaking through. More air pushed right out of my lungs.

She grabs my hand and gently strokes the length of each finger.

I shift uneasily on my feet. "I don't know. I can't really think about that right now." Then I pull my hand away from hers and start down the steps. "Let's go to the beach."

CHAPTER 37

've been waiting for Harper to meet me for the past thirty minutes, and she still hasn't shown. She's not answering her phone or responding to any of my texts, which is strange, because she was texting me like a fiend up until about twenty minutes ago, and then she just stopped. The little bubble said she was formulating a response, and the text never arrived. Like someone ripped the phone right out of her hand.

We haven't talked much since our fight, and for the past week, ever since Mike showed up at my front door with my phone, we've kept our distance from each other. I'm not really sure what to do. Bottom line is we need to talk, which is why I suggested we meet on my father's boat today.

Now I'm just waiting here like a chump.

I check my phone for the tenth time. With a frustrated exhale I finally come to terms with the fact that she's not coming. I tap out one final text to her.

> If you don't want to see me anymore, how about you have the guts to tell me instead of just not showing up?

I hop off the boat and trudge through the marina toward town. As usual, Ocean Avenue is packed with people, every store open and overflowing. The tourists all want to make the most of the last few weeks of summer before Labor Day comes and we all head back to the real world.

It's an unusually hot day today, so the longest line by far is at Scoops, the local ice cream parlor where Harper had a job three years ago. Mike, Ian, and I hung out there every day that summer. Mike and Harper would flirt relentlessly across the counter, and Harper would occasionally dish us out free scoops when her boss was out running errands.

Those were the simpler times. Before life turned into this big hot mess.

Today the line spills out onto the sidewalk and snakes around the corner. I'm just squeezing past the front door when it swings open and two people walk out, laughing and licking ice cream from oversize waffle cones.

I have to do a double take to make sure my eyes are not playing tricks on me, but no. It's them.

Mike and Harper.

Looking like nothing ever split them up.

Harper sees me and freezes. Mike immediately looks to her, then to me, scrutinizing our reactions. I know this is a test. If either one of us reacts strangely, the game is up. He'll know that all the bullshit I dished out about Harper and me being just friends was exactly that—bullshit.

I paint on the breeziest smile I can muster.

"Hey!" I put my fist out for Mike to bump. He does, but it's a measured movement. And he doesn't launch into our secret handshake like he usually does. "What a surprise. What are you two doing here?"

I try to shoot Harper a look of contempt, but I can't

manage to do it. Mike's scrutiny is too intense.

"We just randomly bumped into each other," Harper says with a winning smile. Unlike mine, hers looks 100 percent organic. "And we started talking, and then one thing led to another and we decided to come by Scoops for old times' sake."

Mike takes a lick of his mint chip cone and beams at her.

"So, you two," I begin, but I'm not sure how I'm going to finish. And now I'm just standing here, pointing back and forth between them over and over again like an idiot.

This is why you're supposed to think before you talk. This is why you should plan out entire sentences before you start them.

I clear my throat. "Everything's fine between you?"

Harper bats the air. "Oh yeah. Everything's great. We were just talking about that one time when Mike and I got trapped in the walk-in freezer and had to take off all our clothes so we could keep each other warm with body heat. Remember that?"

And now she's laughing. And Mike is joining in. And they're laughing *together*. Touching each other's arms like they need help staying upright because they're laughing so damn hard.

"When your boss found us . . . ," Mike tries to say, but he can't even finish. He's too bent over in hysterics.

"There went my summer job!" Harper says, practically crying.

I try to join in, but my laugh ends up sounding like a chipmunk with a speech impediment. "That was hilarious!" I say, but it's too loud. Too fake. Both of them stop laughing and shoot me equally curious looks.

"You okay, buddy?" Mike asks.

"Fine," I say, once again trying to make eye contact

with Harper, but she either isn't getting it or is purposefully avoiding me.

"Anyway," Harper says, "we were just going to head down to the beach and hang out. It's so freaking hot! I can't imagine doing anything else. Do you want to come?"

She says this like it's nothing. Like we hang out together all the time. Harper and her ex and the guy she's been secretly hooking up with all summer.

And that's just the thing. Any other summer, this *would* be nothing. This would be normal. This would be just another day on Winlock Harbor. Which is why I really have no choice but to paint on another over-the-top, cheesy grin and say, "Sounds fun! Just like old times."

So it's settled, then. The three of us take off toward the beach. One big happy family. And as we go, all I can think is, *Well, this should be interesting.*

CHAPTER 38

Well, this should be interesting, I think as Harper, Grayson, and I stroll casually to the beach. Harper walks in the middle, and for a minute I'm terrified she's going to link arms with both of us and start skipping merrily down the street like we're characters in *The Wizard of Oz*. Who would that make me? The tin man because I have no heart? The lion because I have no courage? Or the scarecrow, because this might just be the stupidest thing I've ever done?

I wasn't able to follow Harper for long. After a few blocks she popped into another store and started browsing like she had nothing better to do on this scorching hot August afternoon than peruse the shops. And maybe she didn't. Maybe that was her plan along.

Maybe she and Grayson *are* just old friends who occasionally meet up and talk.

Maybe I'm just the suspicious, delusional ex-boyfriend who can't let go.

It's funny, I've never been paranoid before. I'm not really a jealous type of guy. It's not in my DNA. It used to drive Harper insane.

"How do I know that you love me if you never get jealous?" she would always ask.

I would kiss her forehead and tell her that her logic was skewed. It was because I loved her that I didn't get jealous.

She would disagree, and we would almost always eventually end up fighting about it. Sometimes I wondered if she flirted with other guys just to try to make me jealous, and then when it didn't work, she'd start the fight instead. Because at least it was something.

The feeling that has been twisting in my gut all week is so foreign and strange. I hate it. Every time I even consider the idea of Harper and Grayson together, my chest squeezes and my skin flushes with heat and my stomach turns with nausea.

Is this what jealousy feels like? Like you're looking at the world through a fun-house mirror?

But after watching Harper walk into her *third* store since I started following her, I had to entertain the idea that I might have been wrong. That maybe she really was planning to shop all day.

When she came out of the store about ten minutes later, I tried to duck behind a lamppost, but she spotted me and started walking over. I fully expected it to be awkward. We've been avoiding each other for the past two months. And when we have accidentally bumped into each other, it's been all fake waves and averted gazes and pretending we don't have six years of history hanging between us like stale smoke.

Except it wasn't like that this time. Harper was . . . Well, she was Harper. The same old upbeat, funny, bright-eyed Harper. She smiled when she saw me—a real smile. She threw her arms around me and hugged me—a real hug. Her fingers softly rubbed the back of my neck as she told me how good it was to see me.

And then she started doing that thing she always does when she wants to get back together. She started reminiscing about the past. She started finding excuses to touch me. She started laughing way too hard at things I was saying that weren't even that funny.

If you've waited for Harper Jennings to come back as many times as I have, you start to pick up on things. You start to notice patterns. You *look* for them.

And for the past two months, I've been so convinced that this moment was coming. That eventually, Harper would come to her senses once more and we'd be back together again.

The problem is, now that the moment might be here, I'm not sure how I feel about it.

Particularly when Harper, Grayson, and I make it to the beach and I spot Julie waiting there with two reserved chairs. My heart doubles in size and then shrinks to no bigger than a pebble.

I almost forgot about Julie.

When did I turn into such an asshole?

Julie waves her arms wildly in the air to get my attention. I can feel Harper stiffen beside me. After six years with someone, you can just *feel* their energy shift the moment it does.

Unlike me, Harper's DNA is loaded with the jealousy gene. And her finger is always on the trigger.

Not that she has any reason to be jealous now. She's the one who broke it off.

"Hey!" Julie says brightly when we arrive, jutting her hand out. "I'm Julie."

I search for traces of discomfort in her tone, or a flash of annoyance on her face. I search and I search, but I come up with nothing. Julie doesn't seem at all put out by the unexpected additions to our little beach party.

Grayson is the first to grab her hand. He pumps it with way too much enthusiasm. "Nice to meet you." He gives Harper a look I can't quite translate. "I'm Grayson."

"Ah yes," Julie says. "The star quarterback. Mike has told me so much about you!"

I watch Grayson's entire demeanor transform. I have no idea what that's about, but I don't really have time to analyze it right now. I'm too distracted by Harper's reaction to Julie. Harper shakes Julie's hand and introduces herself, but she looks like she wants to throw Julie into the ocean for the sharks to have their way with.

I step in, awkwardly trying to place myself between them. "Julie works at the kids' camp. She's been gracious enough to look after Jasper and Jake this summer while my dad's leg heals."

"Whoa," Grayson says. "Those two? You should get a medal or something."

Julie laughs. "Oh, they're not so bad."

Harper grunts. "They once superglued my shoes to my feet."

Grayson chuckles, which warrants an evil look from Harper. "What?" he asks, holding up his hands in surrender. "You didn't *feel* them gluing your shoes to your feet?

"In her defense," I cut in, "we were really distracted."

Grayson, Harper, and Julie all turn to me at once. Harper looks positively radiant, Grayson looks pissed, and Julie's reaction I can only read as disbelief.

"Watching TV," I'm quick to add. "We were watching a really good paranormal investigation show."

"I *love* those paranormal investigation shows," Julie says in her usual bubbly tone, and I could almost kiss her right there.

We all sit down. Grayson and I offer Julie and Harper the chairs, and we drop down into the sand.

Julie continues to yammer on. "There was this one— What's it called? *Ghost Trackers* or something. It was so good. I'm totally already a believer, but I swear that house was haunted."

"I think I saw that one," I say, trying to keep the conversation going. But I'm getting absolutely no help from Grayson or Harper, who both appear to be sulking. For Harper I can guess at the reason, but for Grayson I have absolutely no idea.

And I suddenly feel bad. I've barely hung out with Grayson or Ian all summer. Between all the extra work and getting the twins to and from the beach club and my late-night walks with Julie, I've hardly had a moment to spend time with the guys.

Sure, Ian talks to me sometimes while I work, but it's not the same. It's not all of us together. Like the old days.

And after that awkward Fourth of July barbecue, I was starting to fear it would never *be* like the old days again.

"Where's Ian?" I ask. "We should text him."

"Probably making out with Whitney somewhere," Grayson grumbles.

"What?" I spit out. "Whitney and Ian? But they hate each other."

He kicks his toe into the sand. "Yeah. They think I don't know. They think they're doing such a good job hiding it—leaving the house separately, late-night swims in the pool—but I know. I live in that house too."

Is that what's bothering him so much? That his sister is dating Ian? His sister could do much worse than Ian Handler. Hell, his sister *has* done much worse.

"So, they're, like, a thing now?" I ask.

Grayson shrugs. "They better be, that's all I can say. He better not break her heart at the end of the summer when he goes off to LA or wherever to be the next One Direction."

"Who's Whitney?" Julie asks.

"Grayson's sister," Harper says, and I hear annoyance in her tone at having to explain something that she finds so basic.

I check my watch. It's almost six-thirty. How much longer are we all expected to hang out here and pretend that this isn't the most uncomfortable situation ever? I consider texting Ian and inviting him to join us, but if that's going to make this even more awkward, then it's probably better that I don't.

I look around at our unlikely foursome—Harper in her lounge chair, looking like she's sucking on a lemon; Julie smiling under her sun hat; and Grayson picking pebbles out of the sand and chucking them at his feet.

"I'm going for a swim," Julie announces, probably as anxious to escape this distorted energy as I am. She jumps to her feet and slips out of her shorts. "Anyone want to join me?"

She directs the question at the whole group, but I know she's really talking to me. I glance from her to Grayson to Harper. Everyone looks extremely invested in my answer. Too invested for my comfort.

No matter what I say, I've made the wrong decision somehow. But I just don't think I can sit here any longer.

"Sure," I say, standing up and pulling my T-shirt over my head. We run toward the surf and jump in. I don't have to glance back at the chairs to know that Harper is pouting. But as soon as the refreshing water splashes up against my legs, I find it extremely difficult to care.

CHAPTER 39

This was a mistake. I don't know why I suggested coming to the beach. I just needed to get away. I was feeling so claustrophobic and trapped back there. With Whitney's probing eyes and words like "girlfriend" floating in the air, it was too much.

But this is the last place I should have tried to escape to. Even this late in the day, the beach is packed with umbrellas and bodies and coolers and tired, wet children running loose like rats let out of a lab cage.

We trudge through the sea of beachgoers, looking for a relatively quiet spot. Yeah, good luck with that.

We traverse half of the damn island before Whitney points to a big yellow umbrella near the next lifeguard stand and says, "Hey! There's Grayson!" She starts to make her way over. I grudgingly follow.

As we get closer, I see that Grayson is not alone. Next to him on a lounge chair is a tall blond girl wearing a purple bikini and cutoff shorts. I stop walking when I realize that it's Harper.

Seriously? *This* is still going on?

I was so convinced that they would have broken it off by now, that it was just a breezy summer fling. But that was more than a month ago, and now it looks like they're in the middle of some heated discussion.

I try to veer off course, but Whitney catches my arm. "Come on, Brooder. Let's go."

"They look like they need privacy."

She scoffs at this. "It's Harper and Grayson. Why would *they* need privacy."

If only you knew, I think as Whitney practically drags me over.

"Hey, guys!" she says, waving.

Grayson glances from Whitney to me, his expression unreadable. I give him an evil glare, which seems to only confuse him.

"What's shaking?" Whitney drops into the empty beach recliner next to Harper, who looks incredibly annoyed by our arrival.

"Nothing," Grayson mumbles. "We were just chatting."

"Is Mike here?" Whitney asks.

Grayson nods toward the ocean. "He went into the water with some chick."

Harper stirs at the comment, but I seem to be the only one who notices. There's something in the air here that I can't quite pinpoint. But it smells.

"Oh reeeaally?" Whitney shields her eyes and tries to peer into the water. "What's her story?"

Grayson shrugs, looking pointedly at Harper. "Don't know. She's hot, though. I'd totally hit that."

Whitney and I both flinch. It's not the playful, charming kind of remark that Grayson is known for when it comes to girls. It goes deeper than that. There's an almost spiteful quality to it.

Harper stands up with a huff, deliberately kicking sand

onto Grayson as she slides her feet into her shoes. "You're a dick."

Then she storms away. I watch Grayson fume for a few seconds before he ultimately decides to follow her, leaving Whitney and me to stare at each other, dumbfounded.

"Okay, we clearly missed something," she says.

I consider telling her what I saw between Grayson and Harper, but decide against it. Whatever is going on between the two of them is their problem. And it looks like a completely fucked-up problem that I don't have the mental or emotional capacity to get in the middle of.

Just then Mike comes running up the beach, shaking water from his hair. Behind him is a cute, bouncy brunette in a one-piece lifeguard bathing suit. They appear to be racing.

"I win!" Mike throws his hands into the air.

"You totally cheated!" she squeals.

Mike grins. "I totally did."

The girl immediately notices that Whitney and I are *not* the people she left on this beach, and she does a double take at both of us. "Hi!" she says, beaming at me. "You must be Ian. I'm Julie."

As I watch her grab a towel from the sand and wring out her short dark hair, I'm immediately struck by how different she is from Harper. Harper, as pretty and free-spirited as she is, always has this kind of heaviness surrounding her. Like a gray cloud constantly threatening rain. While this girl is nothing but clear blue skies.

"I'm Whitney," Whitney introduces herself. "Grayson's sister."

An expression that resembles comprehension quickly flashes over Julie's face as she looks from me to Whitney, her mind putting some kind of puzzle pieces together. "Oh! Right!"

Oh, right?

What's that supposed to mean?

Mike drops into the sand next to me. "How you been, man? I haven't seen you around the house lately."

"Yeah," I say nervously, rubbing the back of my neck.

The truth is, I've kind of been avoiding him. Ever since that day I saw Harper and Grayson in the street, I haven't been able to look Mike in the eye. Whenever I'm around him, I feel incredibly guilty. Like *I'm* the one hooking up with his ex-girlfriend.

"Sorry about that," I go on. "I've been kind of busy."

Mike grins, eyeing Whitney. "I realize that now."

Wait, does Mike know about me and Whitney?

I'm suddenly all kinds of confused.

"Where did Grayson and Harper go?" Julie asks.

I steal a peek at Mike, who seems to be noticing their absence for the first time. I drop my eyes to the sand and start digging a moat around my feet.

"It was really weird," Whitney says, leaning back in her chair. "They had, like, a fight or something."

"A fight?" Mike asks, and I don't miss the suspicion lacing his tone.

"Yeah." Whitney is completely oblivious to his reaction. "He said something totally crass, and she stomped off and he went after her."

Mike immediately starts scanning the beach. "Should I go find them?"

"No," Julie and I both say at once, and for the first time I notice *her* reaction to all of this. Her bubbly demeanor seems to have fizzled just the slightest bit.

"You're right," Mike says with a nervous stutter of a laugh.

"So you work with Mike?" Whitney asks Julie, still apparently unaware of the palpable tension in the air.

"Yeah," Julie says, regaining a bit her of effervescence. "Well, sort of. He does ground maintenance at the club, while I work at the kids' camp."

"Ground maintenance?" Whitney echoes, looking at Mike. "I thought you were doing roofing. Isn't that why you're always banging around on top of my house?"

"I'm doing both this summer. I'm trying to make as much money as I can before I leave for . . ." His voice trails off as he catches himself.

I know exactly what he was going to say. Because it's the same thing he's been saying for the past four summers. Ever since he and Harper came up with their big future life plan. They were going to move to New York together.

But now what?

Harper is having some dramatic fling with Grayson, and Mike seems pretty into this Julie chick.

What's he going to do when the summer is over in a few weeks?

What are *any* of us going to do?

We used to hang out on this very beach at night, talking about the future, thinking we had it all figured out. Grayson was going to play football. Mike was going to move to New York and live happily ever after with Harper. I was going to write songs and travel the country in a beat-up van.

That was back when things made sense. When things seemed easy and simple. Before my world was ripped in half by a suicide bomber.

Mike doesn't finish the thought he started, even though Julie appears to be waiting for the rest. He just lets it hang. Then he clears his throat and sidesteps the whole thing. "That's why I'm totally grateful that your dad has been sliding some extra cash my way," he says to Whitney. "That's really nice of him."

Whitney cocks an eyebrow. "What extra cash?"

"For the roofing job," Mike says. "He's been paying me extra on top of my invoices. I can't tell you how much I appreciate it."

"Huh," Whitney says.

Mike's eyes dart suspiciously to her. "What?"

"Nothing. My dad just hasn't been around much this summer. Does he write you checks?"

"Yeah," Mike replies cautiously. "He tapes them to the front door."

Whitney shrugs, like it's no big deal, but I can tell Mike is still turning this over in his mind.

Then I see Whitney's expression change. It's a dramatic shift. Her mouth falls open and she lowers her sunglasses to stare at something behind me.

Mike must see it too, because his shoulders stiffen. I react to his reaction before I even know what I'm reacting to. Whatever it is, I instinctively know it's not good.

"Isn't that your mom?" Whitney asks.

And just as she asks this, I hear the yelling. I hear her voice. The surrounding area has grown eerily quiet. And I realize that it's not just Whitney and Mike who are staring at the lifeguard tower behind me. It's half the beach.

I slowly turn around, and that's when the hottest day of the summer suddenly freezes over.

CHAPTER 40

I finally catch up with Harper near the beach club snack stand. That girl is in way better shape than I am. Even if I could throw a spiral without doubling over in pain, I would never survive Vanderbilt training camp in this state.

"Don't touch me!" she yells as I try to grab her arm to stop her.

"Keep your voice down."

She only gets louder. "You're a pig."

People are turning to look now. Check out Grayson Cartwright, the island playboy, finally being put in his place.

"Harper," I try, keeping my voice low. "Please. Just talk to me."

"No."

She keeps walking down the beach. I groan and follow after her again. It isn't until we're halfway to the secret alcove that she seems to tire and slows.

"I don't want to talk to you," she says without turning around.

"I'm following after you. I'm *chasing* you. Isn't that what you want? Isn't that why you run?"

This seems to get her attention. She stops but continues to face away from me.

I take a moment to catch my breath. "I'm sorry for what I said back there. I was mad. It was an asshole move."

She spins around angrily. "*You* were mad? What the hell did you have to be mad about?"

"Um, how about you standing me up, for starters? And then when I finally find you, who are you with? Oh right! Your ex-boyfriend! Reminiscing about the past and hanging all over him. You think I don't know how you operate, Harper? You think I haven't paid attention all these years when you've kept my best friend hooked on your line like a damn fish? I know exactly what was happening back there. You were trying to get back together with him, weren't you?"

She looks positively livid. Her nostrils are flaring, and her arms are crossed over her chest, like she's trying to hold herself together.

"Is that really what you think?" she finally roars. "That I was trying to seduce him back?"

I cross my arms too, mirroring her stance. "Yeah. That's what I think."

"You're an idiot." She turns again and starts walking. This time I use every last ounce of wind power left in my lungs to run in front of her, cutting her off, making her look at me.

"I was *saving* you!" she screams into my face.

"What?"

"I was saving your ass. And mine."

Confusion washes over me. Is she crazy? Has she totally lost her mind?

"He. Was. Following. Me." She enunciates every word like I'm hard of hearing. "I was on my way to meet you, and

I sensed he was watching me. And then he actually started following me. He thought he was being so clever, ducking behind poles and buildings like an amateur spy. But I knew he was there from the start. So I had to pretend I was just going shopping. I hoped he'd eventually give up, but he didn't. So I pretended to run into him to try to throw him off the scent. Grayson, he *knows* something. Or at the very least he suspects something. If I had gone to your father's boat like we'd planned, it would have been all over."

I fall silent, completely stunned.

He was following her?

That means he didn't buy my little story about the phone. At least not entirely. He didn't believe me. He doesn't trust me.

The realization hits me like a punch in the gut.

What has happened to us? When did we get to be these people? These strangers? When did we stop being friends?

Maybe about the time when I kissed the love of his life.

I suppose he's right not to trust me. Because that's what I've become. An untrustworthy person. Someone who fools around with my best friend's ex behind his back. Someone who lies to his face about it and then pads his paychecks to ease my own guilt.

Who is this person? I came to Winlock Harbor to find myself again. To escape the stranger I'd become over the past few months. And all I managed to do was get even farther away. To become less recognizable.

Harper is watching me closely, waiting for my response.

"I'm sorry," is all I can think to say. And yet I feel like I'm speaking it to more than just her.

Harper is always surprising me. Always keeping me on my toes. She never does or says what I'm expecting her to do. But the thing that she does next surprises me most of all.

She steps toward me and throws her arms around me. She pulls me into a hug. She rests her head against my chest.

"What are we doing?" she whispers. I can feel her slender body shaking, but I don't dare pull away to see if she's crying. I don't think I could handle it if she were.

"I don't know," I admit.

"You could lose him, you know?" she says. "You could lose your best friend. I could lose mine, too. Is it really worth it? Is *this* really worth it?"

I take a deep breath, inhaling her scent, her warmth, the way she makes me feel when she's this close to me — like no one else has ever made me feel. But that's the thing about inhales. They don't last. You can't keep that air trapped inside you forever. Eventually you have to breathe out. Eventually you have to let it all go.

"I don't know," I say again, and somehow it's the most truthful thing I've said all summer.

CHAPTER 41

an launches out of his chair and stomps toward the life-guard stand, where a small crowd of people has already gathered to watch the commotion. I immediately follow after him. He shouldn't have to do this alone. No one should.

It's not until we're much closer that I can actually hear what's being said, or rather *screamed*, by Mrs. Handler.

"I'm a grown woman! You can't tell me when I can or can't swim! And if you try to stop me, I'll call the police and have you arrested for assault."

Oh no. This isn't good.

This is the drunkest I've seen her all summer. She's stumbling around, sloshing a plastic cup of red wine all over the sand. The tiny droplets at her feet look like blood.

Ian pushes through the onlookers and grabs his mom brusquely by the wrist. "C'mon, Mom. Time to go home and sleep it off."

She shoves Ian away. "No! I won't! You can't make me! Why is everyone trying to make me do things I don't want to do?"

"Mom," Ian says gently but urgently, "you need to calm

down. You've had too much to drink. I'm just going to take you back to the house."

"You're not my son!" she spits, and I can see Ian's face redden with either anger or humiliation. Maybe a little of both. "I haven't seen you all summer. You just left me alone in that house. You're a horrible son. Your father would be ashamed of you, abandoning your mother in her time of grief."

Ian's entire body has gone stone still. He looks like he's about to cry. I push through the crowd and try to take Mrs. Handler's hand. "Jackie," I say in my most soothing voice. "It's me. Mike. We're going to take you home now, okay?"

She glares at me for a good ten seconds, as though she's trying to figure out where she knows me from. It's the longest ten seconds of my life because I know it can only end one of two ways.

It ends the bad way.

She yanks her hand free so hard, I stumble backward. "Get away from me. All of you! Just leave me alone!"

"All right. What's going on here?" A large, booming voice comes from behind me. I turn to find Officer Walton making his way into the circle.

Even though I know this will only further humiliate Ian, I can't help but feel relieved at Officer Walton's arrival. He has been friends with my dad since high school. He's almost like a second father to me.

"She's just had too much to drink," I tell him. "We need help getting her home. She's harmless but she's resisting us."

Officer Walton nods, giving me a sad but understanding look. Then he turns to Ian and his mom. "Okay, Mrs. Handler. Looks like the party is going to have to end early for you. Let's get you home."

I cringe, praying that she'll cooperate. That she won't try to shove him, too. That could get messy.

Officer Walton approaches her cautiously. She watches him like she's a trapped animal. When he tries to take her gently by the arm, she loses it again.

"Don't you dare touch me! My husband is a command sergeant major of the United States Army! He'll eat your face for breakfast!"

"C'mon now." Officer Walton tries to be nice. "Don't be like that. We're all trying to handle this like grown-ups. So why don't you let these nice boys walk you home?"

Mrs. Handler turns her angry glare back to Ian. "Nice boys," she repeats spitefully. "My son is an ingrate. He doesn't care about me. He doesn't care about anything but himself."

I can't bear to look at Ian. The pain on his face is too much. I look to the sand. Fortunately, Office Walton decides that enough is enough.

"Okay," he says, resigned. "I tried to do this the easy way." He walks up to Mrs. Handler, roughly pins her hands behind her back, and secures zip ties around her wrists. She fights him at first, trying to wiggle out of his reach. He has no choice but to wrestle her to the ground until she's facedown on the sand.

The crowd gasps. This is probably the most action Winlock Harbor has seen . . . well, maybe ever. Ian covers his eyes, unable to watch. My stomach wrenches for him.

"Are you ready to go home now?" Officer Walton asks her.

She nods, spitting sand out of her mouth. Officer Walton helps her up and turns to Ian. "Help me walk her down the beach, will you?"

He nods and scrambles forward to take hold of her other elbow. I run to his side. "I'll come," I tell him.

But he shakes his head. "Don't. Stay here."

"I can help."

"Mike," he says sternly. There is no room for argument. "Please. Don't come."

He looks at me then, and I can see the shame and hurt swirling in his eyes like thunderclouds. I know the last thing he wants is for anyone to witness the rest of this debacle, and I can't say I blame him.

He rips his gaze from mine and, with the help of Officer Walton on her other elbow, starts marching his mother down the beach.

I watch them until they've almost completely disappeared around the bend and the crowd has dispersed, returning to their beach chairs and towels. But I can't just sit back down and go on with my afternoon like nothing has happened. My body and mind are too riled up. I need to do something. I need to get away from here.

Julie comes running up to me, but before she can say anything, I blurt out, "Do you want to get something to eat? I'm starving."

She looks concerned for a moment but eventually nods. As we walk toward the clubhouse, I search the beach for Whitney, but she's nowhere to be found.

In the beach club kitchen, Mamma V cooks us up a feast. She even packs it into a picnic basket for us, and we take it to a deserted lawn in the back. When I unpack the basket, I can immediately tell how much Mamma V likes Julie. She would never have gone through so much effort for Harper.

"Are you okay?" Julie finally asks after I've nearly finished off half a rotisserie chicken without muttering a single word.

I'm still completely shaken by the incident on the beach,

and the look that I saw in Ian's eyes as he told me not to go with him.

It was like he had lost. Lost at being a son. Lost at grieving his father. Lost at life. That look has been flashing through my mind ever since, and I can't help shake the feeling that I could have done something. I could have helped. Even though he didn't want me to. Even though he pushed me away.

"I'm okay," I say, gazing off in the direction of the beach. The sun is already starting to set, making for another magnificent Winlock Harbor sunset. "But I'm worried about Ian. He's not doing well. I . . . I feel bad for him, you know? He's been through so much. He doesn't deserve this. I want to help, but . . ."

"But you can't help someone who doesn't want it," she finishes the thought for me, as if she's living right inside my head. As if she can see my thoughts as clearly as she sees her own.

"Yeah," I agree miserably.

She scoots closer and puts an arm around me. I rest my head against her shoulder, and she gently runs a hand through my hair. It feels nice, but it also feels off somehow. Almost foreign. Like it's not the right hand. Not the right shoulder.

"I'm here if you want to talk about it," she says. "Anytime."

"Thanks."

It only takes a few minutes for the emptiness to bloom in my chest. It starts small. A tiny pinprick. Harmless and ignorable. But it quickly grows and grows until it threatens to swallow me whole.

Sadly, I know exactly what this feeling is. It's longing. It's missing someone. It's knowing who you would normally call when something like this happens.

And then it's realizing that person is no longer yours to call.

Julie is sitting next to me, ready and waiting to receive all of my anxiety and thoughts and emotions with open arms and open ears, and all I want to do is talk to Harper. This amazing, beautiful, openhearted girl is right here, right now, and all I want to do is jump headfirst into the past and run back to the girl who has broken my heart a thousand times.

Because she's also the girl who's put my heart back together a thousand times. She knows where all the pieces go. She knows how they fit. How *I* fit.

And right now that familiarity, that sense of belonging somewhere and to someone, is consuming all the space in my mind.

"You know what," I say to Julie, gently taking her hand and giving it a squeeze. "I'm not really feeling well. That whole thing just kind of shook me up. I think I'm just gonna head home."

Julie bites her lip. It's the first time I think I've ever seen a side of her that didn't exude confidence. "Are you sure? Do you want me to come with you?"

I shake my head, but it's too quick, too decisive. "No. That's okay. I just need to be alone."

I cringe at the words. So familiar. Except they were never mine to say. They were always Harper's.

And they're always a lie.

"Okay," she agrees, and I see the disappointment written all over her face. It twists the knife that is already protruding from my gut.

"I'll text you tomorrow," I promise her.

"Okay," she says again, but this time the word feels hollow and meaningless.

I give her a quick kiss on the cheek and jump to my feet. I slide my T-shirt on and start walking down the beach to the Cove. I count my steps and the seconds—127—before I pull my phone out of my pocket and tap out my text to Harper.

> I need to talk to you. Can you meet me at our place?

I hold my breath. I count out another 127 seconds, but she doesn't respond. I stop and watch the screen of my phone, waiting for the little bubble to appear to let me know she's typing, but it never does.

I feel my heart sink. What am I doing?

Julie is back at the club, ready to be there for me, to listen to me, to talk to me, to maybe even be *with* me, and here I am, chasing after a girl who never stops running away.

Grayson was right. When is enough going to be enough?

I stare one last time at my phone and make a decision I should have made months ago.

Today.

That's when enough is enough.

Right now. It ends right now.

With a newfound determination I turn back toward the main beach. Away from the future I always thought I wanted, and toward the future that might have been waiting for me all along.

But I freeze when, out of the corner of my eye, I see that abandoned future. I see Harper. And my heart leaps into my throat.

Because, as usual, she's not alone.

Because every fear and paranoid delusion that I've had for the past week has now been confirmed.

Because she's standing right in front of the entrance to the Cove, kissing my best friend.

CHAPTER 42

B y the time Officer Walton and I get my mother to the house and up the stairs to her bedroom, she has completely passed out. Her head has lolled forward against her chest, and her feet are dragging behind her. I can't decide which version is harder to transport—the ranting, belligerent drunk, or this.

My mother is tiny, but she's heavy. The only reason I've been able to make it all this way is because my rage has been fueling me.

I'm nearly breathless when we finally drop her into bed. Officer Walton rubs sweat from his brow with his handkerchief. I can barely look him in the eye. I'm so mortified.

"Thank you," I manage to say, flicking my gaze toward him just long enough to convey my gratitude. "And I'm sorry for this."

He nods. "Your father was a good man. He served this country well. I would do anything for him. And you two." He nods to me and my mother. I feel my stomach twist. I hate how he says "you two" like we're some kind of team. Like we're in this boat together. My mother has done nothing but humiliate me and herself all summer. I don't want to be anywhere near her fucking boat.

"Thanks," I mutter again, but this one is far less heartfelt.

"Well, I guess I'll leave you. Call me if you have any more trouble."

"Will do, sir."

He turns to leave, but stops just short of the door. "Can I say something to you, Ian?"

I don't know why people ask that. It's such a stupid, pointless formality. It's not like I'm going to refuse. It's not like I'm going to say, "No, you can't say anything to me. Just leave."

I nod.

"I know it's probably not my place, but your mother is hurting. And I'm willing to guess you are too. Maybe you should go a little easier on her."

My fists tighten as another burst of anger hits me.

He's right. It's *not* his place. What the hell does he know about anything?

But thankfully, I'm smart enough not to lash out at a police officer. I mumble another "thanks" before he finally leaves.

And I'm left alone with the sound of my mother's labored breathing.

My phone vibrates in my pocket. It's Whitney. She's left me numerous texts asking if I'm okay, asking if she can help, asking if she can come by.

I don't answer any of them. Because the answer is no.

She can't come by.

She can't help.

And I'm most definitely not okay.

All summer I've tried to convince myself that I could be, but I'm just now realizing how delusional that was.

My father is dead. And that will never be okay.

The house is quiet. Almost too quiet. And it isn't until

this very moment that I realize I haven't heard a single peep from my grandparents. I check the clock on the nightstand. It's barely even eight o'clock. Are they already asleep? Or did they slip down to the beach to watch the sunset?

I would have thought that with all this commotion of dragging my mother up the stairs, they would have emerged to see what was happening.

I creep down the hall to their bedroom and push open the door. The bed is made but the room is empty. I wander down the stairs and stop dead in my tracks when I see what has become of the house. I guess I didn't notice it before because I was too busy shuffling my mother's barely conscious body up a flight of stairs, but the entire first floor is a complete disaster.

It looks like a frat house after an end-of-semester party.

There are dirty dishes overflowing from the sink. There are empty wine bottles scattered all over the floor. And there's trash *everywhere*.

There's no way my grandparents would live like this.

I hurry to the garage door and flick on the light. My stomach sinks when I see that their car is not there.

Where did they go?

How long have they been gone?

How long has my mother been living here by herself?

I never even thought that she might be here all alone. I always just assumed my grandparents were here to watch over her. Now I think back to all those texts I got over the past month. Asking me to come look at home movies. Asking me to visit my father's favorite places on the island.

I just assumed she was trying to get me to reminisce with her. Trying to force me to grieve the way she wanted me to grieve. I didn't realize she was asking because she was lonely.

I glance down to see an empty wine bottle at my feet, and suddenly I can't control the rage anymore. It controls me. It pilots me. It takes over.

I pick up the bottle and hurl it against the wall. It shatters with an ear-piercing crash. I reach for the next one and resign it to the same fate. I'm astonished by how good it feels. How satisfying that sound is.

The sound of things breaking.

The sound of things ending.

The sound of things that will never be put back together.

When there are no more bottles left, I drag myself back up the stairs, my body tired and heavy and out of breath.

I stand in my mother's room for a long time, staring at her unconscious form on the bed. She's completely out, lying at an awkward angle across the comforter, the left side of her face flattened and disfigured against the pillow.

My emotions run the gamut from anger to disgust to pity to guilt, then back to anger again.

Round and round it goes.

Why should I feel guilty? She's the adult here, not me. She's an army wife. Army wives are supposed to be strong. They're supposed to know how to take care of themselves. This is *not* how my father would have wanted her to handle his death.

And what about me?

What would my father have wanted from *me*?

The question plummets the temperature of the room, and I shiver.

He always wanted so much from me. So many things that I wouldn't give him. An army legacy. A soldier. A son who knew how to hold a gun instead of a guitar. And yet he never complained. He wasn't like Grayson's dad, forcing his past on my future. He was always supportive of my aspirations, even if he didn't agree with them.

But what would he want from me now?

And what does it even matter, now that he's gone?

I guess it doesn't.

I shake my head and turn to leave, but my foot catches on something, and I stumble. I look down to see a box filled to the rim with photographs, which have now spilled out onto the floor.

"Shit," I swear aloud, and bend down to scoop them up.

My hand freezes and my stomach turns over when I notice that every single one of these pictures has my father in it. I drop the photographs from my hand like they're made of hot coals.

I'm suddenly paralyzed in my crouch. I want to shove them all away, stuff them back into that box and kick the box under the bed. I don't want to see them. I don't want to be reminded. And yet I can't seem to move. All I can do is stare numbly at the photos. At his cheerful, round face peeking out from every single one of them.

My dad wearing a lobster bib.

My dad and mom holding hands.

My dad in his mess uniform, right before their wedding.

My dad holding me as a baby.

My dad and me fishing on Cherry Tree Bridge.

That's the one that makes my body unfreeze. That returns the sensation to my legs and arms and fingertips. I lean forward and scoop it up, careful not to touch any of the others. I stare at the photo for what seems like forever. It's a close-up shot, slightly off center. I remember my dad held the camera out in front of him with one hand and attempted to capture both of us, but the side of my head is cut off. I try to memorize every inch of it, from the colors of my dad's fishing hat and the shape of the one lone cloud that sits in the sky behind us, to the look of pure joy on both of our faces.

This was our common ground. Of all the things we could never agree on, we could always agree on this.

There was always time for fishing.

Finally the weight of the memories becomes too much and I crumple. I fall back and lean against the side of the bed, pressing the photograph to my chest.

I don't know if my dad would have wanted me to cry.

But like I said, it doesn't really matter anymore what he would have wanted.

CHAPTER 43

I can't remember who started kissing whom first. Harper and I were hugging, then we were just walking the beach talking, and then our lips just found their way to each other. Like they've done all summer. Like they did that one summer six years ago in the garden shed.

Harper and I are complicated magnets.

On one side we attract, on the other we repel. When it's good, it's good, but when it's bad, it's the kind of bad that makes you feel stupid. Like burning yourself on a hot plate that someone already warned you not to touch.

Harper's lips move urgently against mine. I can feel her trying to intensify the kiss. She needs something from it. The way we've both needed something from every single kiss we've stolen over the past two months. But it's something I can't give her. At least not here, just outside the cove. We're too exposed. We're too out in the open.

I pull away. Harper's eyes stay closed for just a moment before slowly dragging open. And then, in a flicker of a second, they're wide. Staring at something just over my shoulder.

A tiny, incomprehensible sound gurgles from her lips.

I'm pretty sure I already know what I'll find when I

turn around. We've had so many close calls this summer, I've come to recognize Harper's reaction to them.

Someone has spotted us. Someone has seen us kissing. Someone now knows.

I just don't know who that someone is and how big an issue it will turn out to be.

Is it as small as an unknown tourist who we've never spoken to?

Or is it as big as someone like Whitney or Ian?

I suck in a breath and turn around.

It's worse.

It's the worst.

It's Mike.

He stands there, staring at us with a closed-mouth, empty gaze, as though he's sleeping with his eyes open. As though he's not even seeing us at all but, rather, seeing through us.

As though we're ghosts.

And I have a feeling that after this moment, we will forever *be* ghosts in his mind.

That's when I realize that my hand is still wrapped around the back of Harper's head. I quickly release it and take a tentative step toward him.

It's the very opposite thing from what my head is telling me to do.

My head is telling me to *run* the other way. But it's as though my brain has been put on mute and my conscience has taken over, guided with some helpful suggestions from my overactive, pounding heart.

"Mike," I say, raising both hands in the air like the surrounded criminal that I am. A criminal who's been on the run for far too long. Who's tired of hiding and lying and disguising himself as someone that he's not.

Who's ready to turn himself in.

Mike still hasn't said a word or moved a muscle.

Is he in shock?

I take another step. Somewhere behind me Harper starts to cry. Her quiet sobs don't deter my course. And they definitely don't do anything to break Mike's trance.

"Look," I say. "I never wanted you to find out this way. I never wanted . . ." I trail off, running out of steam, running out of logic.

Another step.

The statue in the shape of my best friend doesn't move.

"I'm so sorry, man. It just happened. Neither of us planned it."

Two steps. I'm now only a foot away from him, yet he still hasn't fully focused on me. In fact, I can't tell where he's looking. At me? Behind me? Into me?

Now that I'm this close, I can see the subtleties of his expression, the finer details of the sculptor's work. A slight crease below the hairline. A pinching of the jaw muscles. A furrowing of the brow.

His eerie stillness fuels my anxiety, and all I can do to muffle the screaming in my head is keep talking. "I've felt horrible about it all summer. I'm telling you, the guilt has been eating me alive. I've lost so much sleep over this. Because I swear I didn't want to hurt you. Neither of us did. We just—"

THWACK!

Before I can comprehend what has happened, I feel the throbbing in my nose and the blood trickling into my mouth. My face is on fire. My vision swims.

Somewhere behind me Harper lets out a gasp.

I groan as I double over and stare at the ground. Tiny drops of crimson drip onto the sand. It takes my mind a moment to catch up.

Blood.

That's blood.

That's my *blood.*

Mike punched me. In our twelve years of friendship, I don't think I've ever seen Mike throw a punch. And yet he sucker punched me right in the face.

Not that I didn't deserve it. I did. I do.

I deserve all of it and worse.

I take deep breaths, trying to dull the pain. Trying to keep the beach from spinning. When I finally manage to get the disorientation under control, I stand up straight again.

THWACK!

Mike punches me again. This time in the cheek. The same cheek my father smacked only a week ago. My ears ring. My jaw throbs with pain.

"What the hell!" I scream at him.

One punch I deserve. I may even welcome it. But two? Two just seems excessive.

WHAM!

Now he has punched me right in the gut, knocking the wind out of me. I double over again, gagging and fighting for breath.

"Fight back, you asshole!" he yells from somewhere. But through the sound of Harper crying and my ears ringing and the waves crashing, I can't, for the life of me, figure out where his voice is coming from. Is he behind me? In front of me? Towering over me?

"I'm . . . not . . . going . . . to . . . fight . . . you," I manage to gasp out between spasms of breath.

WHAP!

Another solid punch. The pain spreads so fast, I can't even tell where it originated.

"You'll fuck my girlfriend, but you won't fight me?" Mike yells.

"Stop!" Harper screams from somewhere in the dizzying, shrinking void that is my vision. "Please, stop!"

"What kind of a spineless loser are you?" Mike bellows. "The star quarterback. The pride and joy of the Cartwright family. And he can't even throw a fucking punch! What a joke!"

I feel my hands ball into fists. My wounded arm screams out in protest. But the rage wins. It's louder and more persuasive.

"Is that what the extra money was for?" Mike shouts. "Is that why you were padding my checks? To alleviate your own pathetic guilt?" He snorts out a laugh. "I should have known. That's how a pretty little rich boy deals with his problems, isn't it? You throw money at them. You try to buy them off. Because you're too much of a fucking coward to face them yourself."

My muscles coil. My body readies itself to run.

Run.

That's what I've been doing all my life. I've been running. Running away from my father's disappointment. Running away from my future. And what did I do when my mother left? I ran. I ran all the way into that tree.

I'm a quarterback. I'm not supposed to get sacked. I'm not supposed to join the action. I'm supposed to run away from it.

But apparently I'm done running away from the conflict in my life. This time I'm running right toward it. I let out a fierce growl and charge into Mike. He goes flying backward and lands on his back with a grunt. I tumble forward from the momentum and fall on top of him. I scramble to my knees and throw my first punch. It hits him squarely in the jaw. I cock my fist back for another one, but he's too quick. He pushes me off him, and we roll, grappling for control, for the superior position.

Somewhere in the distance I hear Harper calling to us, shouting our names through her terrified tears. But it's too far away to be real, and I'm too far gone to come back.

Mike may be taller than me, but I'm stronger. I always have been. I'm the athlete in the group. I'm the brawn of the Cartwright family. This is what I was born to do. To fight. To be strong. To win.

I manage to get Mike underneath me again, and I pull my fist back, ready to send it flying into his face. But it never gets there.

I feel a fist clamp around mine, holding my arm from moving. Holding my rage in check. And then I feel myself being yanked back with a surprising force, until I'm lying on my back in the sand, breathless and sweaty, with the bitter taste of blood in my mouth.

CHAPTER 44

What the hell is the matter with you two?" There's a voice. It's screaming. But it sounds like it's coming from another planet. Another dimension.

My whole body hurts. My head is vibrating. There's a piercing high-pitched sound in my ears that I worry might never go away.

I lie panting in the sand. Grayson lies a few feet away. I can hear his rugged breathing too.

We were fighting.

I *was fighting.*

I never fight.

The voice is still screaming. I don't know who it belongs to. Harper? Is Harper the one who pulled Grayson off me?

"I've been freaking out! Looking everywhere for you guys! And then I find you brawling on the beach like two wannabe thugs. Are you serious?"

I blink and try to sit up. Bad idea. The beach completes a full rotation around me. I groan and grab my head, right as someone smacks me across the back of it.

"Idiots!" says the voice.

"Ow!" I wail. "What the hell?" I look up to find Whitney

standing between us, glaring down at both of us like an angry mother.

Whitney?

Whitney pulled Grayson off me?

Damn, that girl is strong.

"What do you want, Whit?" Grayson growls from somewhere beside me. I don't dare look at him. I'm afraid if I see him, then I'll see *it* all over again. It'll play in my head like a scene on a scratched DVD. Skipping and skipping and skipping forever.

Grayson's lips on Harper's lips.

Grayson's hand in Harper's hair.

Grayson's tongue in . . .

Rage flares in my chest as I angrily push the thought away.

"What even happened here?" Whitney demands. "You two are best friends!"

I scowl and face away from her. Grayson can explain. Let him admit to his little sister what a douchey asshole he is.

"I've been hooking up with Grayson. All summer."

That would be Harper. I can't bring myself to look at her, either. Her voice sounds so small and broken. She's definitely crying. My heart lurches in my chest, wanting so badly to comfort her the way I always do.

I tell my heart to shut it.

Harper sniffles. "Mike saw us kissing." She stops as a shudder passes through her. "Mikey, I'm sorry. I'm so sorry."

My muscles tighten, but I still won't look at her. I face the ocean instead, the one thing on this island that has always been my friend. That has never betrayed me.

"I never wanted to hurt you," she cries.

"Like hell you didn't!" I snap, whipping my head to her. Dizziness instantly overcomes me, and I have to take a deep breath to regain my grip on the world. "That's all you do, Harper. You hurt me. You pound on my heart like it's your own personal Whac-a-Mole game. Oh! Look! Mike's heart has popped up again, better smash it with my hammer! Bam! Bam! Bam!"

She sobs harder. I tell myself I don't care. Even if I don't really believe that.

The sad truth is, I'll always care. No matter what she does to me, no matter how she hurts me, I'll never stop caring about Harper Jennings.

And that's the problem.

"Mike," Grayson tries to say.

"You shut up!" I snarl.

"No, both of you shut up!" Whitney yells. "We have bigger things to worry about right now than your stupid reality-show drama."

Grayson and I both turn to her with matching frowns.

"It's Ian, you guys," she says, her voice wavering. "He's missing."

Silence falls on the beach. Like the entire world has stopped breathing. Even Harper's blubbering has come to a halt.

"What do you mean, he's missing?" I ask.

Whitney throws her hands into the air. "I mean, he's gone! I can't find him anywhere."

I think back to the last time I saw Ian. He and Officer Walton were walking his drunk, belligerent mother back to his grandparents' house. I offered to go with him, but he shooed me away like I was an annoying fly.

But that wasn't that long ago. An hour?

"I saw what happened on the beach," Whitney continues,

her voice growing more and more frantic by the second. "I tried to text him—"

"Wait, what happened on the beach?" Grayson asks, looking to me.

That guy has a lot of balls, looking to me for anything.

"You would know if you hadn't been off making out with my girlfriend."

"*Ex*-girlfriend," Grayson mumbles.

I let out a growl and lunge for him. Whitney steps between us, kicking sand into my face. "Stop it! We have to focus!"

I spit the sand out of my mouth. "Whitney," I grumble, "I saw him about an hour ago. Why are you so worried?"

"Wake the fuck up, Mike!" she screams.

I stare at her in disbelief. Did she just say that to me? Did that just happen?

"You guys have been so blinded by your own stupid problems this summer, you haven't even noticed that your best friend is drowning. He's suffering. His father died! And he's been hanging on by a thread."

I brave a look at Grayson. He meets my eye. For a tense moment all that passes between us is resentment. I silently berate him for being an inconsiderate, shitty friend. And he silently screams back at me that I don't understand what he's been going through.

And then that moment passes. As moments often do. And all that's left is concern. For our friend.

Did you know? I ask with my eyes.

No, he shamefully admits.

"I tried texting him after he left the beach, but he wouldn't respond," Whitney goes on. "So I went by his house. I knocked on the door for five minutes, but no one answered. It was unlocked, so I let myself in. The place is a war zone. Trash and laundry and dishes and broken glass everywhere. And Ian wasn't there. But I found this by the front door."

From her pocket she pulls out two halves of what used to be a photograph.

I grab the pieces and hold them together, until I can see the full picture. Grayson drags himself closer to me, close enough that he can look over my shoulder. So that he can see what I see.

It's a close-up photograph of Ian and his dad. Ian looks like he's about thirteen. They have their arms around each other, and they're both smiling like idiots.

I look to Grayson, and once again we communicate in silence.

"Cherry Tree Bridge," we say in unison.

"What?" Whitney grabs the photo pieces back from me and studies them. "How can you tell? The picture is so close up, you can't see anything behind them."

"It's the hat," I tell her. "That was his father's fishing hat. He only wore it when they went fishing. It's the one thing Ian and his father had in common."

Whitney has grown quiet, which is unusual for Whitney. I look up at her and notice that her eyes are wide and unfocused. "What?"

"I didn't know," she says quietly, almost as though she doesn't even intend for us to hear.

"What didn't you know?" Grayson is on his feet now, putting an arm around his sister's shoulders. "Whitney. What happened?"

She shakes her head. "We passed by it about a week ago. The bridge. And he . . . I don't know, he just shut down. He barely said a word to me for the rest of the day. I couldn't figure out why."

I get to my feet, ignoring the wooziness that threatens to push me back down again. I give Grayson a worried look. He returns it with just as much intensity.

"You don't think he'd . . ." But I can't even finish the thought. It doesn't matter, though. Grayson understands. Because that's how the three of us have always been.

We just get each other.

"I don't know," he admits. "But we need to get there now."

I start moving, adrenaline and fear powering my sore legs. "C'mon. I know a shortcut."

CHAPTER 45

an you see it now, Ian? Can you see the lure?"

"No, Daddy."

"It's way down there. Stand on your tiptoes."

"I still can't see it."

"Here. Climb up onto this railing. . . . There you go. Be careful. Look down. Can you see it now?"

"There it is! I can see it!"

"That's the deepest part of the creek. That's where the fish are."

"It's so far down. I don't want to fall."

"You won't fall, Ian. I won't let you. Just hold on tight."

I stand on Cherry Tree Bridge and peer over the railing, staring down into the dark ravine. When my father first started bringing me here, I was only six years old. I wasn't tall enough to see over the railing. He let me climb up onto the second rail so that I could see the lure that I had cast so far below.

It's been twelve years since that day. I've grown almost two and a half feet taller, but the ravine looks deeper than ever.

And my dad has never felt farther away.

How did it come to this? How did I even get here? I

thought I had it all under control. I thought my emotions could be sorted into little boxes and stored away to be dealt with later, when I had more capacity to deal with them.

Or to be dealt with never.

My mother was right. I'm a horrible son. I abandoned her. Just like my father abandoned us both. Except I had a choice in the matter. And I chose wrong.

My dad died trying to save someone. Trying to save his friends.

And all I've been is selfish. This whole summer. Thinking that playing songs on my stupid guitar or kissing Whitney's perfect pouty lips would make it all okay.

I miss him.

I miss him so much.

I miss the way he smelled. The way he walked. The way he laughed. The way he lifted me up when I couldn't see.

But who's going to lift me up now?

I'm stumbling in the dark. I can't see anything. And now there's no one to help me. No one to tell me it's going to be okay. No one to make sure I don't fall. No one to remind me to hold on tight.

Because there's nothing left to hold on to.

I step up to the second rail and balance precariously. When I was little, the weight distribution was all different. I was so small. My waist would rest comfortably against the top rail, keeping me stable. And my dad's arms would be wrapped around me from behind. Just in case.

But now I'm too tall. I'm too top heavy. Nothing lines up. My shins hit where my waist used to be. Gravity takes hold of my body and pulls me forward. I have to fight to stay upright.

And there's no one behind me just in case.

For the rest of my life, there will be no one behind me.

I'm alone. Alone on this bridge. Alone on this island. Alone in this world.

"It's so far down. I don't want to fall."
"You won't fall, Ian. I won't let you. Just hold on tight."

What would happen if I stopped struggling? If I stopped pushing against gravity? If I just let myself succumb to its relentless pull?

If I stopped fighting.

Altogether.

It would be easier. I learned that lesson a long time ago, when I lay on the floor of Whitney's bedroom two months ago and let that douche nugget pound on my face. I didn't fight back. I just let it happen. And it was easier.

It's always easier not to fight.

Especially when there's nothing left to fight for.

"Ian!" I hear voices coming from the woods, followed by footsteps. I don't look up from the ravine. I don't want to lose my balance. Not that way. If I'm going to lose my balance, it's going to be my choice.

For once in my fucking life, it's going to be my choice.

"Oh shit!"

That's Grayson. I'd recognize his voice anywhere.

"Oh my God!"

That's Whitney. She's crying. Tough, ballbuster Whitney is crying.

"Ian, what are you doing, man?"

That's Mike.

"Do something!"

That's Harper.

They're all here.

"Ian," Mike says, "talk to me. What's going on?"

I don't respond. I'm too tired. I'm too focused. I'm too done.

"Stay here," Grayson tells someone, and then I hear footsteps. Quiet, tentative, careful. Like someone sneaking up on a scared, trapped animal.

That would be me.

The scared, trapped animal. With nowhere else to go and a useless leg stuck in a snare.

I brave a glance to my left. Mike and Grayson are there, halfway across the bridge, their faces lit up by the small lamps attached to the posts.

"Just leave," I tell them angrily. "I don't even know what you're doing here."

"We're here because we care about you," Mike says.

I snort. "No, you don't."

Mike and Grayson share a glance. "Yes, we do," Grayson confirms. "And we're sorry we haven't been there for you this summer. We . . ." His voice trails off. It almost sounds like it's breaking. Is Grayson Cartwright going to cry? That's an even bigger surprise than his sister.

"We've been preoccupied," Mike says apologetically. "With our own stupid shit. And that was wrong. What you're going through is so much worse."

"You have no idea what I'm going through!" I yell, feeling a sudden burst of rage. Admittedly, it feels good. It feels like *something*. "Because you never asked."

"We did," Mike vows, but there's no conviction in his voice. He knows it's bullshit. "We tried."

"You didn't try," I shout, and the outburst of emotion almost makes me lose my balance. I grip the handrail tighter. "You asked me stupid, pointless questions like, 'Are you okay?' 'How's it going?' 'How are you holding up?'

Those aren't the words of someone who gives a shit. Those are the words of someone who wants to fulfill an obligation. Check something off their daily to-do list so they can feel better about themselves. Of course I'm not okay! Of course I'm not holding up. I'm falling apart. I've been falling apart all summer, and none of you fucking cared enough to ask the real questions. To find out how I *really* felt."

"You're right," Mike says, and I hear the agony in his voice. "You're right. We've been insensitive assholes. I guess we just thought that if you'd wanted to talk about it, you would have."

And I just thought that if you'd cared, you would have asked.

"Yeah," Grayson agrees. "We were just trying to give you space. Because we thought that was what you wanted."

Space.

I stare into the ravine deep below. Into all that space. I wonder if it would hurt. I wonder if I would black out before I hit. It can't possibly be worse than the pain I'm feeling right now. The pain I feel every day.

"I don't know what I want," I admit, and it's the truth.

Actually, no. It's a lie.

I want my father back.

I want my life back.

"You don't want this," Mike says, taking a tentative step toward me.

I feel tears prick my eyes. The ravine is so dark. So vast. Like a black hole. It seems fitting. Since that's what my life has become.

"Just leave," I beg them again. "Please."

They are all silent. I can't even hear Whitney's whimpering anymore. For a minute I think that maybe they really did leave. Maybe they really don't care. Maybe if I go through with this, no one will miss me.

I don't dare look up. Because I'm not even sure what I hope to see if I do. That they're all still there, standing by me. Or that they're gone. And I'm finally alone. Just like I wanted.

For some reason both outcomes make me feel empty.

A stiff wind blows across the bridge. I can actually feel the air moving. Traveling. Crossing to the other side. Banging recklessly through the trees as it goes. It's not a peaceful sound. It's a wild, uncontrollable gust that tears through the island with abandon, leaving behind carnage in its wake.

It's a tornado that takes no prisoners.

It's a hurricane that leaves no survivors.

It's everything I've felt since that harbinger of death called my mother with the news.

I close my eyes, feeling the wind whip past me. Feeling it threaten to take me with it. I could escape into that tempest. I could get lost in that wild breeze. I could let it knock me over and shove me to the ground.

Like I said, it would be *so* easy.

It would be like falling.

But then, as swiftly as it came, the fierce wind is gone. Moved on to ravage another island. Off to torture another soul.

And Mike's voice rings out, clear and unwavering, from the middle of the bridge. "No," he says. "We're not leaving. Not this time. We're staying right here."

I close my eyes tight. But the tears leak out anyway.

"I have nothing left," I whisper. I'm certain the words will be lost to the ravine, swept up in the wind, scattered to the trees. But somehow, by some miracle, Mike and Grayson hear them. Maybe it's the first thing they've heard me say all summer.

But maybe it's the thing I needed them to hear most.

"That's not true," Grayson says. "You have your mom, who loves you." He chokes up, unable to continue.

"And Whitney," Mike says.

"And us," Grayson finishes, getting his voice back.

"And us," Mike echoes softly.

I finally lift my head and look at them again. Something is suddenly different about them. In such a short time something has changed. Just a few moments ago they seemed so separate and distant. So far away from each other. So far away from me.

But now they're standing side by side, like a unified front. Like an army, ready to go to battle.

It's what my father loved most about the military. The sense of comradeship. It was like a family. A brotherhood. That's why he threw himself in front of those men. To shield them from the bomb. He sacrificed himself. Because he loved them.

Staring at my two best friends standing on this bridge, I suddenly realize that I would do the same for them. In a heartbeat. I would throw myself in front of a bullet or a speeding train or a grenade to save their lives. I would rescue them. Just as they've come to rescue me now.

I would *fight*.

Not because it's easy. But because it's what you do. You fight for the things that matter.

My dad always wanted me to enlist. To have what he had. To live the life he loved. But I didn't need to join the army to find that. It turns out I had it right here the whole time.

In Winlock Harbor.

CHAPTER 46

TWO WEEKS LATER

I nervously drum my fingers against the small table at the Winlock Café, glancing up every five seconds whenever I hear the little bell above the door jingle. It took me a week to build up the courage to call, and another week to figure out the scheduling, but now the day is finally here. She's coming. Her ferry docked ten minutes ago. There's no turning back.

Whitney was right. We all make mistakes and we all deserve a chance to fix them.

After the incident on the bridge, I think Mike, Ian, and I started looking at our lives a little differently. Especially when it comes to the mistakes we've made. And we've all made them. Maybe me worst of all.

But time heals a lot of things. It's kind of magic like that. The bruises on my face from the fight with Mike are almost gone. Ian has moved back into his grandparents' house. And Mike has been mostly able to forgive me for everything that happened with Harper. I think if anything, in a strange way, it's helping him move on. He's finally coming to terms with the fact that Harper isn't his future. And she may not be mine, either.

Harper and I haven't talked much since that night

when Mike saw us kissing. We've decided to give each other some space.

The door chimes, and I glance up. My whole body seizes when I see her. She looks exactly as she did the last time I saw her, when she walked out that door with her bags in her hand and an apologetic frown on her face.

"Mom," I say, my voice thick. I stand up, and she immediately rushes over and pulls me into a hug. My body stiffens at her touch. It wasn't what I was expecting. Of all the times I played out this very moment in my mind, touching wasn't part of it. Affection wasn't in the plan.

"Oh, Grayson," she says, stroking my head like she used to do when I was a little kid. But now I'm taller than her and she has to reach up to do it. "I've missed you so much."

She's crying. I can hear it in her voice. Now I suddenly don't want to pull away, because I don't want to see her crying. If there's one thing that I've always had a weakness for, it's my mother's tears. But it doesn't seem to matter, because when she does pull away, she reaches out to wipe my cheeks, and I realize that I'm already crying too.

"I'm so glad you called," she says, her hand lingering on my cheek.

I pull away and sit down. She smiles and sits across from me. For a while neither one of us speaks. I'm not sure how this conversation is supposed to go. All of the scripts and possible scenarios I created in my mind flew right out the window the moment I started blubbering like a baby.

"I guess I'll start," she says after a while, exhaling a gust of air that I'm convinced will start a hurricane on the other side of the world. "I know you must be angry with me."

I feel tears burning my eyes again, but I blink them away and look down at the table.

"I'm angry with me too," she goes on. "I handled the

whole thing poorly. I acted like a child, and I'm sorry. I'm supposed to be the adult here. I'm supposed to make the wise, mature decisions, but, honey, sometimes adults make mistakes too. Sometimes the right decisions are just too scary to face."

My gaze flickers up to her. I think back to what my dad said about genetics. That I got his strength and athleticism, while Whitney got my mother's looks. But her words are hitting so close to home, I'm starting to realize that I may have gotten something from my mother too. An impulsive nature.

She ran.

Then I ran.

And I've been running ever since. Knocking things over in my path. Kissing people I shouldn't be kissing. Jeopardizing friendships. Hiding from the things that scare me.

"I'm sorry," my mom goes on, wiping at her eyes. "I'm so sorry, Grayson. I love you so much. Can you ever forgive me?"

My mind flashes to that night on the bridge. To the way Mike looked at me when we told Ian that he would always have us. No matter what. He forgave me. After I made one of the worst mistakes of my life. Because he knew something that I'm just beginning to see.

We are bigger than our mistakes.

And that's what allows us to rise above them.

"I think I can," I whisper.

My mom lets out a whimper and starts crying again. And before I know it, I'm crying again too. She reaches across the table, grabs my hand, and squeezes it.

"What about Dad?" I ask quietly. "Are you going to talk to him?"

"Oh, sweetie. I *have* been talking to him. Hasn't he told

you? We've been meeting on the mainland every week."

Suddenly I remember all of those times when my father was gone this summer. He kept saying he had business to take care of. I always assumed it was work. I never considered the possibility that he was meeting with my mom.

Were they having romantic rendezvous? Secret affairs in hotel suites? As much as the thought of my parents hooking up repulses me, I feel my hopes rise. The shattered image of our little family slowly starts to piece itself back together in my mind.

"Does that mean you've made up? Are you moving back in?"

She bites her lip, looking anxious. Those short-lived hopes crash and burn in a fiery mess.

"No," she says regretfully. "We've been meeting with a divorce lawyer. We're signing the papers this week."

"But—" I try to say, but my voice threatens to crack again, so I shut my mouth.

I think back to the argument I had with my father in the kitchen. I accused him of avoiding the issue. Of not accepting that my mother was really gone. When the whole time he *was* accepting it. He was dealing with it. He was going through a divorce. And he was probably hurting. He simply hid it all too well. Just as I've been hiding the constant pain in my arm from him.

Fake it till you make it.

I guess I learned from the best.

"Grayson," my mom says gently. "Your father and I just aren't meant to be together anymore. I felt trapped in my marriage for too long, and I finally found the courage to do something about it. Yes, I handled the whole thing terribly. I realize that. But it doesn't change how I feel."

I nod, sniffling. My mom pulls a tissue out of her bag

and hands it to me. I wipe feebly at my nose, feeling more and more like a little child by the second. But maybe sometimes we all need to feel like kids again. To remind us of what's important. To remind us how to get up when we fall.

"But I want to see you," she says earnestly. "I know you're starting football camp at Vanderbilt next week, but I'm still hoping we can be in each other's lives."

I bow my head in shame, thinking about the registration e-mail that's now nothing more than recycled bytes of data. The deadline has long since passed, but it doesn't matter. The truth has been slowly settling in all summer. I've just been too stubborn to see it.

I've been too stubborn to see a lot of things.

I don't know what I'm going to do in the fall, but I know it won't be football.

"Yeah," I say hesitantly, lifting my gaze to look my mom in the eye. "About Vanderbilt. There's something I need to tell you."

CHAPTER 47

Jasper won't get out of his bed. He's on the top bunk, pressed against the wall with his head under the covers.

I really don't have time for this today.

My shift starts in twenty minutes. Now that the roofing job at the Cartwrights' is finished, I've had to double up on my hours at the beach club to keep the bills paid. My dad's leg is finally getting better. He's no longer on bed rest, so he can actually move around the house now, but he needs physical therapy and it's not cheap.

To be honest, I kind of miss the roofing job. Over the summer months, I started to feel more and more comfortable up there. I started to really enjoy it. And there's no better view of the Locks than from the rooftops.

"C'mon," I urge Jasper, losing my patience. "You need to get dressed."

"I don't wanna go!" he screams from under the sheet.

I sigh. "I thought you loved going to the kids' camp. The schedule says today they're doing a snorkel lesson."

His head pokes out from under the sheet. "In the ocean?" he asks, his eyes widening.

I shrug. "I don't know. And neither will you unless you're there."

This seems to do the trick. Jasper leaps from the top to the bottom bunk in a death-defying monkey move that makes me cringe. I fully expect him to cry out in pain. All we need in this family is another broken leg.

But he lands elegantly with a bounce and springs off the bed like an Olympic gymnast, then darts to the bathroom. "I want teeth brushed!" I call after him. "I'll be smelling your breath!"

I pour some kibble into the dish for the dog, who for the past two weeks has been called Jules. I don't have to be a child psychologist to figure that one out.

I get the boys dressed and fed and out the door in record time.

"Bye!" my dad calls from his place on the couch. Then, just as I'm closing the door, I hear him screaming, "A hash! You're making a *hash*? Can you be any less creative?"

When we reach the beach club, I try to scoot the boys in the direction of the kids' camp, but Jake, always the shrewd one, stops and gives me an accusing glare. "Why aren't you coming with us?"

"Because," I tell him calmly—kids can smell fear—"I'm late for work, and it will take me twice as long to get there if I have to walk you through the clubhouse first."

It's not a total lie, but he doesn't buy it for a second. He crosses his arms over his chest. "You never come with us anymore. Did you and Julie have a fight?"

I sigh. "No." At least that much is true. "We didn't have a fight. We just . . ." I trail off. I'm not getting into this with a six-year-old. I can barely understand it myself. "It's complicated, okay?"

"We like Julie," Jake declares.

"Yeah," Jasper agrees, suddenly standing by Jake's side in a matching arms-crossed stance. "Julie is fun."

"I can't argue with you there," I say.

They're right. Julie *is* fun. She's the most fun I've had in a long time. I just haven't been able to bring myself to see her or call her for the past two weeks. Not since I totally ditched her that day to find Harper, who, as it turned out, had found someone else.

At least that question is now answered. Harper always felt like an eternally open-ended parentheses in my life, just waiting to be closed. But I'm starting to realize that the ambiguity of it all was one-sided. Harper closed her parentheses months ago. Maybe even years ago.

I guess I just never believed it. I never wanted to.

Until I saw Grayson sticking his tongue down her throat.

It's been a hard few weeks. I was able to forgive Grayson, but that doesn't mean I don't get a little nauseous every time I think about it. And I still haven't been able to talk to Harper. She texted me a few times after the fight, but I never responded, and eventually she stopped trying.

I have a feeling that wound will heal only with time.

"Why don't you like Julie anymore?" Jake asks, crashing into my thoughts.

"Yeah," Jasper echoes, holding down their unified front.

"I do like Julie," I tell them. "I like her a lot. Like I told you, it's complicated."

Jasper snorts and whispers something into Jake's ear, who in turn snorts as well.

"What?" I ask.

"Nothing," Jasper says, which makes Jake snicker.

"Tell me," I demand, suddenly feeling silly for wanting so badly to be let in on the secret of a pair of six-year-olds. I turn to Jake, giving him a warning look. He's always been the easier one to crack.

"Jasper says you're being stupid," he tells me.

I look to Jasper. He nods tightly. "The stupidest."

I roll my eyes and turn both of them around by their shoulders, give them pats on the back to send them into the club. "Go. I'm late."

They march diligently forward, and I watch them disappear behind the main clubhouse door.

"I'm not stupid," I mumble to myself before turning and stalking off toward the garden shed.

That night the boys and I come home to a loud clattering in the kitchen. "Wait here," I whisper to them in the entryway, convinced that this is the first house burglary in the history of the Locks.

"No!" Jasper whines. "We want to help catch the robber."

Obviously he came to the same conclusion that I did.

"It's not a robber," I say urgently. "Now shush."

"If it's not a robber," Jasper challenges, "then why do we have to shush?"

"Just shush," I tell him. "And stay here."

I eye my father's closed bedroom door and wonder if he took another painkiller. Is he really sleeping through an entire breaking and entering?

I take a deep breath and creep toward the kitchen, realizing way too late that I'm not armed and I'm definitely not equipped to take on a criminal. I could barely hold my own in a fight with my best friend.

I startle when I hear another loud clang, and push myself flush with the wall so I can peer around the corner.

"Where does your mother keep the damn cheese grater?" a voice calls out, and my whole body sags in relief. I walk into the kitchen to find my dad—with his crutches—

rifling through the pantry. The kitchen is a disaster. It looks like he's emptied the contents of every single cabinet onto the countertops.

"What are you doing?" I ask.

He turns to me with a big, impish grin. "I'm cooking dinner."

"*You*?" I ask skeptically. "Are cooking?" My father barely knows how to pour his own cereal. I don't think he's touched a single frying pan in his entire life.

He turns back to the pantry. "Well, I would be if I could find the dang cheese grater."

I pull out a drawer next to the oven and place the cheese grater on the counter for him.

He snaps his fingers. "The one place I didn't look."

"So," I say, treading lightly. "*Why* exactly are you cooking?"

He grabs a chunk of hard white cheese and starts chafing it against the grater with surprisingly decent skill. "Well, I figure if those bozos on the TV can do it, why can't I?"

Ah. The cooking shows. That's what this is about.

Admittedly, I'm really hungry. I haven't eaten dinner yet and I was planning to just fix some sandwiches for me and the twins. I peer curiously over my dad's shoulder, trying to discern what he could be making.

"Nope. Out! Out! Out! I'll call you boys when it's ready." He shoos me out of the kitchen. "Would you watch over Picasso's shoulder while *he* was working?"

I feel the urge to tell my father that he is probably quite far from mastering a blank plate the way Pablo Picasso mastered a blank canvas, but I resist. After all, this new interest in the culinary arts could turn out to be a good thing. It sure beats him sitting around doing nothing.

My mom arrives home a few minutes later while I'm helping the twins change out of their swimsuits. I hear the front door close, followed by footsteps that practically screech to a halt when another crash echoes from the kitchen.

I run out to find my mom clutching her phone in her hand, trying to steady her shaking fingers long enough to dial 9-1-1.

Apparently she came to the same conclusion that the twins and I did. She nearly jumps when she sees me, and I smile and ease the phone out of her hand.

"Dad's cooking," I explain.

She stares at me for a good ten seconds with a blank expression, as though I'm speaking Korean.

"Like, with food?" she confirms.

I raise my eyebrows. "Yeah. Apparently."

Her confusion quickly morphs into panic, and her eyes widen. "He's going to burn down the house."

She marches into the kitchen, only to march back out a moment later when my dad doles out the same order. "Nope! Out you go! Would you hover around Leonardo da Vinci in *his* workshop?"

My mom frowns at me. "Da Vinci?" she whispers.

All I can do is shrug.

An hour later my mother, the boys, and I are seated around a set table, staring blankly at each other while my father yells out, "Five more minutes!"

"He said five more minutes twenty minutes ago," Jake grumbles under his breath so my dad can't hear. Even the twins seem to be respectful of my father's efforts, which I actually find quite fascinating. If it were me or my mom in that kitchen, they would be throwing tantrums at my feet begging to be fed something because they were positively dying of hunger.

"And ten minutes before that," Jasper reminds the rest of us.

I nod, my stomach practically caving in on itself in protest. "I know. Let's just be patient."

"I'm sure it'll be worth the wait," Mom puts in, but I can see in her eyes that she's just as distrustful of this whole escapade as the twins.

Jake sighs and pushes his fork around with his fingertip, while Jasper makes a game out of using his knife to fish out the slivers of ice cubes left in his glass.

Finally, after another half hour of "five more minutes," Dad emerges with plates full of steamy, hot food that admittedly smells amazing. My mom and I share a look of relief across the table.

"What is it?" Jasper says, crinkling his nose slightly.

"Cacio e Pepe!" my dad announces proudly.

"What's that?" Jake asks with a scowl. "It sounds French."

"It's Italian. Roman, actually. And it's delicious."

"What does it mean in English?" Jasper asks, crossing his arms like he's about to stage a formal demonstration.

"Mac and cheese," my dad says, raising his eyebrows in a challenge.

Two sets of genetically identical eyes light up at once, and they immediately dive in with the fervor of a pair of vultures devouring a dead carcass on the road.

"They made it on one of my shows today. It looked so good, I had to have it," my dad explains, watching contentedly as the twins gobble up their creamy pasta. "And after calling every restaurant in town to find out that no one on this island makes it—or has even heard of it—I Googled a recipe, called up Coconut's Market, got Old Man Finn to deliver the ingredients to me, and presto!" He motions toward the plates.

My mom watches me as I wind the pasta around my fork and take a tentative bite. I'm not sure what I'm going to get. I don't exactly trust the twins' culinary palettes. After all, they think the pasta that comes in a can is quality stuff.

To my astonishment and delight, it's incredible. Creamy and flavorful and so divinely rich. I take another bite. My mom joins in.

"What do you think?" Dad asks us.

"Ohmygodsogood," I mumble with my mouth full.

"Wow!" Mom says, doing little to hide her surprise.

My dad claps his hands together excitedly. "Yes! I knew it!"

"You've been holding out on me all these years!" Mom accuses.

Dad looks so damn pleased with himself, I'm afraid he might fall over and break his other leg. "Well," he says, smoothing the sides of his hair like a member of *Jersey Boys*, "I had to make sure you were marrying me for my good looks, and not my culinary skills."

Mom barks out a laugh. "Joke's on you, then, 'cause I actually married you for your money."

"What money?" Jasper asks, and we all burst out laughing.

Dad kisses my mom on the head as she continues to shovel pasta into her mouth. I can't help but smile as I watch them together. No matter what has happened to this family—broken legs and overdue notices and surprise twins—they've never turned on each other. They've always tackled each obstacle as a team. As partners.

"I made plenty," Dad says, sitting down to eat. Enough

for lunch tomorrow." He gives me a pointed look. "I even made enough for Julie, in case she's coming by later."

I don't miss the air of hopefulness in his tone. Or the fact that both twins look up in unison and stare expectantly at me with long strings of cheesy pasta hanging from their mouths.

"Yeah," I say haltingly. "I don't think she'll be coming around."

"Ever?" Dad asks.

I shrug and cast my gaze to my plate. "I dunno."

"He's being the stupidest," Jasper informs our parents.

Mom laughs. "Is that so?"

"Yup," Jake confirms. "We already told him that."

I roll my eyes and keep eating, hoping Dad will just drop the topic. And magically he does.

At least for now.

After the twins are asleep and I've showered all the noxious weed killer and grass smells off my body, my dad knocks on my door.

I'm already in bed with a book, and the lights are off, apart from the small reading lamp on my nightstand.

"Do you want to talk about it?" he asks, and I know he's looking to continue the conversation we half started at dinner.

I shake my head and flip the page. "Not really."

Dad nods, backs out, and starts to close the door again.

"Do you think I'm being stupid?" I ask before the door is fully shut.

He chuckles and limps into my room, then sits down on the corner of my bed. He finds my foot under the covers and gives it a squeeze.

"It depends on the context."

I put my book down, not even sure where to start.

"It's Harper, isn't it?" he asks. "You can't quite let her go. But you have to if you want any future with Julie."

I blink back at him. "How did you know?"

He smiles. "I was eighteen once too."

I look at him, thinking about everything he's been through to get here. He gave up a whole life on the mainland just to be with my mother. One summer vacation here, and he was hooked.

I let out a long sigh. "Dad?"

"Yeah?"

"Do you ever regret moving to the Locks?"

He doesn't even hesitate. "Not for a single second."

"Really? Even though you know how much more there is out there?"

"There's nothing wrong with spending your life here, if it's where you know you belong. I knew I belonged here the moment I met your mother. The question is, where do you belong?"

I don't answer. Because I'm not sure I'm ready to say the truth aloud. For the past six years I thought I belonged with Harper, wherever that led me. New York, Paris, London, Los Angeles, the moon. I would have followed her anywhere. And she probably would have kept doing the same thing to me that she's been doing for six years.

Because even though I always thought I was so sure of her, she was never sure of me. She might not be sure of anything. And I can't hang my entire life on "maybe."

Especially when the certainty of what I want is becoming clearer every day.

My dad squeezes my foot again and stands up. He starts for the door, nearly disappearing into the shadows of my bedroom.

M
I
K
E

301

"I think I could love a life here," I whisper to him. To the shadows. To myself.

Even in the faint light, I can see him smile.

"Then there you go," he says. I hear the squeak of the door opening. "And don't worry about what the twins said."

I tilt my head questioningly.

"They're right. You are being a little stupid." He chuckles. "But I'm sure it's just a phase."

I laugh too as he bids me good night and closes the door.

I set my book on the nightstand and switch off my reading lamp. In the darkness I think about everything that's happened this summer. Harper ending things for good, Julie trying to save me from drowning in the ocean, working on the Cartwrights' roof, long walks around the island with Julie, finding Grayson's phone at the Cove, watching Ian's mother flip out on the beach, seeing Grayson and Harper kissing, punching one best friend in the face, and then saving another best friend's life.

Then I think about what Mamma V said to me in the kitchen that night after the Movies under the Stars party.

"Don't you forget where you're from, mister. There's no shame in working hard. No matter what color your collar is."

And I realize that what I said to my dad is true.

I could have a life I love here.

I think I already do.

CHAPTER 48

The ferry releases a deep warning blast into the early morning fog. Two minutes until departure. Whitney turns to me, her eyes misty. "I can stay another day," she says.

I shake my head. "You should go. School starts next week. And I'm sure you have lots of shopping to do." I flash her a goading grin as she socks me in the arm.

The past two weeks have been tense between us. Between the fight we had and the whole episode on the bridge, neither one of us quite knows what to say or where to step. We texted almost every day, but mostly we've kept our distance from each other. Or maybe she's kept her distance from me. I don't know. I just know that now is not the time to start a new relationship. I'm still trying to mend old ones.

And survive the loss of others.

"I know you don't want to hear it," Whitney says hastily, like she's afraid if she doesn't get it out, she'll lose her nerve, "but I really am sorry about your dad. I just want you to know that. He was a good man."

I feel the tears prick my eyes, and I fight the instinct to blink them away. I've been blinking them away all summer, and it has only led to disaster.

"Thank you," I whisper to her in a thick voice. "And yes, he was."

Then, suddenly her lips are on mine. Warm and urgent. I realize how much I've missed the touch of her kisses in the past two weeks. How much I've missed the way they seem to make all the clamoring and shouting in my head fade to background noise.

I don't know what the kiss means. But it feels unlike any of our other kisses. It feels sad. It feels truthful. It feels like good-bye.

Whitney and I shared a thousand moments this summer. We lay in each other's arms for hours. We talked until we ran out of words. And yet I could never see her as a permanent part of my life. I couldn't allow myself to be someone important to her.

Whitney pulls away first. Tears are already falling down her cheeks. The look in her eyes tells me she gets it. She knows. This isn't going to happen. We aren't going to make empty promises of staying in touch and visiting on weekends and video chatting to get through the lonely nights.

Because we aren't the people we need each other to be. At least not in the long-term.

We were stable bridges when all the others were falling apart.

We helped each other cross the deep ravines that were laid out in front of us, blocking our paths, hindering our views of the future.

I needed someone to distract me from my grief. And she needed someone who could see her as more than just a pretty face and a slutty reputation. Someone who could see the person she's always wanted to be.

And now that we're both safely on the other side, I think we know what happens next.

That's the thing about bridges. Once you cross over, there's no need to go back.

Nobody stays on a bridge forever. Eventually everyone continues to the other side.

Even me.

I watch the ferry pull out of the dock. I watch until it disappears around the side of the lighthouse. I needed to do at least that. I needed to see her until I could no longer see her.

I retreat slowly back to my grandparents' house, taking my time. When I walk through the front door, my mom is sitting on the couch, covered in the afghan that Dad and I used to fall asleep under.

"You're up early," I say. She doesn't respond. I come around the side of the couch and notice that her eyes are closed. She has a cooling mug of coffee on the table in front of her. She must have gotten up and then fallen back asleep.

The living room is clean now. I spent the past two weeks straightening it up and throwing out all the wine. Not that she can't buy more if she wants to, but I guess we'll cross that bridge when we come to it.

After the incident on the beach, I called my grandparents — who, as it turned out, had gone to visit friends on the mainland — and asked them to come home. I told them that Mom needed them. I told them that *I* needed them.

I moved back into my old bedroom. The house finally feels full again. It feels *almost* back to normal. Obviously my father's absence is still a big gaping hole in the center of the floor. We all walk around it, trying not to forget it's there, trying not to fall in. But the difference is, now we talk about it. I make an effort to mention him at least once a day. Either a reference to something he used to like, or a quote he used to say, or sometimes I just admit that I miss him.

It's nice. Saying those things aloud. You can say them all you want in your head, but until you let someone else hear them, they're not quite real. And they're certainly not fixable.

Not that I'll ever stop missing my father. But talking about it somehow makes me miss him a little less every day.

Funny, I always assumed the opposite was true.

I grab my guitar and sit down on the couch. I softly strum the chords of a new song I'm working on. It's about my father. I'm not even close to finishing it. I can only bring myself to write a little bit every day. Who knows? Maybe I'll never finish it. Maybe it'll always be that unanswered question in my life. That great unfinished work that will forever have unlimited possibilities. Unlimited potential endings.

After I've played through the first few bars a couple of times, I set my guitar on the floor, lean it against the couch, and carefully lift the afghan from my mother's body. I scoot closer to her and drape the blanket over both of us. She stirs slightly, mumbling something incomprehensible, but eventually, after I make myself comfortable, I hear her breathing start to settle back to normal. I hear the house start to settle back to normal.

Or whatever this is.

That's the thing about normal. It's a moving target. It changes every day.

With my head resting on the back of the couch, I face my mother, feeling her soft breath on my cheeks. And somewhere, in that space between what we used to be and what we will eventually become, I fall asleep.

CHAPTER 49

My mom took the news about Vanderbilt well. My dad was another story. He yelled at me for a good half hour before he stopped talking to me completely. As I lay on my bed, I could hear him in the living room, shouting into the phone at some poor Vanderbilt admissions officer who was probably telling him exactly what my original acceptance letter had already told us. That if I was going to Vanderbilt, I was going there to play football. That my admission to one of the country's most prestigious schools was fully dependent on my ability to throw a spiral without doubling over in pain.

By the time I manned up enough to tell my father, I had already come to terms with the fact that I was not shipping off to Tennessee this month. The brochure pictures of the college's beautiful redbrick buildings and white columned facades were already fading from my view of the future. Replaced with a big, blank, white space.

My father, it would seem, would require more time to accept this.

And judging from all the sounds of slamming doors that I could hear from my bedroom, it would be a *lot* more time.

Maybe forever. Maybe he would never get over this loss. Maybe he would take it to his grave.

But that's not my problem. It's his.

And this loss is definitely not coming with me to *my* grave. In fact, it almost doesn't even seem like a loss anymore. It almost seems like a win.

"What are you going to do?" Harper asks me as I sit on her bed and watch her haphazardly toss every clothing item she owns into an open suitcase.

I shrug. "I don't know. And I have to admit, that feels pretty damn good."

She smiles, but it looks forced. I know that's not what she was hoping to hear. She was hoping I would say I'll come to New York with her. I'll get on the ferry with her today and never look back.

Harper likes to be followed. Because she likes to run. She just doesn't like to be alone. But maybe that's what we both need. To be alone. To stop running. To stop chasing. To find a place and stay there, without looking back to see who's shadowing us.

She balls up a sweater and throws it into the suitcase. "Well, there's always room for you in New York."

I snort. "You rented a studio apartment the size of this bed. If anything, there's not even room for you."

She laughs, glancing out the window at her view of Winlock Harbor. Or at least this small section of it. "That's okay. I'm used to feeling cooped up. At least there I can walk ten steps and be in the middle of something amazing."

I nod. "Do you have a job lined up?"

She opens a drawer, scoops the entire contents of socks and underwear into her arms, and dumps it into the suitcase. "Yup. You're looking at the newest waitress at the Starstruck Bar and Grill!" Her excitement is paper thin.

"That cheesy place where the servers sing the menu to you?"

She lets out a sad chuckle. "Yeah. A Broadway hopeful waiting tables. I'm a real freaking novelty."

She turns back to her dresser. I stand up and wrap my arms around her waist. She freezes, then spins around and kisses me hard. I kiss her back, just as hard. When the kiss is over, we simply stand there, holding each other. It's nice. The way she feels. The way she smells. It reminds me of the beginning. When I tripped over her on the sand and we sat close enough to touch while she cried.

She's crying again now.

Then she pushes me away, giving both of my arms a squeeze. I wince in pain at the pressure.

"Promise me you'll see a doctor when you get back to Connecticut," she says, turning to empty another drawer.

I sit back down on her bed, cradling my right arm. "My mom already booked me an appointment. She's going to come with me."

"Will it heal?"

I sigh. "Eventually. But it'll never be the same."

She turns and gives me a weak smile. "What fun is the same?"

I smile back. Because it's right then I realize that my broken arm is what brought me to her. Our paths collided because we were both running from futures we knew deep down weren't meant for us. Those futures had been carved out so long ago, by such different versions of ourselves, we barely recognized them anymore.

Harper and I have fought and made up and kissed and sworn to never do it again and stayed up all night talking about how much sense we make, even when saying it aloud didn't make sense.

And now here we both are, on the verge of new horizons, with blank canvases in front of us, and we don't know what to do. We don't know who we are.

And maybe we don't have to know just yet. Maybe that's the whole point.

When she has managed to miraculously fit the contents of her entire dresser and closet into the suitcase, she comes over to the bed and we lie back on the pillows. I scoot my good arm under her neck, and she rests her head on my chest. We melt into each other, like we always do.

We save each other one last time.

Like we always have.

A week later I'm in my room, packing my own suitcase, trying to decide whether or not to go to the final farewell bonfire of the summer. Harper is gone, living it up in the Big Apple. She video chatted with me a few times, showing me around her tiny apartment, gushing about how much she already loves it. The island feels somehow emptier without her.

I spent the past few days packing up the house in silence with my father, in preparation for our big return to Connecticut. The guys came over every night, and we watched the entire new season of *Crusade of Kings*. Ian was the only one of us who had seen it, and he was practically bursting at the seams trying not to give away any spoilers.

We mourned when the characters we loved were offed.

We oohed and aahed like ten-year-old boys every time dragons entered the plot.

We drank when girls showed their boobs.

And then we cried out in agony when the producers left us with yet another heart-wrenching cliff-hanger.

It was just like the old days. Except it wasn't. Because it was better.

Around nine o'clock I'm just zipping up the last of my bags when I get a text from Mike.

Where are you? Bonfire is rocking the house!

I know he's being facetious. The Winlock Harbor bonfires never "rock the house." They're always epically lame. The only reason we go is to make fun of the tourists. And it's this very thought—a last chance to relive a sliver of the past—that eventually convinces me it's exactly where I need to be tonight.

I tap out a quick response.

On my way. Don't let them start the YMCA dance without me! I'll die of disappointment!

Mike sends me back a cringing emoji, and I slide my flip-flops on and start walking down the beach. I can hear the music and smell the smoke in no time. I breathe it in, wondering if it'll be the last time I ever smell it. Who knows what next year will bring. Who knows if my father will even let me come back. I'm surprised he hasn't kicked me out already. He's probably been too busy rewriting his will.

If tonight really is the last night, then I vow to make the most of it.

I find Mike and Ian standing off to the side, watching the spectacle with great amusement. I grab a beer from the bartender and join them.

"Hey, you made it," Mike says. "You're just in time. I sense a conga line forming."

My excitement level skyrockets. "You're kidding."

Mike shoots me a mock glare. "When have I *ever* kidded about a conga line?"

"Well, we need to usher this thing along. Someone has to request 'Celebration' by Kool and the Gang."

"Already done it," Ian says, sipping his beer. "Don't worry. This is happening."

The song comes on a few minutes later, and we watch in delight as the tourists predictably arrange themselves in a long chain of awkward hands-on-hips and start snaking around the bonfire.

"This is amazing," Ian says approvingly.

"This is epic," I agree.

"This is the Locks," Mike says with a sad shake of his head. And all three of us laugh.

I pat him on the back. "Are you sure you want to stay here, buddy?"

He chuckles. "I wouldn't trade it for anything in the world."

We laugh again, but I know he's telling the truth. Mike and Winlock Harbor simply go together. Cheesy tourist dances and all.

"Besides, Ian will help me keep the tourists in check," Mike adds.

I raise an eyebrow at Ian. "You sticking around?"

He shrugs. "I think so. My mom really likes it here, and, I don't know, this was my dad's favorite place in the world. He looked forward to coming here all year." Ian's voice breaks slightly. Mike pats him on the back.

"I think he'd like that you were staying," I offer.

Ian nods. "I think he would too."

"What about you?" Mike asks after a moment. "How long are you going to hang out?"

I shrug. "A few more days, I guess. I think I'm going to check out a few community colleges. Maybe try my hand at the whole getting-smart thing."

Mike laughs. "And what about the old Harpoon? How is she doing?"

I laugh at his use of *my* former nickname for Harper.

"She's having a blast in New York City. Taking the world by storm, like we always knew she would."

I watch Mike's reaction carefully. He gets quiet for a second, staring off into the ocean in front of us.

"Good for her," he whispers, almost inaudibly. And I realize it wasn't meant for us. It was meant for her.

Mike blinks, like he's coming out of a short trance, and takes a sip of his beer. "So, these community colleges you're looking into," he begins, nudging me with his shoulder. "None of them would happen to be in New York City, would they?"

I smile into my cup.

"Hey," Ian says, elbowing Mike. "Isn't that Julie?"

Mike looks up and then awkwardly stares at the ground. "Yeah."

I follow Ian's gaze to see Julie standing on the other side of the bonfire with a man and a woman, presumably her parents. She glances over here for a second before looking away.

My forehead furrows. "What happened? I thought things were going well with her."

He sighs. "They were. But I pretty much screwed it up."

"Oh, I *guarantee* you screwed it up," I affirm. "That's the unfortunate consequence of only dating one girl your entire life. You never learned 'the game.'"

Mike rolls his eyes. "Oh, please teach me, wise master," he intones, and Ian and I both share a laugh.

It feels good. Drinking on the beach, ribbing with the guys again.

I slap Mike on the back. "C'mon. How bad could it possibly be? I'm sure you can fix it."

"Sure," Ian jabs, pointing at me with his beer, "because you are the master at *fixing* relationships."

I kick sand at him, and he protects the mouth of his cup with his hand.

"Actually," Mike says, suddenly growing quiet, "I did have an idea. But I'll need your help."

Ian and I look at each other in surprise, sharing the same silent thought: *Since when does Mike ever ask for help?*

Then, in unison, we turn back to him and say, "Anything."

CHAPTER 50

I wake the twins bright and early the next morning. They grouse and grumble and try to pull covers back over their heads, but I'm not having it. I yank the blankets right off their beds and with a way-too-cheery-for-this-early-in-the-morning voice say, "Come on! Rise and shine! Up and at 'em! The sky's awake! It's a beautiful day!"

Then, when I run out of wake-up clichés, I jump up onto the top bunk, lift up Jasper's pajama top, and give him a big fat raspberry right on his stomach. He giggles and twists and slaps at my face until finally he's up. Then I proceed to do the exact same thing to Jake.

"What's going on?" Jake says sleepily a few minutes later as he squirts toothpaste onto his brush.

"I need your help."

They turn to each other with matching dubious looks. I always wonder what it must be like for them. To feel like you're constantly looking into a mirror. Jasper is silently elected to speak on the duo's behalf.

"What *kind* of help?" he asks with clear skepticism.

"Don't worry," I tell them. "It involves thievery and shenanigans. It's right up your alley."

315

They share another look, this one of surprise, but seem to take my explanation as an acceptable one and start brushing their teeth at warp speed.

My dad has prepared a breakfast feast. I think he's made every single recipe on the Martha Stewart website. The twins sit at the small table in the kitchen, gobbling up their blueberry ricotta pancakes drenched in citrus syrup, and crispy applewood bacon, barely taking time to breathe, let alone chew.

"Easy," I tell them. "I don't have time for you to choke to death. Not today."

"This is really good," I tell my dad as I take a bite of the spinach-and-egg-white frittata. "Like, *really* good."

He beams as he starts rinsing the pan in the sink. "I'm glad you think so. Because I wanted to talk to you about something."

I perk up, continuing to shovel egg into my mouth while keeping my gaze on my father. He dries his hands and tosses the towel over his shoulder. It's a small move, but it strikes me as so professional. So chef-like.

"How do you feel about taking over the roofing business?"

Even the twins stop eating at that one. All three of us look up at him in bewilderment.

"What?" I ask. "But roofing is your life. You love it. Why would you give it up?"

He bobbles his head back and forth. "I'm getting a little old to be skipping around on roofs. As is evident from this." He taps his healing leg. "Plus, I've been talking to Mamma V down at the club, and she wants to retire soon. I think I might be a good replacement. Of course, I'll need some decent training, which she's offered to do. It'll take a few months to get me up to snuff, but—"

He's rambling now, sounding nervous. I ease his anxiety by cutting him off. "Dad, I think that's an amazing idea. The menu down there could use some serious shaking up."

He chuckles. "Right?"

"Will you still cook for us?" Jake asks, his eyes wide with concern.

"Every day, champ," my dad says, ruffling Jake's hair.

This seems to be a satisfactory response, and the boys go back to chowing down on their breakfast.

Dad turns back to me. "I just thought since you've decided to stay, you'll need something a little more full-time. I mean, if you don't like roofing, that's one thing."

Honestly I hadn't quite figured out what I would do once the summer was over. All I knew was that I wanted to stay. The Locks is where I belong. These people—even the terrible villain twins—are my home.

"You can try it out for a few months," Dad offers. "And if you don't like it, we'll sell the business to someone else. What do you think?"

I glance at the two boys, who are both licking the citrus syrup from their plates. Then I turn back to my dad. "I think that's as good an idea as any."

He smiles at me, giving me a firm pat on the back. Then he goes back to the dishes.

I finish my frittata and scoot my chair back. "Okay, boys. Let's get a move on. Someone feed Jules so we can go."

"I fed him last time," Jasper whines. "And his name's not Jules."

I roll my eyes. "Of course it's not. What's his name now? Peter? Paul? Mary?"

Jasper makes a gagging sound. "Mary is a girl's name."

"Never mind," I say, but I get a laugh out of my dad. "Someone just feed him."

"It's Jasper's turn," Jake insists.

"It is not."

"Psst." My dad leans into me as the twins bicker back and forth. "His name is Nike now."

"Nike?" I repeat quizzically. "Like the shoe? I thought they were on an old-man-name trend."

"It rhymes with Mikey," Dad informs me, and then he goes back to the dishes, humming quietly to himself.

I feel a squeeze in my chest as I watch the boys argue. "Okay!" I shout over them, holding up a hand. "Don't worry. I'll feed him. Again."

By the time we get to the Coral Bay Beach Club a half hour later, we've gone over the plan at least three times, and the boys are *pumped*.

"Are you ready?" I ask as we stop outside the front door of the main building.

Both boys salute me in unison. It's about the cutest thing I've ever seen them do. "We're ready!" Jasper says.

"Don't mess it up," I tell them. "And don't start giggling, or she'll know something's up."

Jake slowly lowers his saluting arm. "Is this really going to make Julie come to the house more?"

I reach out and ruffle his soft hair. "That's the plan, buddy."

"Then let's do this!" Jake shouts, adding a kung-fu-style kick. "Hi-YA!"

Jasper and I share a look of befuddlement. Then Jasper takes his brother by the hand and leads him inside. "C'mon, crazy karate kid."

I laugh as I watch them go. My nerves are shot, but I have faith in my little brothers. There are really no two people better suited for the job.

Grayson and Ian meet me on schedule at the beach club snack stand. Grayson is yawning and sipping coffee from a travel mug, while Ian seems bizarrely alert and raring to go. He must be excited to finally have a task.

"Thanks for coming, guys. This beach is just too big to do this alone."

"No problem, man," Ian says, slapping me on the back.

"We're here for you," Grayson says, but he's yawning during the whole thing, so it sounds more like, "Waaah heee fohhhh yoooo."

I check the time on my phone. Any minute now.

"So how do we even know what we're looking for?" Ian asks, and just then, right on cue, Jake and Jasper come running out of the kids' camp building and into the small, enclosed playground. Jasper is covered head to toe in tie-dye, making him look like a member of the Blue-Orange-Yellow-Green Man Group, and Jake, as clean as a whistle, is grinning, with his hand stuffed suspiciously into his pocket.

Things went either terribly well or terribly wrong. Sadly, given the nature of this plan, it's hard to tell just by looking at them.

I run over to the fence. "Did you get it?" I ask, my heart starting to pound in my chest.

Jasper grins wickedly and nods as Jake withdraws his hand from his pocket, pulling out a small white clamshell.

But not just any shell.

Julie's shell.

Jasper chortles giddily. "She had tie-dye everywhere!"

"Jasper got her good!" Jake adds.

"And after she changed her clothes, Jake snuck into the locker room, found her shorts, and got the shell!"

"You guys are awesome!" I praise, giving them both high fives. "Did she seem mad?"

They both look almost confused by the question. "Mike," Jasper explains rationally, "Julie doesn't get mad."

I laugh. "Touché."

"What does that mean?" Jasper raises his eyebrows quizzically.

"It means you're right."

Jasper rolls his eyes. "Of course I'm touché. I'm *always* touché."

"Jasper!" another staffer calls from inside. "Come get cleaned up!"

He shoots me a dirty look. "I have to shower in the men's locker room now. You owe me big-time."

I smile. "I owe you both."

I watch them scamper back into the building, and I carry the magic shell to the beach.

"Pull out your phones," I command our little group. "Take a photo of this shell. We're looking for its *exact* match. Not a close match. An exact match. Every shell has one. The other half of this baby has to be somewhere on this island. Grayson, you go left and cover the area from here to the lighthouse. Ian, you go right and search the area from the marshland to the old docks. I'm going to take the stretch of beach from here to the Winlock Harbor Inn. Meet back here in one hour with every possibility you can find."

The guys nod, and we break apart. I move in a grid pattern, the way I've seen people do in search-and-rescue scenes in movies. I have the original shell, so you would think my part would be easiest, but it's not. It soon becomes evident to me that every single shell on this beach looks nearly identical. It's so easy to be fooled, thinking you've found the right match, when actually it belongs to another half entirely.

As I search, combing through sand and surf, my pants soaked up to the knees, I think about Harper. We talked on the phone last night. After the bonfire I felt the need to call her. She seemed surprised to hear from me, but then we just started talking. About her first week in New York, about the twins, about my father's newfound passion for cooking. It was nice. I'd forgotten how easy it was to talk to Harper. Without all the complicated emotions confusing everything.

It was always too complicated with us.

It was never easy or simple.

For so long I thought Harper was my other half. The shell that made me whole again.

But in the end she wasn't my perfect match. She was just the *first* match that I found. The first shell I picked up off the beach. I had barely been searching at all. But it looked enough like the real thing that I convinced myself it was, for six years. I convinced myself that the shell fit, that the ridges and grooves lined up, when they were always just the slightest bit off.

Maybe Grayson is Harper's other half. Maybe he'll move to New York and they'll continue to fall in love, and they'll get married and bring their children back here on vacation every summer. Or maybe he's not.

Maybe Harper will meet some hot Broadway director in an audition, or a wealthy finance guy on the subway. Maybe she'll fall in love with him instead.

In any case it's just nice to realize that her future is no longer tangled up with mine. It runs alongside it. We are friends, living parallel lives. Maybe our lives will intersect again. Maybe she'll come back to the Locks to visit. Maybe she won't.

But no matter what happens to either of us, she'll

always be that first shell. That first special half I found on the beach.

And that means something too.

When the guys and I meet up again an hour later, my vision is a dizzying blur of seashells and seaweed and pebbles of sand. We dump all of our finds into a huge pile and begin to sift through, comparing each one with the original, trying to fit the ends together to see if they lock. I'm starting to get discouraged. All of these shells look alike, and yet none of them matches up to Julie's.

What if the other half was washed back into the sea?

What if the other half was scooped up by some stupid tourist kid and is now a thousand miles away.

What if I'm too late?

"What are you guys doing?"

I jump to my feet and spin around at the sound of her voice. I try to hide the massive pile of shells behind me.

"Julie," I say, my voice squeaking as I clasp my fist around her shell. I notice she's wearing another cotton polo shirt and shorts that are just a tad too big.

"I was . . . ," I start, unsure of what to say. This is *not* how I imagined my grand gesture playing out. I was supposed to find the shell. I was supposed to ask if I could walk her home after her shift. I was supposed to present it to her in some wildly romantic moment under the stars.

Grayson and Ian share a look and then stand up, brushing sand from their knees. "You got this," Grayson whispers to me. They give me pats on the back and start walking toward the beach club.

Julie watches them go and then takes a step toward me, her expression still demanding an answer to her original question.

"Don't you have to be at the kids' camp?" I ask, trying to stall for time.

"Jasper and Jake said you were out here. They told me you put them up to that little tie-dye stunt."

Traitors.

"What else did they tell you?" I ask, glancing quickly over my shoulder at the shells.

She crosses her arms, looking suspicious. "Nothing. Why? What else should they have told me?"

"Nothing!" I say hastily.

I can tell from her closed-off body language and hesitant stare that she's still not thrilled with me for ditching her on that lawn three weeks ago. And then for avoiding her ever since.

And I don't blame her. That was what this big plan was for. It was an apology. It was something to show her that I care about her. And that I was stupid for not seeing it sooner.

Now I guess I'll just have to rely on words. But I've never been a poet like Ian or a slick sweet talker like Grayson. Rhetoric has never been my strong suit.

"So, then, what are you doing out here?" she demands.

With my body still blocking the pile of shells, I take a deep breath and say, "Julie, I'm sorry. I've been a total ass-hole all summer. You are great. Better than great. The twins adore you. They think you're funny and sweet and pretty. Even my dad adores you."

"Is that what this is about?" she asks icily. It's the coldest I've ever heard her voice. "Is that why you had Jasper stage a tie-dye water gun fight with the other kids? So you could tell me how much *they* like me?"

"No," I say firmly. "That's not what this is about."

I rake my teeth over my bottom lip. I'm already messing this up. How many times have I stood by while Harper said good-bye? How many times have I stayed quiet, pretending it didn't bother me? How many times did I let the opportunity to speak my mind pass me by?

"*I* like you," I finally spit out. "Okay? A lot. *I* think you're funny and sweet and pretty. I also think you're adorable. And sexy as hell. Especially in that uniform, and most people don't look good in those uniforms. Trust me, I worked here through puberty. I know."

She stifles a giggle, hiding her mouth with her hand.

"I adore you too," I go on. "Maybe even more than the twins do. I just got caught up in so much other bullshit that I didn't see it. But now I see it. Like an idiot, I see it right as the summer is ending and you're probably getting ready to leave. But it doesn't matter, because I still see it. And so I wanted to do something for you. I wanted to do this grand-gesture thing. You know, like people do in movies. But it didn't quite work out the way I wanted it to."

With a sigh I step aside, revealing the pile of shells in the sand. Julie lets out a quiet gasp.

"The tie-dye thing was a diversion. So Jake could steal this." I open my palm to reveal her original shell. "I was trying to find the other half for you. I was trying to find your perfect match."

Julie looks from the shells to me. Her eyes are misty with unformed tears. She takes a step toward me and removes the shell from my palm. I feel my heart sink when I realize what it means. She's leaving. And she's taking her half with her.

I let out a loud, surrendering breath and close my eyes. I wait. Wait for yet another girl to walk away from me.

But the longer I wait, the more I wonder why she's

still standing there. Why I can still feel her presence like a refreshing breeze. When I open my eyes again, I see that she's not, in fact, standing next to me. She's crouched down in the sand, rifling through the pile of shells. It only takes her a moment before she finds the one she's looking for. She plucks it from the heap and stands up, facing me. She hands me the newfound shell and holds out her own.

Then slowly we push them together. The ends click into place.

I glance down at our hands, not touching, but each holding our own separate piece, together forming one single shell.

"Smith College is not too far from here, you know?" she says quietly.

I glance up to meet her eye. "Really?"

"Just a train and a ferry ride away."

A smile blooms on my face as I wrap my arms around her waist and pull her into me. "Oh, really?"

"What is Winlock Harbor like in the winter?"

I lean close, our breaths colliding. "It's cold."

"I'd like to see it," she whispers.

"I'd like that too."

Then I press my lips to hers and we join together all over again.

CHAPTER 51

My mom is already seated when I arrive at the Winlock Café. It was my dad's favorite restaurant on the island, and meeting here for breakfast twice a week has become our new tradition.

She's taken the liberty of ordering for both of us. Scrambled eggs with cheese for her, and chocolate chip waffles with whipped cream for me. It's what we always used to order when we'd come here as a family. The only thing that's missing now is my dad's meat-lovers skillet. I make a mental note to order that next time.

Conversation between us is still challenging. There are topics we stick to that feel safe. And topics we avoid that still feel like land mines. We talk a lot about the past, about my father. What he loved, what made him crazy, what made him laugh. But we never talk about the future. I guess we're still taking that one day at a time.

After we pay the bill and leave, my mom suggests we go to the bookstore. "I want to buy some books on home decoration. I think it's time we redecorate the bungalow, don't you?"

This takes me by surprise. I didn't think she'd ever want to redecorate that place. I always assumed the memory of all of it was too precious for her to change.

"What do Nana and Papa say?" I ask.

"Oh, they're fine with it," she assures me. "They agree that it's time."

She must see the concern etched into my face, because she puts an arm around me and squeezes. "Don't worry. We'll keep some stuff the same. I just think if we're going to be here for a while, we should spruce it up a bit."

I nod uncertainly. "Okay."

We walk like that down Ocean Avenue, her arm around me, like we used to do when I was little. The small downtown has mostly cleared out, as the majority of summer visitors have already packed up and left. I'm kind of excited to see Winlock Harbor in the fall.

I pull open the door to Barnacle Books and gesture for my mom to enter. She smiles warmly at me as she passes. I'm just about to follow her inside when I hear a loud catcall from somewhere behind me. "Hey, lover boy! Where you been hiding out?"

I stop in the doorway, my whole body tensing when I recognize the voice. I know when I turn around, he's going to be there. I'm going to see his face.

And I'm right.

It's the douche who attacked Whitney at the beginning of the summer. The one she nailed in the balls. Somehow we were able to avoid him for the past two and a half months. Maybe he hasn't even been on the island. Who knows? But he's here now. And the sight of him, plus the memory of busting through that window and seeing him on top of Whitney, makes my blood boil.

"Go ahead," I tell my mother, and I step back onto the sidewalk, letting the door swing shut behind me.

"She's a little old for you, isn't she?" the guy says, striding up to me and giving my mother a once-over through the window of the shop. He's wearing swim trunks, flip-flops, and no shirt. For some reason the sight of his ripped, tanned abs makes me even angrier. His breath smells like alcohol, even though it's barely eleven o'clock in the morning.

"But I hear she *really* lets loose after she's had a couple." He winks at me, and I don't even give my mind the chance to react. For the first time in my entire life, I let my body react first.

I cock my fist back and rocket launch it into his face.

My hand feels like it's on fire. I shake it out, and tiny droplets of blood—*his* blood—fall onto the pavement. I think I might have broken a few bones in my fingers, but it doesn't matter. The rush I feel at finally socking that asshole is enough to distract me from the pain. It's enough to make me *welcome* the pain.

I've never thrown a punch before. Unless you count the wall in our apartment. Maybe it was beginner's luck, or maybe my dad really did impart some kind of wisdom in the art of combat over all those years, but it was a good punch. The guy is down on the ground, holding his busted nose with his hands while blood spurts through his fingers.

"What the—" he mutters.

"That was for Whitney," I say spitefully. Then, as I stride purposefully into the bookstore, I whisper under my breath, "And my dad."

The next afternoon Mike and I stand on the pier as Grayson's ferry slowly pulls out of the marina. The summer is officially over, but the end has never felt more real than right now. As we watch our friend sail away.

Grayson, Mike, and I met twelve summers ago, when we were six years old. I was building a sand castle on the beach, and Mike came up and asked if he could help.

We worked for hours on that thing. It had everything — pillars, turrets, a moat, even a little drawbridge. Then Grayson, who apparently had been watching us for thirty minutes, came running through like a wrecking ball, and smashed the whole thing.

I cried for more than an hour. Grayson's mother forced him to apologize, and Mike, being true to form, was the first to forgive. But I, also true to form, held on to that anger for nearly a week before I would let Mike bring Grayson to the beach to hang out with us.

Grayson claimed he'd just been playing football and had been running to make a catch when he'd accidentally tripped over our masterful construction. And the football tucked under his arm at the time certainly lent credibility to his story. It wasn't until a few years later that he admitted he'd wrecked the castle on purpose. Because he'd been jealous of it.

And that was the start of us.

Now, as I watch Grayson's ferry steadily move out to sea, I can't help but feel like this might be the end of us. At least, the end of us as we used to be. With Grayson starting community college in the fall, Mike taking over his father's roofing company, and my mom and me moving into my grandparents' house indefinitely, things are not going to be the same.

Sure, we'll all keep in touch. Maybe we'll even continue to spend our summers here, but it will always be different. That's the only thing that I can say for certain.

"And then there were two," Mike says beside me. For a moment I'd almost forgotten he was there.

I let out a sad laugh. "And then there were two."

"Hey, I'm thinking about going to catch some waves. Do you want to come? I have an extra board you can borrow."

I shake my head. "Can't. My mom is redecorating the house. I promised I'd help her search home decorating blogs."

Mike chuckles. "Ouch. Good luck with that."

"Yeah, thanks," I mumble. "But I'm planning to marathon *Crusade of Kings* season two later tonight, if you want to come over."

"Ooh. Season two." Mike feigns getting stabbed in the chest. "The most heart-ripping, soul-crushing season of them all. Definitely count me in for that."

I laugh. "Cool."

"I'll catch you later, then," he says, and I glance down to see he has extended his fist toward me. Without thinking I instinctively bump mine against his, then twice on top, twice on bottom, finishing off our ten-year-old salute with wiggling fingers.

"Have fun," Mike says. Then he jogs back up the dock, leaving me alone on the edge of the pier. I watch him disappear down the beach, before I turn toward the water again, just in time to see Grayson's ferry vanish around the side of the lighthouse.

Then again, maybe some things *will* stay the same.

ACKNOWLEDGMENTS

Thank you to Nicole Ellul, without whom this book would literally not exist. And to Mandy Veloso, Jodie Hockensmith, Carolyn Swerdloff, Mara Anastas, Steve Scott, Bara MacNeill, Russell Gordon, and all the rock stars at Simon & Schuster who send wonderful stories out into the world every single day. Also thanks to my amazing agent, Jim McCarthy; my parents, Michael and Laura Brody; and of course Charlie, who keeps me sane when sanity seems like such an unreachable goal. And finally, overflowing buckets of gratitude to my readers. Your letters, tweets, fan art, gifts, hugs, and unbridled enthusiasm remind me that I have the best job in the world.

JESSICA BRODY

is the author of several popular books for teens, including *52 Reasons to Hate My Father*, *A Week of Mondays*, and the Unremembered trilogy, as well as two adult novels. Her teen diary is filled with boys, most of them appearing in summer months. She splits her time between California and Colorado. Visit her online at jessicabrody.com.

Smart. Funny. Romantic.

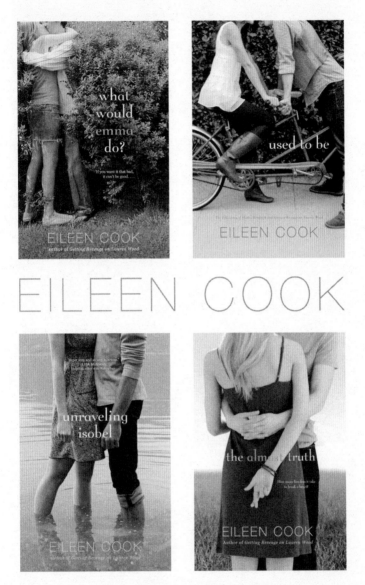

EILEEN COOK

www.eileencook.com

Feisty. Flirty. Fun. Fantastic.

right of way
LAUREN BARNHOLDT
Two-way Street

two*way street
LAUREN BARNHOLDT
The companion novel to Right of Way
A road trip with her ex? Danger ahead.

the thing about the truth
LAUREN BARNHOLDT
author of two-way street and one night that changes everything

sometimes it happens
LAUREN BARNHOLDT
author of two-way street

watch me
LAUREN BARNHOLDT
author of two-way street

one night that changes everything
LAUREN BARNHOLDT
author of two-way street

LAUREN BARNHOLDT

Love. Heartbreak.
Friendship. Trust.

Fall head over heels for
Terra Elan McVoy.